The Fire of Heaven

"*The Fire of Heaven* pulls you in right from the very first paragraph . . . Tom Wallace also created an entire cast of memorable characters without taking the focus off (Jack) Dantzler . . . the author fantastically weaves several murders together in a way that keeps you guessing who the real killer is and what his or her motives could be . . . I can't wait to see who Dantzler tangles with next."

--Natasha Jackson (Readers' Favorite)

The List

"*The List* contains all the must-haves of the thriller genre—danger, intrigue and suspense. Powerful villains. Exciting action scenes. Anticipation. . . Tom Wallace excels is in his ability to make his characters come alive. As with Wallace's previous thriller, *Gnosis*, I ended up finishing this book in less than two days. This book makes for an absorbing and enjoyable read, the kind that had me incessantly turning the pages."

--Mary Fan

"*The List* is a fast-paced, thrilling read. It takes the reader on a journey of intrigue immersed in political and corporate greed. Detective Jack Dantzler's quest to solve the mystery behind his parent's deaths thrusts him into a world of international crime. It has graphic detail but it is perfectly balanced as the story of death, fear and reprisal unfolds. Not a book for the faint of heart."

--Patricia Day (Readers' Favorite)

Gnosis

"A page-turner. *Gnosis* is a book that's virtually impossible to walk away from."

--Mary Fan

"The book features cerebral challenges for readers who like their murder mysteries served Kentucky-style."
--Kentucky Monthly Magazine

The Devil's Racket

"BRAVO!! By far the best book ever. Jack Dantzler is a complicated man and a unique detective with a long shelf life, reminiscent of Michael Connelly's Harry Bosch. *The Devil's Racket* grabbed me from the beginning and it held me to the end. This is a book that you will want to read and pass on to your friends and family. What we have here is a winner."
--MyShelf.com

"Central Kentucky's stunningly beautiful horse farms are the picture of serenity and refinement, but who knows what evil lurks beyond those four-board fences? Enjoy the ride, although it's bumpy and bloody. It just might give you a shiver as you drive past the next pretty horse farm—so pretty, it's, well, scary."
--Lexington Herald-Leader

What Matters Blood

"A masterpiece of murder. Jack Dantzler is a complicated man and a unique detective with a long shelf life, reminiscent of Michael Connelly's Harry Bosch. I suspect Dantzler will be around for quite a while. HIGHEST RECOMMENDATION."
--MyShelf.com

"Tom Wallace delivers a wallop of a thrill with *What Matters Blood*. With masterful characterization, his portrayal of the serial killer is chilling, as well as authentic, enough to elicit goose bumps. The story is fast-paced, the dialogue realistic, and the search for the killer intriguing. One galvanizing read that will hold the reader's interest throughout."
--Midwest Book Review

The Poker Game

The Poker Game

A Jack Dantzler Mystery

By

Tom Wallace

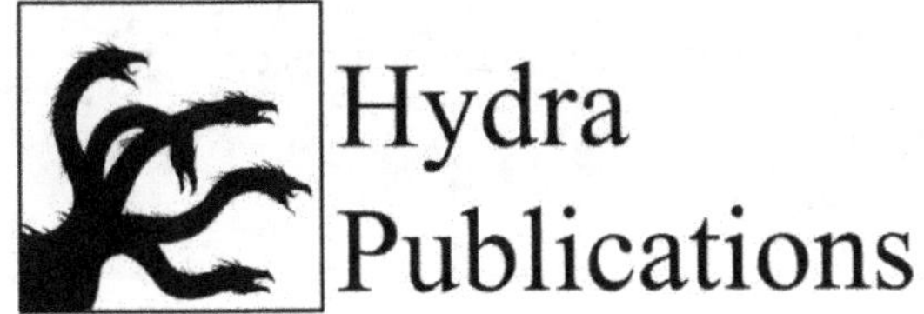

Hydra
Publications

Printed in the United States of America

ISBN-13: 978-1-942212-33-1

Cover by Karri Klawiter

Hydra Publications
Goshen, KY 40026

www.hydrapublications.com

Dedication

This book is dedicated to Sly Douglas (DJ) Norman Jr., the best poker-playing buddy a guy could ever hope to have, and one who beats me on a regular basis.

The Poker Game

CHAPTER ONE

Jack Dantzler stared straight ahead, his thoughts focused on a single question: Exactly when did the world turn upside-down?

He was sitting on a wooden bench outside the courtroom, waiting to testify in a murder trial. This was nothing new; as Lexington's lead homicide investigator for more than two decades, he'd testified on at least seventy-five previous occasions. But this time was different, and for a reason he simply could not fathom.

He had been called to testify *for* the defense.

That fact in itself was a puzzler. Making it even more curious was a second fact—he had not been the lead investigator on the case. He had been out of town when the crime was committed. In his absence, Eric Gamble handled the investigation. And as always, Eric did outstanding work.

Not that Eric needed to do too much. Based on the circumstances, this was a simple and clear-cut case of first-degree homicide. The facts: In the early morning hours of April 4, 2015— the medical examiner estimated the time of death to be around one-thirty a.m.—Morgan Ballard went into her bedroom, put a .45 pistol to her husband's temple and pulled the trigger, scattering his blood, brains and pieces of his skull over the bed, floor and walls. According to Arnie Edwards, the M.E., death for thirty-one year old Deke Ballard was instantaneous.

When Eric took the witness stand, he told the jury that the police were notified of the incident at four-ten p.m. Two uniformed officers arrived at the Ballard home at four twenty-two. Eric and Jake Thomas got there at five twenty-three. Arnie Edwards was already on the scene.

"I estimate the time of death to be around one-thirty," Arnie told Eric and Jake at the time. "Pretty straight forward, too. Your only question is why?"

"Any sign of a struggle?" Eric asked Arnie.

"Nope. The man was sound asleep. Dreaming one minute, surrounded by darkness a second later."

The 'who' was never in question—Morgan Ballard admitted pulling the trigger. Still, there were a few questions Eric wanted answered, beginning with why she did it, and why did it take almost three hours before authorities were notified?

Although Morgan was said to be too traumatized to respond to an interrogation at this point, Eric didn't need her to give him the answer to his second question. He already knew the answer to that one. Morgan's first phone call went to her father, Richard Chambers, a call later verified by both father and daughter.

Richard Chambers was one of the wealthiest, most influential men in the commonwealth, having made untold millions in real estate, banking and coal mining. Knowing she was in deep trouble, daddy's precious little girl reached out to the one man she knew could save her. The one man who had always been there for her when times were tough.

At the Ballard house on the morning of the killing, as the sun was coming up, Richard Chambers behaved like a man annoyed at all the people coming and going, at the crime scene folks traipsing from house to car carrying bags of evidence, at the guy with the camera capturing it all on video. In his mind, they were nothing less than leeches prying into his daughter's private world. Into *his* private world. Arrogance dripped from him like water.

Richard Chambers was a big man, thicker than he was tall, perhaps once a sleek linebacker who now had the physique of a defensive tackle. He had gray hair, wore glasses, and was dressed in a very expensive suit, the trousers held up by red suspenders. A white silk shirt open at the collar, pricey Italian shoes and gold cufflinks rounded out his death-scene ensemble.

Eric and Jake had immediately sized him up as an asshole and a prick, one of those rich bastards who feel superior to anyone who lacks their financial wherewithal. Which happened to be approximately ninety-nine percent of the world's population.

Now, six weeks later, sitting on a bench outside the courtroom, Dantzler looked at his watch. He'd been told that he would take the stand no later than one-thirty. That was fifteen minutes ago. He'd been in situations like this enough times to know that things rarely go according to plan during a big trial. There were always bumps in the road that slow down the wheels of justice. Still, the bench wasn't getting any softer, and his growling stomach kept reminding him that he had not eaten since finishing off a bialy and some orange juice at a little past seven.

Dantzler had another reason to be antsy—he was scheduled to meet with Captain Richard Bird, head of the Homicide Unit, at three-fifteen. Things had changed within the department during the past few weeks, and those changes needed to be discussed. Milt Brewer had finally called it quits after four decades on the force, Scott Crofton left to fulfill his dream of working for the FBI, and Laurie Dunn, Dantzler's on-again off-again love interest had taken a job with the Justice Department.

Losing them cut the homicide squad by fifty percent, leaving only Dantzler, Eric and Jake to handle things. Making matters worse, Bird said budget cuts precluded him from hiring replacements for at least another couple of years. Dantzler wasn't too concerned about the manpower shortage, not as long as he had Eric and Jake on the team. Eric was now a seasoned veteran, a top-notch investigator and, in the eyes of many, a future Police Commissioner. Jake was a war hero who left the Marines to become a cop, and had in a very brief period of time distinguished himself as a true up-and-comer. Dantzler was convinced that he, Eric and Jake could handle most investigations without difficulty. His one concern was how that trio would handle something really big and, if such a situation arose, how fast could he get the extra support?

It was now a little past two and Dantzler was getting pissed off. Even if he took the stand at this moment, and even if it went smoothly and quickly, there was no way he could make a three-fifteen meeting with Captain Bird. And it wasn't like Bird didn't have other matters on his plate that had to be addressed. At best, Dantzler knew the meeting would be pushed back an hour or so, but more than likely it would have to be rescheduled for tomorrow.

What the hell am I doing here? he kept asking himself. *Testifying for the defense in a trial that shouldn't even have happened in the first place?*

Based on the circumstances, everyone in the homicide unit and the D.A.'s office agreed that the wisest thing Morgan Ballard could do was to admit her guilt, then seek the best plea deal she could get. However, no one was shocked or surprised when Morgan, no doubt following her father's orders, quickly rejected that notion. She was innocent, she said, adding, "I am certain jurors will agree with me once they hear the evidence."

Which could be tricky, since none of the evidence worked in Morgan's favor.

When questioned by Eric and Jake two days after the incident, Morgan said she killed her husband because she feared for her life. According to Morgan, Deke Ballard had been systematically abusing her—mentally and physically—for the past five years. She said the physical beatings had grown much worse, and had occurred with greater regularity in recent months. Morgan went on to say, "Deke threatened to kill me on multiple occasions, and I had become convinced that he would go through with it."

Then Jake asked the most logical question of all: Why not simply get a divorce?

"He would have killed me for sure if I had done that." Morgan's take on the situation. "It was him or me."

But there was one problem with Morgan's story—it was all bullshit.

There was simply no evidence to support her claims of having been abused by her husband. None. Nada. Absolutely zilch. No emergency room visits, no doctor's office visits, no X-rays, no photos, no written documentation . . . nothing. In addition, none of her family or close friends claimed to have seen any signs of abuse.

Except for her father, who was quick to take her side. Richard Chambers swore that his daughter was telling the truth, that Deke Ballard had been a bully who consistently inflicted physical pain and psychological abuse on his precious child.

Chambers' account was judged to be another heavy load of bullshit that was quickly dismissed by the detectives and those in the D.A.'s office. It was so off-base as to be almost comical. Richard Chambers was a bulldog of a man who had a reputation for having an extremely aggressive personality. Like many self-made men, he carried a heavy chip on his shoulder, one that manifested itself in a combination of paranoia and a quick temper. If anyone was a bully, it was Richard Chambers.

Had he known Morgan was being beaten he would have taken care of the situation before the day was through. Deke Ballard would either have been beaten to a pulp or, more likely, killed. To think that a hothead like Richard Chambers would allow his daughter to be abused for five years without intervening stretched believability to the breaking point and beyond.

Four days after the event, Morgan Chambers Ballard was arrested and charged with pre-meditated first-degree murder. At her arraignment, the Chambers family attorney asked for bail, which, over the strenuous objections of the prosecutor, was granted. Bail was set for two-million dollars, which Richard Chambers posted in less than an hour.

Having secured his daughter's temporary freedom, Richard Chambers then did what only the rich and powerful can do—he hired one of the most famous, most high-priced defense attorneys on the planet.

For the past fifteen years, Grace West had carved her reputation by successfully defending famous clients in highly watched trials all across the country. A native of Chicago, Grace had authored several books, was a familiar face on the TV talk show circuit, served as a legal analyst for CNN, and had been written about and profiled in virtually every popular magazine. When People Magazine did a cover story on Grace, they dubbed her "the Barracuda Barrister" for her ferocious and relentless interrogation tactics. It was a well-deserved, well-earned moniker.

Standing just a shade shy of six feet tall, more beautiful than most Hollywood starlets, Grace West had proven herself to be a formidable challenge for anyone unfortunate enough to be sitting in the witness chair.

A chair whose next occupant would be Jack Dantzler.

At exactly two-fifteen, the courtroom door opened and Dantzler was beckoned in. He stood, straightened his tie and headed toward the door, again asking himself, *What the hell am I doing here?*

He was about to find out.

CHAPTER TWO

As he walked down the aisle toward the witness stand, Dantzler felt like a condemned man heading toward the electric chair. If Grace West was only half as good as advertised, his time in that chair might be particularly painful. Right now, he'd rather be anywhere but here.

Overseeing the proceeding was Judge Leonard Kurtz, who, with his head of unruly white hair and his mustache, always reminded Dantzler of photos he'd seen of Einstein. Kurtz was a veteran on the bench, and a judge considered to be fair-minded and impartial, although most defense attorneys swore that the vast majority of Judge Kurtz's rulings on close calls tended to go in favor of the prosecution. He was also known for running a tight ship, and for reigning in long-winded attorneys on either side of the aisle.

At the witness stand Dantzler was sworn in, asked to give his full name, and then spell his last name. With those preliminaries out of the way, he took his seat and adjusted the microphone in front of him.

Looking up, he was somewhat surprised to see a full house. He wondered if it had been this way from day one, or if his presence on the stand was the big drawing card. Either way, there were few empty seats in the spacious room. Among those sitting together in the crowd were four familiar faces—Eric and Jake were sitting between David Bloom, the psychiatrist and Dantzler's college tennis teammate, and Sean Montgomery, an ex-cop who left the force, went to law school and became a defense attorney.

Each man wore a bemused look. Clearly, curiosity was the honey that drew those four bees.

Dantzler cut his eyes to the defense table, getting his first look at Grace West. She was indeed an impressive-looking woman, and a beautiful one at that. Dantzler judged her to be far more beautiful in person than she was on TV, or from photos he'd seen in various magazines. She had dark hair and green eyes, wore a simple but elegant blue pants suit, white blouse and black shoes. Earrings and a gold necklace completed her ensemble. Sleek, professional and pricey.

Grace West picked up her yellow legal pad, nodded and smiled at Dantzler. "I apologize for the delay in getting you on the stand, Detective Dantzler. Your patience is greatly appreciated. I promise to do everything I can to make this as short and painless as possible."

"*That* would be greatly appreciated," Dantzler replied.

"Would you tell the jury what you do for a living?" Grace asked.

"Homicide detective for the Lexington Police Department."

"And how long have you been a detective?"

"Almost twenty-five years."

"Are you the lead detective?"

"On most cases, yes."

"Because you have the longest tenure, correct?"

"Correct."

"Isn't it true that you were the youngest detective to earn a gold shield?"

"Yes."

"In your twenty-five years as a homicide detective, approximately how many murder cases have you worked?"

"I can't say for sure, but it's a fairly high number."

"A hundred?"

"I'd say that's a fair estimate. But we investigate all suspicious deaths. Some turn out to be suicide, some are accidental. The degree of our involvement rests on the medical examiner's ruling."

"You were not the lead detective on this case, correct?"

Dantzler nodded, said, "Correct. I was out of town when the murder occurred."

"Objection, Your Honor," Grace West quickly responded. "I object to the detective's use of the word murder."

"Sustained," Judge Kurtz said. Turning to the jury box, he addressed the jurors. "You are to disregard Detective Dantzler's last statement. Proceed, Counselor."

Grace West said, "Detective Dantzler, are you familiar with the facts of this case?"

"Yes, I am."

"Are you familiar with the defendant, Morgan Ballard?"

"Not really. I've seen her around, but I don't know her."

"Isn't it true that you are an outstanding tennis player? That you have professional-level talent?"

Dantzler chuckled, said, "Maybe once upon a time, but not anymore."

"Oh, come now, Detective, don't be so modest. I've heard that you are the best tennis player this town has ever produced."

Before Dantzler could respond, Bryan Richmond, the assistant D.A., stood and said, "Objection, Your Honor. What could Detective Dantzler's tennis talent possibly have to do with this case?"

"That's the most intelligent question I've heard all day," Judge Kurtz said. "What about it, Miss West? Where are you going with this?"

"If you will bear with me, Judge Kurtz, I will show you where I'm heading."

"Well, head in that direction with great haste, Miss West. I am not inclined to waste the court's time with irrelevant inquiries."

"Thank you, Your Honor." Looking back at Dantzler, Grace West asked, "Detective Dantzler, isn't it true that you own the Lexington Tennis Center?"

"I'm a one-third owner. David Bloom and Sean Montgomery are my partners."

"Now, you previously stated that you are familiar with Morgan Ballard, correct?"

"Correct."

"Where do you know her from?"

"The Tennis Center. I've seen her around there a few times."

"Ever had a conversation with her?"

"Not that I remember."

"Never interacted with her in any way?"

"Nothing more than a nod and a hello."

"What about Deke Ballard? Were you familiar with him?"

"I was better acquainted with him than with the defendant."

"From the Tennis Center, correct?"

"Correct."

"Did you ever have any dealings or conversations with Deke Ballard outside the Tennis Center?"

"No."

"Did you ever play tennis with Deke Ballard?"

"Once again, I must object, Your Honor," Bryan Richmond protested. "Who Detective Dantzler plays tennis with is not relevant to this case."

Judge Kurtz looked down from the bench. "Take us somewhere in a hurry, Miss West, or change your line of questioning."

Grace West said, "Yes, Your Honor." Then to Dantzler: "For the record, did you ever play tennis with Deke Ballard?"

"Doubles on a few occasions. As an opponent, not a partner."

"How would you rate Deke Ballard as a tennis player?"

"This is absolutely my final warning, Miss West," thundered Judge Kurtz, before the prosecutor had time to object. "You are trying the court's patience."

"Your Honor, it's important that Detective Dantzler answer my last question. Once he does that, I promise you that this line of questioning will begin to make sense?"

"For your sake, Miss West, I certainly hope you can deliver on that promise," Judge Kurtz said. "Answer the question, Detective Dantzler."

"Deke Ballard was a slightly above average player. Better at doubles than singles."

"Certainly not in your league, correct?" Grace West said.

"Correct."

"Talent aside, would you say he was a hot-headed player?"

Now Dantzler understood where this was heading, and why he was here. "No, I wouldn't say he was a hot-headed player."

"Are you sure about that, Detective Dantzler? Isn't it true that Deke Ballard had a bad temper?"

"Objection, Your Honor," Bryan Richmond said. "Mr. Dantzler is a homicide detective, not a psychiatrist."

Judge Kurtz put his hand to his chin and thought about the objection for almost a minute. Finally, he gave his ruling, "No, I'm going to allow Detective Dantzler to answer that one."

"I really can't answer that. I didn't know him away from the Tennis Center, so I don't know how he behaved in other venues."

"Fine. Then let's stick with the venue where you did know him," Grace West said. "Isn't it true that on the evening of June four of last year, sometime around eight-thirty, Deke Ballard was involved in an altercation with another player?"

"Yes."

"Are you familiar with the details that led up to that altercation?"

"Deke Ballard objected to several close calls made by his opponent. When the match was over he made his feelings known."

"Come now, Detective Dantzler, there's more to it than that. Isn't it true that Deke Ballard followed his opponent into the locker room, accosted him, and threatened him, saying, and I quote, 'I will bash your fucking brains in'?"

"I didn't hear him say that, but I later learned that he did say it."

"But you did eventually arrive in the locker room, correct?"

"Yes."

"And isn't it also true that when you arrived on the scene, Deke Ballard had the man pinned against the lockers, had one hand on the man's throat, his fist drawn back, ready to hit the man?"

"I can't say for sure what he was going to do with his fist, but everything else you described is accurate."

"Isn't it true that you had to quickly intervene and pull Deke Ballard off the man?"

"That's correct."

"So, Detective Dantzler, you want us to believe that a man who verbally trashes an opponent, then follows him into the locker room, where he physically assaults the man, then threatens to bash his fucking brains in is not a hothead with a bad temper?"

"He was definitely angry that night, yes. But that's the only time he ever acted in such a manner."

"How can you be sure of that, Detective? Isn't it possible that he lost his temper on other occasions and you didn't hear about it?"

"I doubt it. If there had been other incidents, I would have been made aware of it. But none were ever reported to me, or to my partners."

"His behavior was such that you felt the need to punish him, correct?"

"Yes, he was suspended for two weeks. He also apologized to me, my partners and to the gentleman he had the altercation with. His apologies were accepted and the incident was forgotten."

"One final question, Detective Dantzler. Wouldn't you agree that if Deke Ballard was hot-headed enough to threaten a tennis opponent, he was capable of abusing his wife?"

"Objection, Your Honor," Bryan Richman shouted.

"Sustained," Judge Kurtz responded.

"No further questions for this witness, Your Honor," Grace West said, taking her seat at the table.

"Witness is excused." Judge Kurtz banged his gavel. "Court is in recess until Monday at nine a.m.

*****

When Dantzler exited the courtroom, he saw his four compatriots standing across the hallway. Those earlier bemused looks had been replaced by shaking heads and wry smiles.

"Not as bad as I thought it might be," Dantzler said, loosening his tie and unbuttoning his shirt.

"Hate to tell you this, Ace, but if that had been a tennis match, you just got bageled," David Bloom said. "She handed you your head on a platter."

"What are you talking about?"

"Tell him, Sean."

"She got you to contradict yourself. That's an automatic win for her."

"How do you figure that?"

"Come on, Jack. You denied that Deke Ballard had a hot temper, then turned around and admitted that he choked a guy and threatened to bash his brains in. That's a contradiction, my friend."

"No, what I said was, I didn't interact with the man outside of the Tennis Center, so I had no clue how he behaved in other venues. What I did say was that he was definitely angry that night."

"Parse the words any way you want to, Bill Clinton," Sean said, grinning. "The Barracuda clearly won that round. Chalk up a big W for her."

"Screw you, Montgomery. You know, once upon a time you were one of the good guys. But that was before you sold out and went over to the dark side. Tell me again how you can take money from those scumbags you defend."

"With both palms wide open, Jack. With a smile on my face and joy in my heart."

Bloom said, "Let's walk down to McCarthy's. We could all use a pint or two of Guinness. Drinks are on me."

Sean draped an arm around Dantzler. "After suffering through that humiliating debacle, Jack probably needs something a lot stronger than Guinness. Right, Jack? A couple of shots of Jameson, maybe? Something to wash out the bitter taste of defeat?"

"She didn't win, Sean."

"Okay, you cocky prick, have it your way. Score it any way you want to."

"Thank you."

"No problem, Jack. But she did beat your ass. Live with it."

CHAPTER THREE

The empty chair to Dustin Ridley's right might as well have been occupied by a giant question mark. Each time he glanced at it, he wondered what was going on. In all the years Dustin had been coming here, six men sat around the table. Always. Yet tonight, for whatever reason, only five men were present. Dustin wanted to ask why one of the regulars was missing, but knew better than to pose the question. If the others—and Judge Leonard Kurtz in particular—wanted him to know, they would tell him. Otherwise, he would keep his mouth shut.

The men were in Judge Kurtz's recreation room to play poker. But this wasn't just any poker game. Far from it. This was a game with great history and tradition. Rules were strict, and so was entrance into the group; getting accepted was a long and arduous process that could last several weeks. When a member died, or became too old to participate, each remaining player was allowed to nominate up to three men to fill the vacant chair. Each candidate was grilled by the five members, who then voted for their top choice. The top two vote-getters were invited back for a second interview. Only after those interviews was a final selection made. In the event of a tie the Judge would cast the deciding vote.

The Judge had been a member since the initial group was formed more than forty-five years ago. The man who started the weekly game was Charles Minton, a wealthy investment banker. When he died in nineteen eighty-four, the Judge took over as leader, moving the game to the recreation room in his massive home located in The Woods, one of Lexington's most upscale enclaves.

The men gathered every Saturday night, the first hand dealt at exactly seven p.m. The game lasted until seven a.m. the next morning. There were bathroom breaks every two hours. The Judge provided a full bar, with a heavy emphasis on scotch, which seemed to be the preferred choice among the men. Initially, the Judge's wife Ginny took care of the food and drinks. Since Ginny's death nine years ago, the Judge handled everything. Smoking was allowed. Cigarettes, cigars, pipes . . . all were accepted. For the men at this table health concerns and political correctness held no sway.

Nor did an empty wallet. Each player had to bring a minimum of ten-thousand dollars with him each week. Paper money was used in lieu of chips. That was another tradition the players refused to break. The only game played was five-card draw, Jacks or better to open, nothing wild. The rest of the poker world might have fallen in love with Texas Hold 'em, but that game, which these men all loathed, would not be played here. To do so would be sacrilege.

As the youngest player by at least two decades, and the latest to be granted a seat at the table, Dustin was aware of the good fortune that had come his way. He wasn't positive but he'd heard a rumor that he beat out thirteen other individuals who also went through the vetting process. Whether it was two, or thirteen, or fifty really didn't matter. He won—survived was the more accurate description—and that victory earned him a chair at a poker game he'd heard about since he was a teenager.

Dustin loved being part of this scene. He loved everything about it: the game, the players, the atmosphere, the tradition, the competition. This was no-nonsense, no-bullshit, high-stakes poker. Save for a few bits of gossip and an occasional crude joke tossed in along the way, there was virtually no idle chatter. These men did not deal in the mundane. The time-honored poker language was what they spoke, and Dustin loved hearing it. To him it was poetry.

For exactly twelve hours each week, fifty weeks a year, he was as close to heaven as he could ever hope to be.

Despite the time spent with these men, Dustin knew virtually nothing about any of them. He knew their first names and that was it. Save for Judge Kurtz, Dustin had no clue what any of the others did for a living. No doubt, based on their age, some, perhaps all, were retired. But how they made their money—and they all had plenty of it—remained a mystery.

He knew the Judge was a widower, but what about the others? Were they married, divorced, widowers, had secret lovers, gay . . . none of that information was known to him. Of course, they all knew about him from the vetting process, that he was single, and that he owned five McDonald's franchises in the area. But work, past or present, was never discussed. Same for politics and religion. Those subjects were taboo. At this table, God and the president took a backseat to a full house or a straight flush.

Even during bathroom breaks, or when the players were re-filling their drinks, there was very little small talk. In those ten minutes or so, the men tended to go about their business without speaking. The number of complete sentences spoken during any given break could be counted on one hand. Dustin learned early on that when the men did converse, there was one question that was absolutely verboten—*never* query another player about how he was faring that night. To do so was viewed as bad manners. If a player paid attention—and these men certainly did—then he knew how the others were doing at any given moment. Whether an opponent was up or down was none of anyone else's business. Worry about your own pocketbook; let the other guy worry about his.

At the one a.m. break, Dustin was stunned when Judge Kurtz tapped him on the shoulder and pulled him aside. This had never happened in the seven years he'd been a member of the group. His immediate thought was that he had done something wrong, broken protocol in some way, and was now about to be read the riot act. His stomach was suddenly filled with a swarm of butterflies.

"How has life been treating you, young man?" Judge Kurtz asked, smiling. "Are you making a decent living under those golden arches?"

"Yes, sir. The world is not lacking for hamburger lovers."

"I'll confess I'm not much of a burger guy, but I damn sure

like your French fries. I have them quite often for lunch. I always get the large order, too. None of that small or medium size for me. Most folks eat fries with ketchup. Not me. I prefer to dip mine in ranch dressing. Probably makes me seem strange, doesn't it?"

"Not really. You would be surprised how many customers ask for ranch with their fries."

"Well, I don't know if that makes me feel better or worse. I always liked the notion of being something of a renegade. Being one of the masses never held much appeal for me."

"Rest easy, Judge. Ketchup is the clear winner with fries. You're definitely in the minority."

Judge Kurtz put an arm around Dustin. "Are you enjoying being a member of our little cabal?"

"Yes, sir. Very much, sir. I'm honored to be a member."

"How long have you been with us now?"

"Seven years."

"And has being a member fulfilled your expectations?"

"More than fulfilled them, sir."

"Just so you know the others are quite fond of you. They all agree that you are a superb player, a worthy opponent, and you have great respect for our traditions. That is all any of us can ask of a new member."

"I am very pleased to hear that, sir."

"Kind of strange only having five players, isn't it? Throws off the balance in some peculiar way, like a spoke is missing from the wheel."

Dustin wanted to ask the Judge why the player was absent, but thought it unwise to do so. "Yes, sir. The game does have a different feel to it."

"Well, there is nothing we can do about it, so let's get back to business."

Conversation concluded, the Judge moved back to the table and took his usual seat. The others quickly followed, and within twenty seconds the cards were being shuffled.

Dustin looked at his watch. It was now one-twenty, meaning there were just under six hours remaining until the game ended. He was having a great night—up approximately eight grand—and if his cards kept running hot he could easily walk away with twice that amount or more. The most he had ever won was thirteen thousand, an amount he had every intention of surpassing tonight.

Poker players, like virtually all human beings, tend to be creatures of habit. Every player has his own unique way of doing things, his own idiosyncrasies, his standard trademarks. Very rarely do they stray too far off the familiar path. Like the way in which they receive their cards. Some pick up each card as it is dealt, while others—like Dustin—wait until all five cards are on the table before picking them up. There was no right way or wrong way; it was just each player's preference. And for Dustin, seeing them all at once was what he preferred.

Dustin was the only player in this group who always waited until all cards were dealt before checking to see what he had. His reason for doing so was simple—it gave him an opportunity to closely observe his opponents. For Dustin, being able to read an opponent was just as important as knowing when to bet, when to bluff, or when to fold. More often than not, a player's facial expression when he looked at each card was a clear indicator of whether he was pleased or pissed. That's known as a "tell" in the poker world. And any player with an obvious "tell" was likely to see his finances shrink in a hurry.

Dustin knew that two of the four players were pleased with what they had been dealt, while the other two weren't. The Judge, in particular, wore the happiest expression. Clearly, he was holding a potentially strong hand.

He had better be.

Because when Dustin picked up his five cards and looked at them, he saw the faces of four Kings staring back at him. A near-perfect draw. Only four aces or a straight flush could beat him, and he doubted that the Judge would be that lucky. Dustin knew he was holding a winning hand.

What he didn't know was that it would be the last hand he was ever dealt.

CHAPTER FOUR

Dantzler leaned against the marble bar and surveyed the carnage. Five adult males, all deceased, were slumped over in chairs situated around a poker table, victims of what appeared to be a single gunshot to the back of the head. Each man was bent at the waist, his head, arms and upper torso lying flat on the table. Dantzler calculated the odds of them all ending in the same position as something like a million to one against, which meant the killer—or killers—probably arranged the bodies after the fact.

Pushing away from the bar, careful not to step in blood or touch areas likely to be dusted for fingerprints, Dantzler eased a few steps closer to the poker table. Arnie Edwards, the M.E., was somehow miraculously managing to avoid stepping in the pool of blood surrounding the table while making a closer examination of the head wounds. Two crime scene techs were in the huge room, dusting for prints and spraying luminol in other areas, checking for blood spatter. David Bennett, looking very green around the gills, was getting it all on video.

You're shooting one helluva horror movie, David, Dantzler thought to himself. *You have good reason to look like you're about to toss your cookies.*

Not much more than an hour ago Dantzler was having lunch with David Bloom. The two men met early in the morning at the Tennis Center, played some doubles with another couple of guys, showered and then went to Ramsey's for lunch. When they finished eating, Dantzler took Bloom back to the Tennis Center, dropping him off at his car. Then Dantzler drove to his house on

Lakeshore Drive, opened a can of Diet Pepsi, went out on his deck that overlooked the small lake that bumped up against his back yard, and sat there enjoying the scenery, the sun and the quiet.

It had been a fairly typical Sunday.

Until . . .

Sunday's beauty quickly turned ugly.

At a few minutes past two, a 911 dispatcher received a call from a frantic, screaming woman who said something horrible had happened at the home of Judge Leonard Kurtz. According to the caller, several men appeared to be dead or badly injured. No one was moving, she said, and there was a lot of blood. Despite the caller's hysteria and her heavy Hispanic accent, the dispatcher was finally able to ascertain the location of the Kurtz home. Within minutes a patrol car was heading in that direction.

When the uniformed officer arrived at the location, he was met by a middle-aged man comforting a woman who was sobbing uncontrollably. The man, who said he was a neighbor, told the officer that the woman entered the residence through a sliding door located at the rear of the house. He went on to tell the officer that the sliding door was the back entry into the recreation room.

The officer walked to the back of the house, found the sliding door completely open, went inside and immediately saw the bodies. Backing out of the room, he put in a call for back-up, quickly adding, "You'll need to get in touch with Homicide and with the coroner's office. We've got a friggin' slaughter here."

By the time Dantzler arrived an hour later, the place was a buzz of activity. Five patrol cars were there, strategically parked in such a manner as to keep the growing crowd of curious neighbors from encroaching on the scene. The coroner's van was parked closer to the house, along with several other vehicles Dantzler recognized, including those belonging to Eric Gamble and Jake Thomas. Yellow crime scene tape ringed the entire house, the definitive clue that something very bad had indeed happened here.

Never in his wildest imagination would he have guessed it would be *this* bad.

"I would never presume to tell you how to do your job, Jack, but I think you can safely rule out robbery as a motive,"

Arnie Edwards said, pointing at the poker table. "That's a huge amount of cash for anyone, especially a killer, to simply walk off and leave. I would estimate that we're looking at fifty or sixty grand. In addition to that, several of these unfortunate gentlemen are wearing watches that cost more than I make in a year."

"I recognize Judge Kurtz; any ID for the others?"

"So far, no," Arnie answered. "I haven't been able to get to their wallets just yet."

"Let me know when you get those names."

"Will do."

At the top of the stairs, Dantzler looked to his left, into what appeared to be the den, where Jake was sitting next to a small, dark-skin woman, doing his best to take some notes. He wasn't having much luck; the woman was sobbing so hard she could barely speak.

Jake stood when he saw Dantzler approaching. "This is Maria Ramirez," he said. "I'm sure you can tell from looking at her that she's the one who found the bodies. Between her crying and her thick accent, it's been difficult getting much from her, though I did manage to learn a few details."

"Enlighten me."

"Every Sunday, right after Mass, she comes here to clean the recreation room. She usually gets here about one or one-thirty, works for a couple of hours, then leaves. She . . ."

"Just the rec room?" Dantzler asked.

"On Sundays, yes. She also works for him two days during the week."

"If the Judge was dead and couldn't open the door for her, how did she get in?"

"There's a sliding door that opens directly to the recreation room. She said the Judge always leaves that door unlocked for her."

"I'd say right about now she wishes this was the one time he forgot to unlock it. To walk in and see something that horrific will likely mess her up for years." Dantzler looked around the room. "Where's Eric?"

"Still checking out the rest of the house."

"See what else you can get from Maria, but don't push her too hard. Schedule a time tomorrow for her to come in and talk with us. If you think we need a Spanish interpreter, I'll have one available. When you're done here make sure she has a ride home."

Leaving the den, Dantzler saw Eric and a uniformed officer coming down the stairs. Dantzler nodded to the officer, then said, "Find anything up there, Eric?"

Eric shook his head. "Nothing. Whoever did this had only one thing on his mind—take out those guys downstairs. Nothing else interested him. Did you check out the cash on that poker table? We're talking some serious dough. If the killer was willing to walk away from that, then I can't imagine that there is anything else in this house that he'd want."

"You're probably right, but I still want each room dusted for prints. With the Judge as one of the victims, this is going to be high profile. We can't risk the possibility of overlooking something that might come back to bite us in the ass."

"Wouldn't you agree that the timing of this is rather interesting?" Eric asked. "I mean, with the Ballard trial going on? And a guilty verdict the likely outcome?"

"Yeah. Interesting."

"Think a guy like Richard Chambers might do something like this? Or have it done? Let's face it. After what happened here they'll have to declare a mistrial."

"It's way too early to make any assumptions, Eric. Keep in mind that five people died in that room downstairs. At this stage we can't be certain that Judge Kurtz was the primary target. There's only a one-in-five chance that he was. The devil is always in the details. And in the details is where we'll find our answers."

Dantzler remained at the Kurtz house for the next five hours, carefully observing the collection of potential evidence and the work performed by the crime scene people. Although he had complete faith in their ability to do their jobs properly, as lead detective on the case he was the one who would eventually have to answer for any mistakes or oversights that occurred during the collection and processing of any evidence. Plus, he had always believed that the more he knew about every detail of an investigation, the odds of apprehending the person or persons responsible were greatly improved.

At some point in the afternoon, he took a tour of the Judge's house, which consisted of four upstairs bedrooms, each with its own bathroom. There were two bathrooms on the main floor and one in the recreation room. He spent almost an hour in what he assumed was the Judge's office. Most of the important items had already been removed by Eric, including two laptop computers, an appointment book, cancelled checks, a Rolodex and several boxes filled with letters, cards and various other pieces of correspondence. There really wasn't much left that interested Dantzler, but he somehow found it useful to sit in the big leather chair at the Judge's desk. It gave him the feeling of seeing the room the way Judge Kurtz saw it.

As Dantzler was rising from the Judge's chair, a uniformed officer poked his head into the room. "A gentleman is here who says he works with Judge Kurtz," the officer said. "I thought you might want to speak with him."

"What's his name?"

"Devon McIntyre."

"Is he with you now?"

"Yes, sir."

"Send him in."

Devon McIntyre was a chunky fellow dressed in an outfit that screamed golf course. Checkered slacks, blue Polo shirt with the familiar crocodile logo, loafers with no socks. He had dark hair, a deep tan and a look on his face that was stuck somewhere between hope and fear, with fear holding a slight lead.

"Has something happened to Judge Kurtz?" Devon asked. "No one will tell me anything. Is the Judge all right?"

Dantzler pointed at the Judge's chair. "Why don't you take a seat, Mr. McIntyre?"

"I don't need to sit," Devon responded, shaking his head. "I need to know what's happening. Why are so many police officers here?"

"I'm sorry to have to tell you this, but Judge Kurtz is dead."

"Oh, God, no." Devon's eyes filled with tears. "How?

What happened?"

"I can't get into specifics right now, but I would like to ask you a few questions if you don't mind."

"Yes. Sure. Whatever."

"What's your relationship to Judge Kurtz?"

"I'm his clerk. I have been for twelve years." Devon suddenly perked up. "Has anyone informed Josh yet?"

"Who is Josh?"

"The Judge's oldest son. He lives in Louisville. Maybe I should contact him. Josh is the reason I came by this afternoon. He'd been calling his father all morning and didn't get an answer. The Judge has had some heart issues in the past, so Josh was concerned that maybe his father had suffered a heart attack. He asked me to check on him."

"I'll take care of that, Devon. Do you have his number?"

"Yes."

"Is Josh the Judge's only child?"

"No. There's another son, Andy, but I don't know where he lives. Josh can probably tell you."

"Are you aware of any threats Judge Kurtz has received recently?" Dantzler asked. "Anything out of the ordinary? Phone calls, letters, cards, e-mails?"

"Questions like that indicate the Judge was murdered. Is that what happened?"

Dantzler nodded. "What can you tell me about this poker game?"

"Oh, my God, don't tell me it happened during the poker game. Did it?"

"It appears that way."

"What kind of a monster can come into a room and murder six innocent people? Who can do something that evil?"

"Why did you say six people?"

"Because the Judge once told me the poker group consisted of six players."

"Do you know the names of the group members?"

"The Judge never shared that information with me," Devon answered, shaking his head. "All I know is they met every

Saturday night and there were six players. Why? Didn't you find six victims?"

"Only five."

"Well, at least one of the players was very lucky," Devon said.

Lucky, or he was the killer. "Give me Josh's number and I'll make the call." Dantzler closed his notepad, took a card from his shirt pocket and handed it to Devon. "Call me sometime tomorrow and we'll get you in for an official statement."

"Yes, yes, I'll do anything to help. The Judge was like a second father to me. I worshipped that man."

After Devon left, Dantzler closed the door and made the call to Josh Kurtz, giving him the grim news that this father was deceased. Dantzler supplied only the briefest details, but Josh figured it out pretty quickly his father had not died from natural causes. Josh said he would come to Lexington immediately, and that he'd meet with Dantzler first thing in the morning.

It was almost nine-thirty when Dantzler left the Kurtz house and headed for his car. As he opened the car door, his cell phone rang. Flipping it open, he saw an unfamiliar number.

"Detective Dantzler," he said.

"How about I buy you a drink, Detective? I suspect you could use one right about now."

Grace West.

"Are we even allowed to be communicating with each other, Miss West? Isn't that a violation of protocol?"

"I hardly think anyone is going to give a shit, given the circumstances. Do you?"

"So, you've heard?"

"Yes."

"Where are you?"

"At an establishment called Cheapside."

"Give me fifteen or twenty minutes."

"See you then."

*****

Grace West was sitting at the bar when Dantzler entered Cheapside. She immediately finished her drink, moved to an empty booth and took a seat. Dantzler sat down across from her.

"What's your poison, Detective?"

"Jameson and Diet Coke."

"Sounds like a winner; think I'll have one myself." Grace went to the bar, ordered the two drinks, came back and handed one to Dantzler. "See, even a defense attorney can be a gracious host."

Taking the drink, Dantzler said, "My friends are in agreement that you won our little skirmish Friday afternoon. Naturally, I disagree with them."

"Naturally." Grace clinked her glass against Dantzler's. "But I'm sorry to inform you that your friends are correct. You lost big-time. And to be quite honest with you, Detective, you weren't that much of a challenge."

"Can't see it."

"You know, Detective, I'm a damn good tennis player. But if I played you, it wouldn't be close. You'd win easy. Well, a courtroom is a long way from a tennis court, and in the courtroom I'm the heavyweight. That's where I dominate."

"It's for sure the Barracuda Barrister doesn't lack for confidence," Dantzler said.

"God, I hate that nickname." Grace took a drink. "Thought about suing People Magazine, but . . . what the hell? I suppose bad publicity is better than no publicity."

"You don't fool me, Grace. You loved it. You love anything that strokes your ego."

"You're wrong, Detective. I love hearing a not guilty verdict."

"What happens now? Mistrial?"

"Has to be."

"Which is a good thing for Morgan Ballard and Grace West, right? She stays out on bail until a new trial date is set, while you get to squeeze more money out of Richard Chambers. I read that as a real win-win situation."

Grace sipped her drink and shook her head. "I seriously doubt I'll be hired a second time around. Papa Chambers and I didn't always see eye to eye on several important matters. He's not a man who likes to be challenged, especially by a female. I suspect he'll bring in someone who is more compliant than I am. A yes person, essentially."

"Morgan Ballard is guilty of first-degree murder, regardless of who defends her."

"Well, fortunately for all of us, juries make that call, not detectives."

"What's next for Grace West? Pack up your suitcase and head back to Chicago?"

"Funny you should ask, Detective Dantzler. I'm thinking seriously about opening an office here in Lexington."

"Just what this city needs, another lawyer."

"Would you be terribly offended if I chose to stay in your fair city?"

"Correct me if I'm wrong, but barracudas are rumored to be quite dangerous."

"Depends on the barracuda, wouldn't you say?"

"I don't know. I'm not an expert on barracudas."

She took hold of his arm, pulled him forward, leaned across the table and whispered in his ear. "You want to know a little secret, Detective?"

"Sure."

"You like me."

"That's it? That's your secret? I was hoping maybe you would give me something important, like the name of Judge Kurtz's killer."

"Can't help you with that." Grace finished her drink, stood and placed two ten-dollar bills on the table. "Based on what I've seen during my short stay in Lexington, people tend to get murdered at a rather alarming rate. Given that, I would feel much safer if accompanied by a big, strong man like you. Walk me to the Hyatt, Detective."

"Be more than happy to, although I don't think you scare very easily."

"Admit it, Detective," Grace said. "You like me."

CHAPTER FIVE

Dantzler left the Hyatt a little before sunrise, feeling exhausted and spent but with no complaints. He'd discovered—happily—that the courtroom wasn't the only venue in which Grace West excelled. He drove home, took a shower, dressed, gulped down a glass of orange juice and headed for the office, arriving a few minutes past eight.

An hour later, Dantzler was sitting in the War Room eyeing the box of assorted pastries on the table. The voices in his head were waging a fierce battle; one side telling him to go ahead and satisfy his sugar fix, the opposing side reminding him of potential land mines like clogged arteries and heart attacks. Opting for health over a sugar rush, he ignored the land mines and sipped from a bottle of water. Jake Thomas went the other route, quickly putting away two chocolate-covered doughnuts, while Eric split the difference, eating a single crème horn. The three men watched as Richard Bird completed his task at the chalkboard.

"Here are the names and ages of our five victims," Bird said, putting down the chalk. "As you can see, with one exception we're dealing with a group of senior citizens."

Leonard Kurtz	73
John Dawkins	71
Sahid Hassaine	67
Carl Banks	71
Dustin Ridley	45

As the three detectives began writing down the victims' names, Bird continued, "It's also something of a multi-national group. Kurtz was Jewish, Dawkins an African-American, Hassaine a Muslim. At least, I'm assuming from his name that he's Muslim. Don't know about the other two victims yet, except to say they appear to be typical white-bread Caucasians. Bottom line is we have plenty of digging to do. And, Jack, I'm wondering if the three of you can handle it. That's a lot of bodies."

"True. But I'm betting there's only one killer," Dantzler answered. "I'm confident the three of us can find him."

"Or her," Jake chimed in.

"No way did a female do this, Jake. We're definitely looking for a male."

Bird said, "At any rate, back-up is available if you ever need it. I can bring in a couple of guys from Robbery or Special Victims. Also, Glenn Rigby says the FBI will assist if we need them. So, additional resources are at your disposal. All you have to do is ask."

"Maybe down the road we'll take you up on it, Rich. But for right now we need to get started on this. Any preliminary thoughts, guys?"

"I know I'm sounding like a broken record here, but we gotta start with Richard Chambers," Eric said. "He has to be the first guy we talk to."

"Why are you so hot for him, Eric?" Dantzler asked, leaning back in his chair.

"Isn't it obvious? The Judge presiding over the trial of Chambers' daughter is murdered just days before a verdict is rendered, causing a mistrial. She was going to be found guilty, and it would be Kurtz who sent her away for life. Now everything is on hold. Richard Chambers bought his daughter some time. My hunch is he'll send her to another country, one with no extradition process. She'll skate on this, wait and see."

"Lot of assumptions in that little sermon, Eric, beginning with your certainty that Morgan Ballard would have been found guilty. Grace West informed me that she contacted every member of the jury, and according to her, the vote was seven to five for guilty. That's a long way from unanimous."

"Deliberations hadn't begun yet," Eric said. "Those five

voting not guilty could've changed their minds."

"That works both ways, Eric. Maybe the seven would switch sides. Either way there was likely to be a hung jury. That would probably mean a second trial." Dantzler took a sip of water. "Here's my main problem seeing Richard Chambers as the shooter. Why kill four innocent men if his goal was to take out Judge Kurtz? Why all those extra victims?"

"So we would ask that very question," Eric quickly replied. "He hides the diamond among the glass stones."

"What do you think, Jake?" Dantzler asked.

"I'm not as glued to Chambers as Eric is, but I do agree that he's the starting point. He would be the first one I bring in."

"Agreed," Dantzler said. "But we don't bring him in; we pay him a visit. If he shows up here he'll have a lawyer with him. I'd rather catch him by surprise. You two go see him right after we break up here. After that, you guys need to find out everything you can about Dawkins, Hassaine, Banks and Ridley. Divide them up any way you see fit. I'm meeting with Josh Kurtz in fifteen minutes, so hopefully he can fill me in on what we need to know about the Judge. Later this afternoon, Maria Ramirez and Devon McIntyre will be in to give us a full statement. Captain Bird will handle that for us."

"You might need a Spanish interpreter for Miss Ramirez," Jake advised. "Her accent is really thick."

"I'll have Emily Martinez sit in with us, just in case," Bird said.

"We also need to dump phone records for all victims," Dantzler said. "Maybe that's where we'll find some connections that will lead us somewhere. That may also be our best shot at learning the name of the missing player."

Eric picked up his notepad and stood. "I'll do the background stuff, Jake. You look at the phone records."

"Roger that."

You guys have anything else we need to discuss?" Dantzler asked Eric and Jake. Head shakes from both men. "Okay, then let's go catch a five-time murderer."

*****

Josh Kurtz showed up accompanied by his wife Hannah. Josh stood about six-two, an inch or so shorter than Dantzler. He was dressed casually in Levis, black T-shirt and loafers. At first glance Dantzler thought the guy looked like a refugee from some old '60s rock band. It was a look that hadn't happened by accident; he'd probably spent a good deal of time creating this image. Hannah's attire also had that I'm-trying-to-look-young-and-cool thing going for it, with washed-out jeans, blue denim shirt and sneakers, but she couldn't quite pull it off. Slumming just didn't work for her, regardless of how much effort she put into it. Dantzler figured those jeans probably set her back a couple hundred bucks, and there was no telling how much the sneakers cost. She had blond hair, wore little noticeable make-up and, save for a Star of David medallion dangling on a gold chain around her neck, no jewelry. An attractive, classy lady, Dantzler decided.

"Would either of you care for something to drink?" Dantzler asked, after ushering them into the War Room. "Coffee, water, a soft drink?"

Josh looked at his wife, who shook her head. "No, thanks," he said. "We're good."

"First, let me say how sorry I am for what happened to your father. I didn't know him personally, but I have testified at several trials he presided over, so I had some contact with him. I can tell you that he was highly regarded and well-respected within this community. And I can promise you that we will bring to justice the person or persons responsible for his death. You have my word on that."

"Thank you for those kind words, Detective," Josh said. "And I'm certain you will do what it takes to find his murderer."

"Were you and your father close?" Dantzler asked.

"Yes. Very much so."

"What do you do for a living?"

"I'm an attorney. Hannah and I are both attorneys. Corporate law. We each have several big clients that we represent exclusively."

"In Louisville, correct?"

"Our office is in Louisville, and we do have several clients there, but we also have clients in other locations."

"Any clients in Lexington?"

"Not at the present time, no."

"When was the last time you saw or spoke to your father?"

"Well, I speak with my father almost every day. The last time was Saturday morning, a little before noon. The last time I—we—saw him was, let me think, about two weeks ago. Isn't that right, Hannah?"

"Yes. We came to Lexington on Sunday and had dinner with him at The Chop House."

"The Judge is a widower, correct?" Dantzler said.

Josh nodded. "Yes. My mother passed away nine years ago."

"I understand you have a brother. Andy. "

"Yes."

"Are you close?"

"We have the same father, Detective. Does that answer your question?"

"Where does Andy live, and is he aware of the situation?"

"Andy calls Louisville his home, but in reality he's something of a nomad. And yes, he has been made aware of what happened. Whether or not he shows up for the funeral is anyone's guess."

"What does your brother do for a living, Josh?"

"Great question, Detective. The honest answer is I don't have a clue. Andy is ten times more intelligent and more talented than my father or me, yet he has nothing to show for it. If you want an example of a wasted life, look no farther than my brother."

"Is he older or younger than you?"

"Younger by three years."

"What was his relationship with your father?"

Josh shrugged, said, "Dad tried to get along with Andy, to accommodate him, but . . . he never really succeeded. He loved Andy, wanted the best for him, gave him money—I gave him money—but getting close to him, reaching him, was impossible. I'm convinced that my father's heart troubles can be directly traced to his concern for Andy."

"The money you and your father gave to Andy . . . any idea why he needed it?"

"My brother isn't a drug user, but he does drink quite a bit. The hard stuff. I'm sure some of the money was spent on alcohol. However, I suspect that much of it was used to gamble and/or to pay off gambling debts."

"Do you have a number where I can reach Andy?" Dantzler said. "I do need to speak with him."

"He rarely answers his calls. Probably because he fears it will be someone calling about a gambling debt. But there is a woman he lives with off and on who will answer his phone. Her name is Tricia. She seems like a pretty decent woman. She'll make sure he contacts you. If he does surprise us by attending our father's funeral, I will personally see to it that he gets with you."

"Thanks." Dantzler flipped the page in his notepad. "Let's stick with the subject of gambling. What can you tell me about your father's poker game?"

"It was like a religious ceremony to him. He loved it, couldn't wait for Saturday to roll around. You know, that game was played fifty times a year. There were two weeks each summer when the game wasn't played. I think my father was bored stiff during that time."

"Were there different players each week?"

"No. There was a set group. And getting into the group wasn't easy. When a player died, or became too old to participate, the remaining members nominated and voted on a replacement. According to what my father told me, it could be a fairly lengthy process."

"Were there always six members in the group?"

"Yes."

"Did you know any of them?"

"No. My father never mentioned their names."

"Are you aware that there were only five victims?"

"Yes. And that can only mean one of two things: Either the person was ill and couldn't attend, or didn't have the money to play that night. You see, Detective, each player had to put ten-thousand dollars on the table prior to the first hand being dealt. I'm sure the person or persons who committed this horrible crime were aware of how much money was on hand."

"The money wasn't taken."

"You're kidding." Josh looked at his wife, then back at Dantzler. "I can't believe that. Why else would they do it if not for the money?"

"That's one of the two key questions we need to answer. That . . . and the name of the man who wasn't at the table that night."

"Are you positive the missing player was a man?" Josh asked.

The question startled Dantzler. "I was under the impression that it was a male-only game. Are you saying women were involved?"

"All I can say for sure is that my father once told me he was thinking of possibly opening up the game to women."

"Did he give you any names?"

"No."

Dantzler scribbled something in his notepad before continuing. "Your father was Jewish. Any anti-Semitic threats he may have told you about?"

"No."

"Your father was a judge, and while I'm sure judges make a good living, I wouldn't think they made enough to participate in a ten-thousand dollar a week poker game. How did he manage that?"

"My father got his money the old-fashion way—he inherited it. His father was an extremely wealthy man, like, a multi-multi-millionaire. The family had money going back decades. My mother's family was also quite well off. While we didn't live an opulent lifestyle by any means, money was never an issue in our family."

"One of the items we found in your father's office was a zip drive with a copy of his will on it. Did you know your father had a will?"

"Sure. I have a copy of it in my office."

"Then you know that you and your brother are about to become very rich men?"

"Where are you going with this, Detective? Are you insinuating that my brother and I had our father killed so we could collect an inheritance that we would eventually get anyway, when he passed away of natural causes? That's a stretch, wouldn't you agree?"

"People have been murdered for much less money than you and your brother stand to inherit."

"Detective Dantzler, I did not murder my own father. I loved the man more than you could ever imagine. Knowing I will never see him again, never hear his voice again, fills me with a sadness I never thought possible."

"Do you think Andy feels the same sense of loss? The same level of grief?"

"I can't speak for my brother, Detective. But like I've already indicated to you, his relationship with our father was somewhat complicated. But . . . the idea that Andy murdered our father is simply ludicrous."

"The money he's going to inherit will certainly pay off a lot of gambling debts."

"Don't head in that direction, Detective, it would only be a waste of time. My father gave Andy untold thousands of dollars over the years. Andy knew that all he had to do was ask and father would help out. Andy didn't need to kill him."

"I will still need to speak with him, so if you do see him, make sure he gets in touch with me."

"Is there anything else you need from us, Detective?" Josh said, taking his wife's hand. "If not, we need to start making funeral arrangements."

"No, you've been a big help." Dantzler took out a card and handed it to Josh. "If you think of anything you deem important, you can contact me at either of those numbers. And once again, I am very sorry for your loss."

After escorting Josh and Hannah Kurtz out of the building, Dantzler went back up the stairs and knocked on Captain Bird's door. Bird was sitting at his desk, pencil in hand, hard at work on the crossword puzzle.

"Israel's first king?" Bird asked, looking up. "Four letters. Thought it was David, but unless the Israelites called him Dave, that ain't right."

"Saul."

"Yeah, that works." Bird wrote down the letters. "What's your take on the Kurtz couple?"

Dantzler shrugged. "Sad. Genuinely grieving."

"Learn anything worthwhile?"

"I'm not sure."

CHAPTER SIX

Arnie Edwards was sitting at his desk eating a hot dog when Dantzler showed up. Having witnessed more than his share of autopsies, Dantzler couldn't imagine how anyone could partake of food in the very place where desecration of the human body was conducted. He hated everything about this room, most of all the smell. It was a place he never would get used to, regardless of how many times he was here. How Arnie—or anyone for that matter—could carve up a human body one minute then put away a hot dog a few minutes later was something Dantzler simply couldn't comprehend. An autopsy room should not be used as an eating joint.

"Detective Dantzler," Arnie said, wiping a smudge of mustard from his face, "why am I not surprised to see you here? To be honest, I thought you would've been here sooner. With what's happened, I'm sure you are looking for helpful details. Unfortunately, I don't have much to offer."

"Okay, then tell me what you *do* have."

"Five deceased males, all victims of a close-contact gunshot to the back of the head. Killer used a forty-five caliber pistol. That's the full extent of my knowledge thus far."

"What about drugs or alcohol?"

"Full tox results won't be ready for a week or so, but the preliminary results show no signs of illegal drugs and no substantial amounts of alcohol. I would say, booze-wise, it's about what you'd expect from men playing poker. All were slightly above the legal limit. However, that doesn't necessarily mean they were inebriated."

"Nothing interesting, is that what you're telling me?"

"Well, not quite. One victim," Arnie checked his notes, "Banks. Yeah, Carl Banks. Seems he had more than a small trace of sildenafil citrate in his system."

"What the hell is that?" Dantzler asked.

"Viagra. Apparently, the late Mr. Banks was raising the dead for someone. And I'm fairly certain that someone wasn't Mrs. Banks."

"Why do you say that?"

"She's confined to a wheelchair, the result of a massive stroke suffered several years ago. No way that poor woman is having sexual relations with anyone."

"When did you meet her?"

"When she came in to ID her husband's body."

"So Carl was having his fun elsewhere?"

"Would certainly seem that way. At his age—seventy-one—the hydraulics didn't work like they once did. So he used the little blue pill to achieve liftoff."

"The question is, did he have a mistress, or did he meet with hookers?"

"That's two questions, Detective Dantzler. And sadly, I can't answer either one."

"Well, let me tell you something, Arnie." Dantzler headed for the door. "It's a pair of questions that need to be answered."

*****

Richard Chambers had his main office in a large brick building he owned on Executive Drive, which was located off Winchester Road. That's where Eric and Jake found him. They had been informed by Mrs. Chambers that Richard had gone to the office for the purpose of catching up on projects that had been neglected because of the trial. She said her husband would likely be in his office until nine or ten o'clock that evening.

Chambers was standing next to his desk when Eric and Jake walked in. He was holding a large glass in one hand and a bottle of Maker's Mark in the other hand. After filling the glass, he placed the bottle of bourbon back on the desk.

"Care for a snort, fellas?" he asked, holding up the glass. "Might knock that serious look off your faces."

"Thanks, but we'll pass," Eric answered. "We didn't come here to drink."

"No, I don't suppose you did. Not after the slaughter at the judge's house."

"That's what we want to talk to you about."

Chambers sat in the chair behind his desk. "I was wondering how long it would take before you guys showed up. I'd say you're right on schedule." He cut his eyes up to Jake. "I recognize you from somewhere, don't I? Let me think. Aren't you the big war hero? Won a bunch of medals, got wounded? Had a big story written about you in the paper? That's you, right?"

"That's definitely *not* what we're here to talk about," Jake said, leaning against the wall.

"Did you kill any of those crazy towel heads?" Chambers asked. "I sure hope you did. Far as I'm concerned, all those desert tribes should be wiped out. Drop a couple of the big ones on them, that's what I say. Turn that sand into an ocean of blood. Then we can go in and take over the oil production. Make every country around the world depend on us for that black gold. That would be my strategy."

"How about we stay on point here and discuss the incident that took place in Judge Kurtz's house?" Eric said.

"And what about your tribe, Detective?" Chambers said, shifting his attention to Eric. "The *African*-Americans? Want to know what I think about them?"

"No doubt, you'd have us all go back to Africa so you could drop one of the 'big ones' on us," Eric answered. "That sound about right?"

"No, no, no, Detective, I have nothing against black folks. I just wish they'd work a little more and not always have their hand out waiting for government assistance. I mean, look at you. You made it, you're successful. That's a credit to you. My question is why can't more of your brothers and sisters rise to your level? The answer is they don't want to. And why should they when they know the government is going to take care of them? They're just riding the big gravy train as far as it will go."

Eric glanced at Jake, smiled and looked back at Chambers. "You're one racist prick, you know that?"

"Don't kid yourself, Detective, we're all racist. It's as much a part of our DNA as the color of our eyes, or how tall we are. If you believe otherwise you're just fooling yourself. Like all those bleeding-heart liberals who think they have answers for everything. Hell, most of them are just educated idiots. If an all-out war between whites and blacks breaks out, which side will you fight for? Blacks, of course. And I will be on the other side aiming a rifle right at your heart. Everyone will fight for his or her own race. That's the natural law of the jungle. A lion and a tiger will never fight on the same side. If they cross paths it'll be a fight to the death. The human animal is no different, trust me."

"Fortunately, the majority of human animals don't think the way you do," Eric said. "Most of us are far more enlightened than a Neanderthal like you."

Chambers laughed and took a big drink. "Relax, Detective. I would never drop the big one on your race. Hell, if I did there would be no more NBA or NFL, and I can't live without my hoops and my football. So, your people are safe."

"That's comforting," Eric said. "Now if you don't mind moving away from your bigoted views on race relations, we'd like to ask you about your whereabouts on Saturday night and early Sunday morning."

"I was at home," Chambers replied, after taking a drink of bourbon. "We had a few guests over for dinner and cocktails. I will be more than happy to provide their names if you need them."

"How long did this get-together last?" Jake asked.

"Until about two, I would say. My wife and I were in bed by two-fifteen."

"Was your daughter at this gathering?" Eric said.

"She was."

"Did she go to bed at the same time you and your wife did?"

"No. She told me the next morning that she went to bed around four."

"Two hours after you and your wife, right?"

"Damn, you're good at math, Detective. Yes, that's two hours. But in case you are harboring the notion that she snuck out of the house and killed five men, you can forget it. When I got up at a little past three to take a leak, I could hear her talking on the phone. She was most definitely in the house when those men were killed."

"Who was she talking to at three in the morning?" Jake said.

"I couldn't say. You would have to ask her."

"When did you learn that Judge Kurtz had been murdered?"

"Around noon on Sunday."

"How did you hear about it?"

"From a newspaper reporter. He called wanting to know if I felt the trial would continue. I told him I had no clue what would transpire, but I didn't see how it could go on without the trial judge."

"I can't imagine that you were too disappointed to learn that Judge Kurtz was dead."

"Why would you say that, Detective? Truth is I was disappointed. Now, because of what happened to Judge Kurtz, we have to suffer through a new trial. That's time-consuming and very expensive. Morgan is innocent, and had the trial continued she would have been acquitted."

"You sure about that?"

"Yep. She killed her abuser, a wife-beater. What she did was absolutely justified."

"Do you own any guns?" Eric said.

"What are you looking for, Detective? Rifle, shotgun, pistol . . . I have just about anything your heart desires."

"Well, Mr. Chambers, what about a forty-five?"

"Sorry, Detective, can't help you. I've got a twenty-two, a thirty-eight and a three-fifty-seven Magnum. Can't say I ever owned a forty-five."

"Were you familiar with any of the other four victims?"

"Carl Banks and Dustin Ridley. Neither one was what I would call a friend, but I did know them."

"How?"

"Carl was the best architect in this area at one point. In fact, he designed this building. So I knew him through work. With Dustin it's kind of a reverse situation. My construction company did some remodeling work for a couple of his McDonald's franchises. But like I said, neither one was a close friend."

"Didn't know Dawkins or Hassaine?" Jake asked.

"Nope."

"A Negro and a Muslim," Eric pointed out. "Why am I not surprised?"

"See that door, Detective?" Chambers pointed across the room. "Take your sarcasm and your war-hero partner and vamoose. I've already spent far too much time with you two asswipes. If you want to speak with me in the future, contact my attorney. Same goes for Morgan. No attorney present, no questioning. Got it?"

"You may as well go ahead and provide us with your attorney's name and number," Eric said, as he opened the door. "Because you can damn sure count on us questioning your daughter."

"Get out of here," Chambers barked.

Offering his best angelic smile, Jake said, "You have a pleasant rest of the evening, Mr. Chambers."

*****

"Okay, guys, what have you got for me?" Dantzler asked Eric and Jake. The trio was sitting in the lounge area of the Tennis Center. "Begin with Richard Chambers. How did that go?"

Eric answered quickly. "He's a racist and an arrogant jerk, but he has a solid alibi for the night of the murders. That doesn't mean he didn't farm it out to a hired gun, which I could see him doing. But he didn't pull the trigger."

"What's his alibi?"

"A get-together at his house that lasted until around two in the morning. We spoke with three of the people there, and they verified that Chambers was present and never left the house."

"Was Morgan there?"

"Yes. And here's where we run into something interesting. According to Chambers, when he went to the bathroom at three o'clock, he heard Morgan talking on the phone. He had no idea who she was talking to."

"Okay, that's good to know," Dantzler said. To Jake: "How about you? Get anything from the phone records for the five victims?"

Jake shrugged. "Won't have them until sometime tomorrow. There was a glitch, and it's taking longer than we thought."

"Push hard to get them sooner rather than later. That's probably our best bet for finding a link among any of these five guys. Also, we might learn the name of that sixth player. And while you're at it, dump phone records for Morgan Ballard and Richard Chambers. I would like to know who Morgan was chatting with at three in the morning."

Turning to Eric, he said, "Tell me what you know about Hassaine, Banks, Dawkins and Ridley."

"Ridley was the only one still actively working," Eric answered, after thumbing through his notes. "He owns five McDonald's franchises: three in Lexington, one in Georgetown and one in Richmond. The three older men were all retired. Hassaine taught Philosophy at the University of Kentucky, Banks was an architect—he also owned a lot of rental property—and Dawkins was a thirty-year military man. He was in the army, retired as a master sergeant. Banks, Dawkins and Hassaine were married, Ridley was single. None of the four had any criminal record, not even a speeding ticket. All in all, a squeaky-clean group."

"Squeaky-clean guys don't normally get gunned down in cold blood," Dantzler said.

"*Executed* in cold blood," Jake corrected.

"Something's bothering you, isn't it, Jack?" Eric asked.

After taking a sip of Pepsi, Dantzler nodded, said, "The money. With the exception of Judge Kurtz, who inherited a fortune, where did an architect, a college professor and a retired military guy come up with enough money to support participation in a ten-thousand-dollar-a-week poker game? That game was played fifty weeks each year, which computes to half-a-million bucks per man. That's serious money. Same goes for Ridley. Okay, he owns five McDonald's franchises. He'll make good money, sure, but not *serious* money."

"If Banks owned rental property that could translate into big money," Jake noted.

"It would have to be a lot of rental property," Dantzler replied, shaking his head.

"They were old guys, they worked hard all their life, they were frugal," Eric said. "They saved, or they invested wisely. That would account for a nice bankroll."

"Eric, I make about the same amount of money as a college professor. I also make decent money from the Tennis Center and from giving the occasional tennis lesson. And I consider myself to be a fairly frugal guy. But there is no way I could afford to play poker for ten grand a week fifty times each year."

Eric looked at Jake, said, "Well, he's honest about being frugal. He never picks up the check."

"Yeah, I've noticed that."

"We need to really take a close look at their finances," Dantzler continued, ignoring the dig. "Finances and phone records are critical areas at this stage."

"And identifying that sixth player," Eric added.

"Yeah, getting that name would definitely be a step in the right direction."

CHAPTER SEVEN

His eyes moved quickly, constantly scanning left to right, then right to left, over and over, always on the lookout for danger. In the past he had often heard it said that he had "shifty" eyes, whatever the hell that meant. Didn't really matter to him, because it was an inaccurate description. He had observant eyes.

And that's what he was doing now, sitting at a rear table in a dinky little pizza parlor located in a crappy run-down strip mall. His eyes danced around the small room, closely checking out each of the customers seated at the tables in front of him, constantly wondering which one might be trouble in disguise.

Could it be the heavy-set man two tables away, the one who had tucked his tie inside his shirt to protect it from his meatball sub? He looked like a banker or a real estate agent—one of those cushy jobs—but who could ever really be sure? Who can afford to take chances? The man might be a professional killer. Hell, killers come in all shapes and sizes.

Never take anything—or anyone—for granted. That was his motto.

Or what about the woman seated next to the front window? Was she worthy of his wariness? There's no rule that says a female who looks like a typical grandmother can't be a cold-blooded murderer. Same goes for the young couple who just walked in. Assassins can work as a team, one serving as the shooter, the partner serving as spotter. And just because they're young and look like college kids doesn't mean they aren't worth observing.

Everyone is a potential threat, and if you fail to recognize the one coming for you, then you are asking for a one-way ticket to the bone orchard.

Sitting there, sipping a Sprite, he couldn't help but wonder if any of the others were observing him the way he was eyeing them. Probably not; they were too busy stuffing their faces with all that nasty-looking food served by this pitiful joint. He wouldn't eat that crap if they paid him.

But what if one of these local yokels, say, the heavy-set man, was eyeing him with the same intensity, the same wariness? What would the heavy-set man be thinking? What would be his assessment? Would he suspect potential danger?

No, he wouldn't. He would see a small man in his late thirties, neatly dressed, quietly sipping a Sprite and minding his own business. Yes, he might notice the man's eyes, which were constantly in motion, or the fact that he has very fair skin, but other than that, nothing of consequence. Just another customer who dropped in for something to drink.

In short, harmless.

The man smiled at the notion that someone would assess him as harmless. He was anything but harmless, and if the heavy-set man was truly observant he'd realize that in about two seconds. Because a really observant individual would notice the bulge just above the right ankle and recognize it as a holstered pistol. The heavy-set man would instinctively know that he was looking at a dangerous person. Most likely, his initial thought would be that this dangerous man was a member of law enforcement, probably an undercover narcotics officer. Given that the heavy-set man lived in a safe world, it's doubtful that his thoughts would drift in the direction of hired killer. In his world, that shit only existed in the movies and on TV.

But the man with the watchful eyes knew better. That shit existed in the real world. He knew, because he was a hired killer.

When the waitress noticed his empty glass, she asked if he wanted a refill. He really didn't, but he said yes anyway. She took his glass, went behind the counter, filled the glass with ice and Sprite, and then brought it back to his table.

He watched her every step of the way. She was beautiful

and sexy, and she had a great smile, but . . . who knows? She might be the one paid to put a bullet in the back of his head.

"Would you care for something to eat?" she queried, setting the glass on the table. "Our food is really terrific, especially our sub sandwiches. If you're interested I'll fetch you a menu."

"No, I'm fine," he answered, keeping his eyes on hers. Most people watch the hands when looking for the first sign of imminent danger. Not him; he always watched the eyes. They will invariably give the signal that your opponent is ready to strike.

"Well, if you change your mind let me know," she said, walking away.

He hadn't come to eat, and even if he had been starving to death he certainly would have never eaten in this crummy dump. His purpose for being here was to meet someone—though he didn't know who—and receive a considerable sum of money. The meeting had been set for noon, which was thirty minutes ago. He didn't like waiting—more specifically, he didn't like being stationary for any length of time—and he didn't like being stood up. When a meeting is set be on time. Being tardy is unprofessional and disrespectful.

At twelve-forty a very tall, very skinny young man barely out of his teens came in and began searching the room, his eyes finally landing on the man. He smiled, nodded and began walking toward the back table. The man's right hand instinctively grabbed the handle of his pistol.

"Are you Max?" the young man inquired, taking a thick envelope from each hip pocket of his Levis. "If you are I'm supposed to give these to you."

The man's name wasn't really Max, but that's the one he had given. "What makes you think I'm Max?" he asked. "Could be that guy over there."

The kid looked at the heavy-set man, shook his head and said, "Nah, he don't fit the description I was given. You do."

"What description?"

"Well, you know, thin, wiry, light-brown hair, very alert eyes. You, you're Max, am I right?"

"Yeah, kid, I'm Max. You should be a detective."

"Nah. You gotta go to school for that, and I ain't much for the education thing," the kid said, handing over the two envelopes. "Book learning ain't exactly my forte."

"Good word, forte. And used properly."

"Ah, hell, I've heard others say it. Probably on TV. Ain't got a clue what it actually means."

"What's your name?"

"Gary Brown," the kid told him, "although everyone calls me Stick, 'cause I'm so tall."

"You live around here?"

"Yeah, me and my girlfriend live in a duplex on Lansdowne. Directly across the street from the post office."

The man held up the envelopes, said, "Thanks for bringing these to me, Stick. You can go now."

"No prob, man. Take care, Max."

The man left one envelope on the table, lowered the second one under the table and opened it. Inside was twenty-five grand, all in hundred-dollar bills. He did the same with the second envelope, which contained the same amount of money. Fifty grand in all. Not a bad haul, but still a long way from what he would eventually rake in. He was thinking more along the lines of half-a-million, which was, of course, an amount those doing the paying would never agree to pay. But they would, because failure to pay left them with two choices, neither of which is particularly pleasant.

Prison or death.

Present people those two options and they'll always pay up.

But what the man didn't know was the identity of the person doing the paying. Whoever it was had been cautious and professional, and that impressed the man. No doubt he had been contacted by an intermediary and not by the person calling the shots. That person was creating layers separating him from past or future crimes. Smart.

What this meant was that he had some work to do if he was going to remove those layers. Doing so was the only way to uncover the identity of the person at the top of this pyramid. It wouldn't be easy, but that didn't matter. For the kind of payoff he envisioned, any amount of effort was worth it.

And he knew right where to begin looking.

*****

Dantzler took out his cell phone, punched in a number and waited. The call was answered after the first ring.

"Detective Dantzler," Arnie Edwards said. "I hope the purpose of your call isn't to acquire new information, because, sadly, I still don't have anything new to tell you."

"No, that's not the reason for calling. I need a name, if you have it."

"Fire away and I'll tell you yes or no."

"When Carl Banks's wife showed up to ID her husband's body, did she come by herself?"

"Oh, heavens no. The poor lady is in no shape to drive a vehicle. She was accompanied by a woman, who, if I recall correctly, was a niece. Or perhaps a cousin. I got the impression she was related to Mrs. Banks."

"Do you happen to have the woman's name?"

"I think so. Hold on for a sec and let me check my notes. Yep, got it right here. Her name is Rosemary Belcher."

"What about a phone number?"

"For her or for Mrs. Banks?"

"Rosemary. I need to ask some delicate questions, and I'd rather go around Mrs. Banks, if possible."

"Who might be the beneficiary of the Viagra Carl Banks was taking, right?" Arnie asked.

"You got it, Doc. I may end up having no alternative but to ask Mrs. Banks about it, though I'd prefer not to."

"Well, you came to the right place, Detective. I have Rosemary's number right here."

Dantzler jotted down the information, thanked Arnie and ended the call. He then punched in Rosemary's number, which went straight to voice mail. Deciding against leaving a message, he closed the phone, stood and left the office.

*****

Grace West was surprised to get a call from Morgan Ballard, and even more surprised when Morgan asked if they could get together for drinks. She had become convinced that she would never hear from Morgan again, that it would be Richard Chambers calling to say her services as defense attorney were no longer needed. That call would have come as no surprise. This one did, and it caused Grace to wonder just what in the hell was up.

During the pre-trial work, and throughout the trial itself, Grace had hit it off well with Morgan. Under a different set of circumstances, Grace could envision the two women becoming good friends. True, they came from very different backgrounds, and lived different lives, but there were enough similarities in taste, style and attitude to overcome those differences. Still, Grace knew, there was a huge roadblock that would hinder friendship, both physically and emotionally, and that was the presence of Richard Chambers.

The man was an asshole personified, a bully and, though he would never admit it, a woman-hater. He was one of those men who didn't want women to succeed, especially in any business where men have traditionally ruled. Yes, his love for Morgan was unequivocal, yet he kept her under his thumb like she was still a little girl. Morgan Ballard was a bird who would never be allowed to spread her wings and fly. Not as long as Richard Chambers was still alive.

Thinking about it now, Grace had to admit to herself that perhaps her feelings for Morgan were based on sympathy more than anything else. If so, then there was no reason to accept Morgan's invitation to meet. Sympathy was not a sound basis for friendship.

But Grace did accept the invitation, and after closing her phone and tossing it on the bed, she wasn't sure why she had.

*****

Eric sat on a comfortable couch waiting to speak with Sahid Hassaine's widow. Her name was Amelie, and based on her looks and accent Eric quickly decided that she probably wasn't a native of the Middle East. France was Eric's first choice, a guess that turned out to be accurate.

"Sahid and I met in Paris, which is where I'm from," Amelie said, her voice barely above a whisper. "That was in nineteen-ninety. We fell in love immediately."

"Pardon me for asking, but . . ."

"Yes, there is an age difference," she offered. "That is what you were going to inquire about, wasn't it?"

Eric nodded.

"He was forty-two when we met, I was nineteen," Amelie continued. "So if you do the math, it comes to twenty-three years. Age difference is much more of an issue in the States than in many other countries around the world. It never presented a problem for us."

"Any children?"

"No."

"Your husband was a Muslim, correct?"

"Yes."

"And you?"

"Catholic. But religion was never a problem for us."

"He taught Philosophy at UK. Are you also a teacher?"

Amelie shook her head. "I'm a pediatrician. I work at the UK hospital."

"Mrs. Hassaine, I need to ask some very sensitive questions. I apologize in advance, but it pertains to information that might help us find the person or persons who committed this crime."

"Ask me anything, Detective. I have nothing to hide."

"According to tax records, your husband's income from his pension and retirement added up to just over eighty-thousand dollars last year, correct?"

"Yes."

"What did you make last year? Approximately?"

"Somewhere in the neighborhood of two-hundred-thousand. Why are you interested in our finances?"

"Did either you or your husband inherit money?"

She snickered. "No, Detective, we were both very poor

growing up. Neither of our families had any money."

Eric said, "I'm sure you knew about the Saturday night poker game your husband was involved in, right?"

"Of course. He had been in that group for more than twenty years. Playing poker with those men was one of the great joys in his life."

"Mrs. Hassaine, were you aware that each of those men, prior to the first card being dealt, had to show that he had ten-thousand dollars in cash? Ten grand, fifty weeks each year, comes to a total of half-a-million bucks. That's a lot of money."

"I do not believe that," Amelie said, shaking her head. "Sahid did not have that kind of money. *We* didn't have that kind of money. Ten-thousand dollars a week . . . that's, that's preposterous."

"I'm afraid not, ma'am. That was one of the hard rules. No ten grand, no seat at the table."

"You have to be mistaken," she insisted.

"Did you and your husband have a joint bank account?"

"Yes, we did. At Central Bank."

"Is there any chance that he had a separate account somewhere that you aren't aware of?"

"I've seen no evidence to indicate that he did. And we didn't keep secrets from each other. We had an open, honest marriage."

"And yet you didn't know about the ten grand required to participate in that poker game fifty weeks a year."

"That absolutely cannot be true, Detective Gamble. Sahid did not have that kind of money."

"Did he have any outside income at all?"

"No."

"No tutoring, no writing, no lecturing?"

"No, nothing."

"Did you happen to see the names of those men who were with your husband that night?"

"I did, yes."

"Did you know any of them?"

"No, although I had heard of Judge Kurtz."

"Had you ever met him?"

"No."

"One final question, Mrs. Hassaine. Normally, there were six players at the table. But as you know, there were only five victims. Do you by any chance know who that missing person might be?"

"I have no idea," Amelie said. "But whoever he is, he's alive. And that means he's a lot better off than my husband."

CHAPTER EIGHT

"That's a Purple Heart," Millie Dawkins said, handing the framed medal to Eric. "My husband was wounded while serving in Vietnam. Took a bullet to his chest. Missed his heart and his spine by inches. That happened during his second tour, back in nineteen-seventy."

Taking the medal back from Eric, she asked, "Have you ever seen one of these before?"

Eric nodded, said, "One of my fellow detectives was wounded twice in Afghanistan. He showed me his medals."

"Did you serve in the military, Detective?"

"No, ma'am. High school, college, then the police department."

"In much the same way you're doing what my husband did in the military—keeping the peace by fighting the bad guys," Millie said. "But the military isn't for everyone. You do get to travel, see some of the world, but it can be a difficult life for those who are serving, and for their families."

"Other than being in Vietnam, was your husband ever stationed overseas?"

"We lived in Germany for four years. Loved the country, the people not so much. Here, let's have a seat," Millie said, heading toward the living room. "These feet and legs aren't as sturdy as they once were."

Millie Dawkins was a small woman with skin much darker than Eric's, and a tender, gentle smile that somehow failed to hide her hauntingly sad eyes. She appeared to Eric as a woman who was hurting, and would be for a long time. And for good reason.

After waiting until Millie sat on a recliner, Eric took a seat on the couch across from her and opened his notepad. "I'm terribly sorry for your loss, Mrs. Dawkins. But I give you my word that we are doing everything possible to find the person or persons responsible for this crime."

"I'm sure you will, Detective. I know you have questions for me, but do you mind if I ask you one first?"

"Absolutely not. What do you want to know?"

"Was your mother a Givens by any chance?"

"No, ma'am. My mother was a Jefferson. But my grandmother was originally a Givens."

Millie smiled, said, "Beatrice, but everyone called her 'Beetle', right?"

"That's her . . . Granny Beetle."

"She and I went to high school together," Millie remembered, her thoughts going back to decades long past. "Dunbar High School—the original one, not the new one. You bear a strong resemblance to her, young man. She was a beautiful girl and you're a handsome man. I was very sad when I heard she passed."

"Thank you, ma'am."

"Now, you go ahead and ask your questions, Detective. I will tell you everything I know."

"For starters, was your husband having problems with anyone that you know of?"

"If he was he never said anything to me about it."

"No one had done anything to you that might have angered him?"

"No."

"Did he have any big debts?"

"No. We are in good shape financially."

"Your husband was a career military guy, correct?"

"Yes, the army. Joined up two days after he graduated from high school. Served thirty years."

"Retired as a sergeant major, right?"

"No, he was a master sergeant. That's a rank or two below

sergeant major.”

“Never had any desire to become an officer?”

Millie laughed, said, “Never. He considered most officers to be rockheads, especially the younger ones. No, Johnny was perfectly content being an enlisted man.”

“As I’m sure you know, your husband was involved in a regular weekly poker game. Turns out, it was a very expensive game. In fact, each player had to have ten-thousand dollars in cash before being allowed to participate.”

“So . . .?”

“Well, ma’am, that’s a lot of money. And it’s my understanding that the game was played fifty weeks each year. That adds up to five-hundred-thousand dollars per man.”

“And you’re wondering how a retired military veteran can have that kind of money, aren’t you?” Millie asked.

“It is a question we need answered.”

Millie rose from her chair, went back to the wall where the framed Purple Heart was hanging and took down the photo of a young man wearing a baseball uniform. Walking back, she handed the framed picture to Eric. “That was our son, Derek. This picture was taken when he was sixteen. Johnny was stationed in Fort Knox at the time. Derek was a standout athlete at Elizabethtown High School. Played baseball, basketball and ran track. He was . . .”

Seeing Millie’s eyes fill with tears, Eric asked, “Are you all right, ma’am?”

Millie took a tissue, dabbed her eyes and replied, “Three days after Derek graduated from high school he was killed in an automobile accident. It happened in Louisville. The driver of the other car, who was only nineteen at the time, was intoxicated and high on drugs. He ran through a red light at almost a hundred miles per hour and slammed into Derek’s car. Derek died instantly.”

“I’m very sorry.” Eric handed the photo back to Millie. “Losing a child . . . I don’t see how any parent gets over that.”

“You don’t. And contrary to what the so-called experts tell you, time doesn’t heal all wounds. That’s simply a crock of shit, pardon my French. Not a day goes by that I don’t think of Derek. And it was the same for my husband. We never really got over losing our son."

"Was the driver of the other car prosecuted?"

Millie snickered, said, "Slap on the wrists, is all. Five years' probation and community service? Would hardly call that justice, would you?"

"No, I wouldn't. How did he get off with such a light sentence?"

"The oldest reason of all—his family had plenty of money and influence. Just happened to be one of the wealthiest, most powerful families in Kentucky. I mean, the boy's father had friends in the White House. No way a man with those connections is ever going to let his son go to prison for killing a black kid."

"Did you sue?"

"Didn't have to," Millie answered, shaking her head. "They came to us, wanting to settle. Offered us five-million dollars. Our attorney advised us to reject their offer, and to let them know that we were following through with the lawsuit. Well, I suppose they feared that we'd come back and ask for the world, because they immediately upped the offer to twelve million, which we agreed to. Don't get me wrong, Detective. No amount of money could ever make up for the loss of our son. But we didn't want to go through the hassle of a big lawsuit, which, given that family's wealth and power, would have dragged on for years. It wasn't justice for Derek that much I can tell you."

She gently ran her fingers across the photo of her son, stood and carefully hung it back on the wall. "So you see, Detective," she said, sitting in the recliner, "we were very well off financially. My husband had plenty of money for poker. And from what he told me, he was normally the big winner."

Millie looked away, her eyes again filling with tears, then quietly whispered, "Until Saturday night."

*****

As she watched Morgan Ballard enter the bar and begin walking toward her, Grace West was struck by how beautiful the woman was. And how confident looking. Morgan wasn't simply walking; she was striding with confidence and authority, like she was royalty. Grace had spent countless hours with Morgan during the lead-up to the trial and during the trial itself, but that Morgan had been quiet, tentative and subservient to the point of coming off as almost mousy. The Morgan that Grace was seeing now was a different woman entirely.

"I am so pleased that you agreed to meet with me," Morgan said, sliding into the booth. "Because of the trial we never really had an opportunity to socialize, something I've wanted to do since we first met. Now we can."

"Does this mean your father has decided to replace me as your attorney?" Grace asked.

"Who know what that jackass will do," Morgan replied. "But if I have anything to say about it, you'll remain on the job."

"If your father is paying the bill, he'll make the call. And based on my gut instinct, he'll bring in someone else."

"Well, I'll fight him on it. I will insist that he keeps you on board. The jackass doesn't get to win all the time."

"Richard Chambers doesn't strike me as a man who readily accepts not getting his way. I don't see him as being a gracious loser."

"He's not gracious. He's selfish, egotistical and overbearing."

"I never expected to hear that coming from you."

"Just telling it like it is."

Grace was stunned that daddy's little girl was suddenly showing such fire and grit. This was a far cry from the meek Morgan she had been accustomed to seeing. Grace couldn't help but wonder if this was the real Morgan, or if she was acting so brave and strong simply because Richard Chambers wasn't around.

Jackass? Would Morgan dare say that to her father's face? Doubtful, regardless of how brave she was sounding right now.

"What are you drinking?" Morgan asked.

"Jameson and Diet Coke."

"Never had one. Is it any good?"

"Very good."

"Then I'll have one, too." Morgan beckoned the waitress

over. "I would like what she's having. And bring her another one as well. Thanks."

Neither woman spoke until the drinks arrived. After taking a tentative sip, Morgan commented, "Wow, this really is tasty. Has this always been your drink of choice?"

Grace's thoughts immediately flashed on Dantzler, then she smiled, shook her head and said, "Actually, a guy I just met introduced me to Jameson. I tried it and found that I liked it."

"What about the guy?" Morgan said, grinning. "Like him too?"

"He seems like an okay guy."

"Just okay? Come on, give me more than that."

"There's really not much more to give."

"That's not the vibe I'm getting," Morgan countered. "I think maybe you like him more than you're letting on. Come on, girl, fess up."

"He's practically a stranger," Grace said. "So you might want to reassess that vibe you're getting."

"What does he do for a living?"

"Homicide detective."

"No shit. That's way cool." Morgan laughed. "That means if you have sex with him, you'll be getting a dick from a dick."

"Never thought of it that way."

"That's what they call cops, isn't it? Dicks?"

"More in movies and books than in real life, I think."

"Math-wise, if you do get it on with him, would you be getting dick times two, or dick squared?"

Grace said, "I have to tell you, this is a version of you that I've never seen before. I mean, you are far bolder, more assertive and out there than the Morgan I've known for the past few months. Which one is the real you?"

Morgan laughed and took a drink. "We're all actors. The roles we play depend on the situations we're in. I'm sure the Grace West who works her magic in the courtroom is far different than the Grace West who shares a drink with a homicide detective. We play different parts for different audiences. That's how we survive."

"And the role you play for your father? Daddy's meek and precious little girl, right?"

Morgan snapped her fingers and said, "You got it. Gets me what I want, so why change?"

"So he's dear daddy when you're with him and jackass when you're not?"

"No, he's a jackass all the time. I just refrain from calling him that to his face. That wouldn't fit with my role as precious little girl, now, would it?"

"No, I don't suppose it would."

After Morgan ordered two more drinks, she said, "Just for the record, the Morgan you're seeing now is the real me. Much like you, Grace, I am a strong woman. And I have a life far removed from my father."

"What does that life entail?"

"Doing my own thing."

Nice dodge. "That's known as a non-response response. Maybe you should be a politician."

"Oh, no. I know too many of them, and they are all greedy pricks and scumbags."

"How do you know politicians?"

"My late departed husband was a bona fide prick and scumbag," Morgan said.

Another nice dodge. "What role did you play for him?"

"Not one he was ever very happy with."

Listening to *this* Morgan Ballard, Grace couldn't help but wonder if the woman was schizophrenic, or was one of those rare individuals who suffered from multiple personality disorder. With each passing minute, Grace was finding it virtually impossible to reconcile the Morgan sitting across from her now with the Morgan she had been representing for the past three months. The two versions belonged in different solar systems."

As she observed the woman sitting across for her, Grace was hit with a sudden epiphany: This Morgan Ballard was a keeper of dark secrets.

CHAPTER NINE

Rosemary Belcher agreed to meet Dantzler at the YMCA off Harrodsburg Road, saying she would be there at approximately eight p.m. She arrived two minutes past eight, dressed in gym shorts, a T-shirt and sneakers, obviously there to workout. Dantzler had told her he would be standing by the front desk, and that's where she found him.

"I apologize for being late," Rosemary said, checking her wristwatch. "I'm notoriously famous for being early, but there was a wreck on New Circle that slowed traffic to a standstill. I'm also notoriously famous for not making excuses, so I'll simply say again that I'm sorry for being late."

"Don't apologize. I've only been here a few minutes myself. And I know you told me you're crunched for time, so I'll try to keep it short." Dantzler led them into a room with a sign above the door that said Staff Only. "We can talk in here."

"There just doesn't seem to be enough time anymore," Rosemary said, taking a seat at the long table. "That's why I enjoy working out so much. Sure, it's healthy and keeps me in relatively good shape, but more importantly, it's my time. I don't have to share it with anyone else."

"What do you do for a living, Rosemary?"

"I'm a nurse, an RN. I work midnights at Baptist Health. Then for several hours during the day I help out with Norma Banks. Originally, I would stay with her a couple hours each afternoon. However, since her husband's death I've practically been a full-time caretaker. She has a neighbor who stays with her while I'm at work, but she leaves the instant I show up, which is usually around eight-thirty. So, as you can see, I don't have much time for myself."

"I'll be honest with you, Rosemary. I'm not sure I have what it takes to be a good caretaker."

"I love Norma to death, and want to do what I can to help, but, yes, it is very difficult, especially for someone who also works full-time. That's doubly true for someone who is a nurse. It's like I never get a break from working with the sick, the injured or the infirmed. Oh, well, I shouldn't be complaining. Norma has agreed to move into a nursing home. When that happens I'll probably miss spending so much time with her."

"Nursing homes can be extremely expensive. Will that be a problem for her?"

"Not at all. She is very well-off financially."

"How well did you know her husband?" Dantzler asked.

"Not as well as I know Norma. Carl wasn't around that much; he was kind of an absentee spouse. Prior to Norma suffering her stroke, I would give Carl a B as a husband. After the stroke, a D. He was good to her when he was around; it's just that more and more he was around less and less."

"Did they have any kids?"

"They didn't, but Norma did tell me that Carl's nephew lived with them for a brief period shortly after their marriage."

"Did Norma have any contact with the nephew?" Dantzler asked, scribbling in his notepad.

Rosemary shook her head. "No. And she also never talked about her first marriage."

"I wasn't aware that she had been married before."

"She lived in Nashville at the time. Norma once told me that he was several years older than she was, and that they never really got along. She indicated that he had a serious drinking problem."

"What about the ex-hubby? Did Norma have any contact with him?"

"No. I think Norma had closed the book on that chapter of her life. She only spoke to me about it on a couple of occasions, and she always made it clear that it wasn't a particularly happy time."

"You said Norma is in good shape money-wise," Dantzler said. "How do you know that?"

"Norma showed me a copy of Carl's will. She inherits his money, his rental properties, his stock certificates and several IRAs. I'm certainly no expert in such matters, but from what I could ascertain, she's worth somewhere between ten and fifteen million dollars."

"Carl was an architect, correct?"

"Not *just* an architect; he was at one time *the* architect for Central Kentucky. From what I've heard, he was the best of the best. He had his own firm, which was very successful. He sold that for a small fortune in the early nineties. Plus, he owns a lot of rental property that brings in big bucks each month. No, Detective Dantzler, money is the last thing Norma Banks has to worry about."

"Did Norma have to worry about other women? I mean, prior to suffering her stroke?"

Rosemary pondered the question for a few seconds before answering. "Yes, Detective, she did. A few months ago Norma told me that she was certain Carl was having an affair, and that over the years there had probably been many women in his life."

"Do you think that's true, or was she just being overly suspicious?"

"Well, I can't say for sure that there were a lot of women, but I do know for a fact that there was at least one. I happened to see Carl and a very beautiful, very young woman at a restaurant in Louisville. And they were being quite cozy with each other."

"When was this?"

"About ten or eleven years ago."

"Before Norma had her stroke, right?"

"Yes."

"What about more recently?" Dantzler asked. "Any hint that Carl was still playing around?"

"My goodness, Detective, the man was in his seventies. Surely, he'd slowed down by now."

"The medical examiner found Viagra in his system during the autopsy."

"How pathetic. What is it about men that they want to remain sixteen all their lives? Give it a rest, already. But given what Norma said about Carl, I'm not the least bit surprised."

"Did Norma ever mention the names of any women?"

"No."

"Can you think of anyone—any enemies—who might have wanted to murder Carl?"

"When a man chases women, especially younger ones, or those that are married, he runs the risk of pissing off boyfriends or husbands. Maybe he pissed off the wrong one."

"Maybe."

*****

Dantzler left the YMCA and drove back to his office. Arriving, he was surprised to see Eric sitting in the War Room, typing on a laptop. Dantzler grabbed a bottle of water from the refrigerator and took a chair across from Eric.

"Detective business, or are you hard at work on your next novel?" Dantzler asked. Eric's first novel, a mystery, had been published a year ago, and Dantzler knew Eric had been talking about a follow-up. "If it's your next novel you need to give me a bigger role."

"You had no role in the first one," Eric countered.

"And that's why it will never be regarded as a classic. In this one, make the lead detective a Caucasian and base him on yours truly. That way, if they make it into a movie, someone like Sean Penn or Russell Crowe can play me."

"I keep telling you, Jack, the lead character in any book I write will be black, and if they ever make one of them into a movie, it's Denzel Washington or it's nobody."

"And I keep telling you, if the money's right you'll agree to let John Goodman play the role. Besides, Denzel is getting some age on him. Who do you want if he turns you down, or if he's too old?"

"Idris Elba."

"Hey, now, there you go. He was great as Stringer Bell on *The Wire*. Good choice."

"I cannot believe that you watched *The Wire*," Eric said, shaking his head.

"Second-best TV show ever. Topped only by *The Sopranos*."

"In my book, it's a coin toss between those two." Eric turned the laptop around. "Just so you'll know, I'm not working on my next novel. I would never do that on company time. These are notes from my interviews with Mrs. Hassaine and Mrs. Dawkins. The only one I've yet to speak with is Mrs. Banks. I will try to hook up with her tomorrow."

"Don't bother; she had a stroke and is in no condition to answer questions. Anyway, I just came from speaking with Rosemary Belcher, a long-time friend who has been helping take care of Mrs. Banks for the past few years. She told me all I needed to know about Carl Banks."

"Were his pockets deep enough to handle a ten-grand-a-week poker game?" Eric asked, turning the laptop back around.

"Money wasn't a problem for Carl. Neither was adultery, apparently. Seems the man was a serial cheater. That might be an area we want to explore more fully."

"That leaves us with Dustin Ridley," Eric pointed out. "His parents are deceased, and he's an only child, so the only family member I contacted was an uncle on his father's side. He said he hadn't seen Dustin in fifteen years. Didn't even know Dustin had those five McDonald's franchises."

"The guy had to have a will, something in place to handle his estate in the event he died. A guy in his position would certainly want to have his affairs in order. No way would he be that irresponsible."

"He was only in his forties . . . maybe he still thought he would live forever."

"Surprise, surprise, Dustin." Dantzler leaned back and ran his hands through his hair. "Wait. Someone had to claim the body, right?"

"Right."

Taking out his cell phone, Dantzler said, "I'll call Arnie, find out who it was."

"Now?"

"Why not? It's only ten-fifteen. If we're working, he should be working."

"He'll love you for this," Eric said.

"Arnie, Jack Dantzler. Didn't get you out of bed, did I? Yeah, I do know what time it is. Of course I need information, Arnie. Much as I like you, I'd never call this late just to chat. What I need is this: Who came to ID or claim Dustin Ridley's body? No, I couldn't put this off until tomorrow. Wait, slow down while I get a pen. Okay, go ahead. Got it. Thanks, Arnie. Yeah, yeah, I know. I need to get a life. I'll start on that first thing in the morning."

Dantzler closed his cell phone and laid it on the table. "Suzanne Worley. She's the one who claimed Dustin's body."

"She an attorney?"

"Arnie didn't say."

"If she's not family, she'd almost have to be an attorney. Unless, of course, she was his girlfriend."

"I'll contact Sean Montgomery. If she's a local attorney he'll know her."

"You gonna call him now?"

Dantzler chuckled, said, "No, I happen to know Sean's indisposed at the present time."

"A woman, right?"

"With Sean, you can count on it."

*****

Dantzler swung by the Liquor Barn and bought a bottle of Pernod before heading home. When he arrived at his house, a red BMW with Illinois license plates was parked in his driveway. Leaning against the trunk, arms crossed, was a grinning Grace West.

Climbing out of his car, Dantzler asked, "How'd you find out where I live?"

"You're not the only good detective in Lexington." She

pointed at the bag he was holding. "What's in that? More Jameson?"

"Pernod."

"Hmm, another one I'm not familiar with. Any good?"

"Only one way to find out," Dantzler said.

"Then let's go give it the taste test."

Once they were inside, Dantzler made their drinks while Grace spent ten minutes touring the place. When she concluded her walk-through, she came back into the kitchen, immediately picked up her glass and took a sip.

"Ah, the jury is still out on this one," she said, grimacing. "I'm thinking this might be one of those drinks you have to develop a taste for. Never been a big fan of licorice."

"Leave it; I'll drink it later. Don't have any Jameson, but I do have Guinness and Smithwick's. Want one of those?"

"No, I'm gonna stick with Pernod and orange juice. I don't want to come off as a wuss."

"I don't think you have to worry about that. Come on, let's go out on the deck."

"Judging by all those trophies in your den, I think I underestimated your skill as a tennis player," Grace said, sitting in a wicker chair. "I didn't see a single trophy that had runner-up on it. They all said first place or champion."

"I knew how to pick the right opponents."

"Why are you so modest? Come right out and say it—you were damn good. Nothing wrong with bragging about your accomplishments, especially when you have the talent to back it up. I'm damn sure not reluctant to toot my own horn."

"So I've noticed."

Grace said, "It's really nice out here; quiet, peaceful. And the lake, with the moon's reflection in it, is beautiful. I could get used to hanging out here."

"I'll make you a deal, Grace. You can have an open invitation to come by here any time you want, so long as you acknowledge that you didn't beat me when I was on the witness stand."

Grace barked out a loud laugh, said, "Detective, your ship

of hope left the dock ages ago, carrying with it a final verdict that says, 'Grace one, Dantzler zero.' If they were handing out trophies, mine would say 'champion' and yours would say 'runner-up.' This would be one instance where you picked the wrong opponent."

Dantzler took a drink and grinned. "And they say I'm cocky."

"Changing the subject, Detective. What . . ."

"Don't you think you should be calling me Jack by now?"

"Okay, Jack, what is your impression of Morgan Ballard?"

"Cold-blooded killer."

"Let's agree to disagree on that, okay? I'm talking about her personality, her demeanor. How do you see her in that light?"

"Meek, spoiled to the nth degree, a classic daddy's girl. Why are you asking me? You spent hours with her. I don't even know the woman."

"Everything you said about her, being meek, spoiled, daddy's girl, well, that's a perfect description of how I viewed her. But I'm not so sure either of our assessments is accurate."

Leaning forward, interest piqued, Dantzler asked, "Why do you say that? What caused you to change your mind and see her differently?"

"Earlier this afternoon, out of the blue, I received a call from Morgan saying we should get together for a drink. We did, and it was like I was sitting with a complete stranger. I'm not exaggerating when I tell you that this Morgan was so different from the one I had come to know that I couldn't help but wonder if she was maybe suffering from multiple personality disorder. I'm telling you, Jack, the change was so startling it was almost spooky."

"Was she drunk? Or high on drugs?"

"We only had a couple of drinks," Grace said. "And she didn't give the appearance of being on drugs. She was just . . . different."

"Different in what way?"

"Bold, assertive, aggressive, fearless . . . she kept referring to her father as a jackass. The meek, mild Morgan I knew would *never* say that. She. . ."

"Look, she's acting brave because daddy's not around. That's no big deal."

"No, you weren't there, Jack. It was more than that. She was quick to talk about sex, to make off-color jokes. Said she knew a bunch of politicians, and they were all greedy pricks and scumbags. Said her late husband was a prick and a scumbag. When I pressed her for details she cleverly dodged answering. She did tell me that the Morgan I was with this evening is the real Morgan. I'm inclined to agree with her."

"So what does all this mean?"

"I don't know. All I can say is that thinking about her now causes chills to run down my spine."

Dantzler stood and took the still-full glass from her hand. Helping her out of the chair, he said, "I have the perfect antidote for those chills."

"I was hoping you would say that."

CHAPTER TEN

At a few minutes before midnight, the man known as Max knocked on the front door of a duplex across the street from the Lansdowne post office. Almost instantly an overhead light came on, and the front door opened maybe four inches, just wide enough for him to see the right side of a woman's face.

"I need to speak with Stick," Max said, smiling.

"Gary is not here right now," she answered. "He went to the store to get us some milk."

"Milk, huh? Must have a baby in there."

"No, no baby. We needed milk for cereal."

"When do you expect him back?"

"Shouldn't be too long. If you come back in an hour he'll probably be here."

Max put his shoulder against the door and nudged it open. "No, I think I'll wait for him inside." Taking her by the arm, he locked the door behind them, led her into the living room, then said, "Have a seat on the sofa. We'll wait for him together. Cozy, like old pals."

"Are you going to hurt us?"

"Wouldn't think of it, Miss . . ."

"Darlene."

"I'm not here to hurt anyone, Darlene. Just need to ask Stick a few questions, is all."

"Mind if I smoke?"

"I'd rather you wouldn't."

"Where do you know Gary from?" Darlene asked, her

voice trembling. "I know most of Gary's friends, but I've never seen you before."

"He did me a favor; I want to thank him."

"You couldn't do that tomorrow?"

"I was in the area, thought I'd go ahead and do it now." Max surveyed the room, which he judged to be a dump. "Are you Stick's wife?"

"Girlfriend. We've been together for six years."

"You love him?"

"Yes, very much."

"Does he love you?"

"Yes."

"You sure?"

"Yes, I'm sure. Gary loves me."

"Is Stick the jealous type?"

"No."

"Good." Max sat in the chair across from her, said, "Take off your shorts and your underwear, Darlene."

"What?"

"You heard me. Take off your shorts and underwear."

"I will not."

Max reached behind him, took out a pistol and waved it at Darlene. "Do what I told you," he ordered.

Darlene's eyes filled with tears. "Please, mister, don't make me do that."

Max pointed the pistol at her. "I won't ask again."

Darlene stood, unhooked the button on her shorts and slowly slid them down. "Please, mister, don't . . . ."

"You're halfway home, Darlene. Finish the job."

Sobbing, Darlene lowered her underwear and looked away.

"Nice bush," Max said. "Hard to find one of those anymore."

"Are you going to rape me?" Darlene managed to say.

"Nah, I like women with more meat on their bones than you have. You're too skinny for my taste. My advice would be for you and your boyfriend to stock up on candy and ice cream. You both could stand to put on a pound or two."

"Can I put my clothes back on?"

"Sure."

"Why do you have a gun?" Darlene asked, after sitting back on the sofa.

"Person sees a gun, arguments and debates end rather quickly. I'm not one for long conversations."

Hearing the front door rattle, Darlene jumped to her feet and started across the room. Max stepped to her left as she unlocked the door and opened it.

"Why was the door locked?" Stick inquired. "I told you I'd be back in a few minutes."

"I didn't lock it—he did."

Closing the door, Stick looked up at Max. It took a few seconds for recognition to hit. "Hey, I know you. You're the guy I met in the pizza place. Gave you a couple of envelopes. Right?"

"That's me."

"He has a gun, Gary," Darlene said. "He made me undress."

"He what?"

"He ordered me to get undressed."

Taking out the gun, Max said, "Technically, I only made you partially undress. If you're going to tell him what happened, be accurate." Max pointed the gun at the sofa. "Put the milk down, Stick, and take a seat next to Darlene."

"Why are you here?" Stick asked, after putting the milk on an end table. "And what do you want?"

"Who lives next door?"

"No one lives there now. A Mexican couple did, but they moved out last week."

"Those envelopes you gave me. Do you know what was in them?"

"No. I was ordered not to look, and I didn't."

"Describe the person who gave you the order."

"I can't. I never saw him."

"How did he contact you?"

"Called me on my cell phone."

"What did he tell you to do?"

"He told me there was a car parked at Kirklevington Park—a white Toyota Avalon—and that the envelopes would be under the driver's seat. He told me to take them to the pizza place, and then he gave me your description. And that I shouldn't check to see what was in them. That's it."

"Why did this guy pick you, and how did he get your cell phone number?"

"I ain't got a clue."

"Stick, those envelopes contained fifty-thousand dollars. It's hard to believe that this man would trust a job involving that much cash to a total stranger." Max aimed the pistol directly at Stick. "Now, the truth. You know this man, don't you?"

"Yes, I've run some errands for him in the past."

"Describe him for me."

"Tall, but not quite as tall as me. Wiry, maybe forty, kinda scary looking."

"See, honesty is always the best policy," Max said, seconds before squeezing the trigger and blowing a hole in Stick's forehead. He fired a second bullet into Darlene's face before she had time to scream. "Lights out, kids."

Driving away, Max opened his cell phone and sent a single-word text message: Done. Almost instantly, he received a single-word reply: Excellent.

Max didn't need to prod Stick to cough up the name of the man who sent the fifty grand. He already knew—it was the man who hired Max for the earlier job. They met for the first time four days ago and the meeting went well. Both men were professionals who understood that certain things had to happen if the final outcome was to be successful. Given that, Stick's death was preordained; he was a possible liability, and neither Max nor the man could afford to have any loose ends out there that might come back to hang them. The stakes were too high to take any unnecessary risks. Stick's voice had to be permanently silenced.

Max wasn't blind to the fact that he could also be viewed as a risk. After all, he was now the only person other than the man who paid the cash who knew the whole truth. Could be he was next on the hit list. That's why Max knew he had to be wary, to be constantly alert. You can't see the hit man coming if you're not on the lookout for him.

That's also why Max needed to quickly move things along. Deep in his gut he didn't think the man who paid the money had any desire to eliminate him. They seemed to hit it off well, and Max got the feeling that the man might have more work for him in the future.

But . . .

Max also had the feeling that there was someone higher up who was actually calling the shots. Or if not higher up, at the very least an equal partner.

And that's the man Max wanted to meet.

*****

Unable to sleep, his thoughts racing at warp speed, Dantzler eased out of bed, careful not to wake Grace. He slipped on a pair of jeans, went into the kitchen and opened a can of Pepsi. Grabbing a legal pad and pen from the counter, he went into his den, sat and began writing down what he knew—and what he needed to know—about the murders at the Kurtz house.

- Killer used a .45
- Multiple killers?
- Deke Ballard killed by a .45 (any connection?)
- Victim Hassaine—how could he afford game?
- Learn more about Ridley
- Who is missing player?
- Banks' lovers
- Study phone records
- Speak with Andy Kurtz
- Morgan Ballard????

Dantzler put the pen down and took another sip of Pepsi. He studied the list, and immediately judged it to be incomplete. Something crucial was missing, a key piece of the puzzle necessary for solving the crime. It was out there. He could feel it waiting to be discovered. All he had to do was find it.

"Do you ever give your mind a break?" Grace asked. She was standing in the doorway, wearing one of Dantzler's shirts. "I'm a maniac when it comes to work, but I have a feeling you're an even worse maniac than I am."

"Here's the difference, Grace. You're trying to free the bad guys, I'm trying to put them away. The terrible irony is, if you do your job well enough, you eradicate what I do. The killer I catch is then set free to kill again."

"That makes me sound like one of the bad guys. Is that how you see me?"

"Look, I know you're only doing your job. And I know every person deserves legal representation. I get all that. It's just that sometimes your job sucks, especially when you get a guilty person acquitted."

"Want me to let you in on a scoop, Jack? If I get a client acquitted, then that client isn't guilty."

Dantzler laughed. "We both know that's bullshit."

Grace stood over Dantzler's shoulder, looking down at the list he had written. "Why do you have four question marks after Morgan Ballard's name? Why would you even include her name on a list that pertains to the murders at Judge Kurtz's house? You don't suspect her of being involved in that, do you?"

"Not really, no. But I am intrigued by what you told me earlier. If what you say is true, and I don't doubt for a second that it is, then . . . I don't know. There's just something in my gut that's bothering me, something I'm remembering."

"What?"

"When Eric interviewed Morgan after she shot her husband, he said there was just something 'off' about her. He said there were times when she'd get this strange look in her eyes, like there was a second person inside her ready to break out. Eric's no psychiatrist, but he's sharp as hell. If he saw something, it was there. I should've paid more attention."

Grace said, "Based on what I saw tonight, and judging by the Morgan Ballard I was accustomed to seeing, I think the second person has been set free."

CHAPTER ELEVEN

All killers fuck up. That had been Dantzler's firm belief since his earliest days as a homicide detective. Most criminals, especially those that commit murder, don't rate high on the IQ scale. If they did they wouldn't kill in the first place. But they do kill, and always will, for reasons that date back to antiquity, with anger, greed, jealousy and hate ranking as the big four. Given the sheer stupidity of these animals, if they do manage to escape capture, it means law enforcement folks failed to do their job properly. Simple as that.

True, some crimes are more challenging than others. The toughest to solve are random killings, where there isn't—or doesn't appear to be—any connection between killer and victim. Those are the ones that keep homicide investigators up at night. If no link can be found, the odds against solving the case skyrocket.

On the surface, the murder of the five poker players appeared to be random. No connecting link could be found among the victims. Outside of the weekly game, none of them socialized together. They weren't buddies in the traditional sense. But why would a killer come in and murder five people? What was his motive? And if only one victim was the true target, which one was it? Based on occupations, Judge Kurtz was the obvious choice. Did someone he sent to prison come back to exact revenge? But if so, why murder four innocent men? Why not get the Judge alone and simply take him out?

Why, why, why?

Dantzler pondered these questions as he drove toward

town. He left the house at eight-fifteen (late for him), leaving Grace sleeping in his bed. Grace West. She triggered yet another series of questions hard at work inside his brain. Where was that going? Was it smart or dumb? Did he even want it to go anywhere? That's the question that lingered at the forefront. Was he ready for a serious relationship, or should he do what was necessary to keep things on a casual level? He and Grace certainly got along well, and bedroom activities had been exceptional, yet doubts persisted. Of course, it was also possible that all his questions were moot. Could be Grace wasn't even contemplating a relationship. Maybe she was only looking for companionship, a good time while she was in Lexington. But is that what he wanted? Or did he, somewhere deep in his heart, want something more? Those were questions only time could answer.

Ten minutes from his office, Dantzler got a call on his cell phone. It was from Bruce Rawlinson, the veteran desk sergeant. A call from Bruce this early was never a good thing.

"Got another one for you, Ace," Bruce said. "A double on Lansdowne across from the post office."

"Anyone there yet?"

"Jake."

"All right, I'm headed that way."

When Dantzler arrived at the scene, he parked in the big lot across the street. Already, a gaggle of curious onlookers had gathered on the sidewalk in front of the duplex. Dantzler worked his way through the crowd, ducked under the crime-scene tape and went inside. Arnie was examining the two victims, Jake was making a drawing of the living room, and one of the CSU guys was working on extracting a bullet from the wall behind the female victim.

"Got any IDs, Jake?"

"Gary Brown and Darlene Johnson, both twenty-three years old."

"Got a time of death?"

Dantzler's question was directed at Arnie, but Jake answered.

"There is a receipt inside the bag," Jake said, pointing at

the end table. "According to the time stamp, the milk was purchased at eleven fifty-eight last night."

"Therefore, my preliminary guess as to TOD would be between twelve-fifteen and twelve-thirty." Arnie nodded toward the male victim. "He took a bullet to the forehead, no exit wound. She was hit in the eye. As you can see, the bullet exited the back of her head and imbedded in the wall."

"It's in deep," the tech informed them, "but I should have it in a few seconds."

"Okay, let's think this through," Dantzler said. "He's wearing shoes, she's not, so we can assume he went out for the milk. He comes home and . . . what? He either lets the killer in after returning home, or the killer is already inside when Gary gets back. If he let him in, it means they probably knew each other. If the killer was already inside, then it might've been a friend, or it might not have been. Whatever, he makes them sit on the couch, then he shoots them."

"*Executes* them," Jake said. "But why?"

"Situation like this, drugs are my first thought."

"I don't think this is about drugs. I found a very small amount of pot in the bedroom, not much more than enough to roll a couple of joints. And if these two were selling drugs, then judging by the dump they're living in they would have to be the worst drug dealers in history."

"Got the bullet, Detectives," the tech announced, dropping it into an evidence bag. "Damaged pretty badly, but if I had to make a guess, I'd say it's a forty-five."

"Same caliber as the ones retrieved from the victims at the Kurtz house," Jake said.

Richard Bird came into the room, took a quick look at the two victims and turned away. Bird had always been a better administrator than a homicide detective. He had no stomach for the ugliness that went with the job.

"We now have seven bodies, Jack. I think it's time we call in reinforcements."

"Not yet, Rich."

"Why not, for Christ's sake? Don't let your pride get in the way, Jack. After this, the heat to get results is going to crank up. I'm just not convinced that you, Eric and Jake can handle this. If we bring in help it makes life easier for everyone."

"Give me a day or two, Rich. At least until we find out about the bullet used here."

"What about the bullet?"

"We think it's from a forty-five. That's the same caliber used by the killer at the Kurtz house. I have a gut feeling they are going to match."

"Jesus, Jack, that's a stretch, don't you think?"

"Maybe so, but it's intriguing."

"Want to hear something else that's intriguing?" Jake asked, coming out of the bedroom with a piece of paper in his hand. "According to this receipt, the landlord for this place was Carl Banks."

"Come on, Rich," Dantzler pleaded. "Give us some time."

Bird rubbed his eyes with his hands. "All right, Jack, even I find that intriguing. I'll give you a couple of days to see what fruit you can shake from the tree. If nothing falls I'm calling in help."

Bird left the room, was outside for only a few seconds, before stepping back inside. "There's a lady out front who says her daughter lives here," he told the detectives. "You'd better speak with her."

"Want me to?" Jake asked.

Dantzler shook his head. "No, I'll do it. You were first on the scene, Jake, so you take the lead on this one."

"Roger that."

The woman claiming to be Darlene's mother was standing in the yard next door speaking with a female officer. She wasn't crying or acting upset, but she wore a look of concern that Dantzler had seen far too often in his career. He knew that the next few minutes would be the worst in this lady's life.

"My daughter lives in that duplex," she said, as Dantzler approached. "Has something bad happened to her?"

"Miss. . .?"

"Trudy Spears. Darlene Johnson is my daughter. Is she all right?"

"Miss Spears, Darlene and Gary were attacked sometime last night or early this morning. I regret having to tell you this, but both of them are dead. I'm very sorry."

"Dead? How?"

"At the present time we're looking at it as a possible homicide."

Trudy Spears's eyes turned stone cold, her face set in a frozen mask, not a tear in sight. "Do you know who did it?" Her voice was hard as steel. "And how was it done?"

"We don't know who did it, but we'll find out. That much I can promise you."

"You didn't answer my second question, Detective. *How* was it done?"

"Gun. Miss Spears, do you know of anyone who would want to harm your daughter and Gary Brown?"

"*Harm*? You mean murder, don't you?"

"Yes. Can you think of anyone who would want to murder them?"

"No. They were just two innocent, dumb kids who were madly in love with each other."

"Were they married?"

"Might as well have been, long as they've been together. They hooked up when they were fifteen or sixteen. Talked about getting hitched, but never got around to it. Now they never will."

"Did either of them work?"

"Darlene worked for a vet on Reynolds Road. Been there for three years. Gary worked mostly odd jobs. Some construction, some roofing . . . things like that. He was really good at fixing things. If something was broke, Gary was the person who could fix it. He also made a lot of money playing pool."

"Where did he usually play?"

"Couldn't tell you."

"Were they having any money problems?"

"Look at this place, Detective," Trudy answered. "It's not exactly the Taj Mahal. Sure they struggled. But they got food stamps, and I helped out when I could, so they managed to get by."

"Where do you work, Miss Spears?"

"I tend bar at a place called The Pit Stop."

"What about drugs? Either of them big users?"

"They smoked a little pot, but, then, hell, everybody does that nowadays. But the heavy stuff? No . . . no way."

"What about Gary's parents? How well do you know them?"

"His parents are dead. He was raised by his grandmother. She passed a couple of years ago."

"Does he have any family we can contact?"

"I'm the closest thing to family Gary had. I'll be the one who sees that he and Darlene get a decent funeral."

"That can be costly. If you need financial help, there are some organizations that . . ."

"No, Detective, I'll handle it. I don't want help from anyone."

"Well, if you change your mind, let me know," Dantzler said, handing her one of his cards.

Trudy took the card and barely glanced at it. "You just find the son of a bitch who did this to my daughter. That's all I want from you."

"You have my promise."

As she turned to walk away, Dantzler saw the tears begin to run down her cheeks.

*****

After finalizing things with Jake, Dantzler got in his car and headed for the office. As soon as he entered the building, his phone buzzed. The caller was Sean Montgomery. Dantzler had phoned Sean before leaving his house, got no answer, so he left a message.

"About time you got out of bed, Sean. She must be wearing you out."

"You got it all wrong, Jack. It's the other way around."

"I doubt it."

"Well, it's in your nature to doubt everything. Calling so early must mean you want information. What can I do for you?"

"You know a lady named Suzanne Worley?"

"Yeah. Had a class with her in law school."

"So she's an attorney?"

"She passed the bar, but I don't think she's a practicing attorney. If she is, I'm not aware of it. Why are you asking about her?"

"She's the person who handled Dustin Ridley's affairs. I need to speak with her."

"Dustin Ridley was one of the five poker players who were murdered, right?"

"Right."

"Well, Jack, things are getting stranger and stranger for you," Sean said, laughing.

"Why do you say that?"

"Because Suzanne Worley is best buds with Morgan Ballard."

"That's not strange, Sean. That's very fucking interesting."

CHAPTER TWELVE

Sitting in the War Room, across the table from Eric, Dantzler shuffled through a stack of papers until he found what he was looking for. He extracted it from the stack and held it up. It was a photo of Sahid Hassaine.

"This is who we need to be looking at," Dantzler said, sliding the photo to Eric. "He's the only one of the five who, on the surface at least, doesn't appear to have the financial resources to participate in such an expensive weekly poker game."

Eric shook his head, far from convinced that Dantzler was right. "He's one of the victims, Jack. Why zero in on him?"

"Where did he come up with that kind of cash, Eric? That's what I'd like to know. What did his wife tell you—that they both grew up poor? Okay, so no big inheritance on either side of the family. And not many retired college professors I know have big-time bank accounts when they call it quits. So . . . how was he able to afford a seat at the table?"

"According to his wife, they had about sixty grand in a savings account. She also said they had a few stocks that would probably cash out at fifty grand. Plus, he did get retirement money."

"Add all that up, Eric, and he has about enough to play maybe nine times, ten tops. And that's only if he robbed those accounts, which he didn't."

"He did have an insurance policy for a million dollars, which his wife will receive."

"Now she has more money than he had. If they start up a

new game, she can play."

"I hope you aren't thinking that maybe she . . ."

"No, no way," Dantzler interrupted. "But what I do think is that Sahid Hassaine had money his wife knew nothing about. I'd like to know where the money is, and how he got it."

"I'll try to find out who his close friends were. Maybe one of them knows something." Eric slid the photo back across the table. "Any early thoughts on the two victims found this morning?"

Dantzler shrugged, said, "Not really. Too soon to say."

"But you gotta be thinking something. Carl Banks is a murder victim *and* their landlord? All seven victims killed by a forty-five? That's either seriously random, or a serious coincidence."

Dantzler went to the chalkboard and drew six circles. "We have five murder victims," he said, marking the first circle. "Then we have two murdered today, a forty-five used in both crimes, Banks as landlord to our latest victims, Suzanne Worley's connection to victim Dustin Ridley, and Suzanne's close friendship with Morgan Ballard. That's six stars floating in their own orbit. We need to bring them together, combine them into a single galaxy."

"Among all those stars, this Worley woman is the most mysterious," Eric pointed out.

Dantzler picked up his cell phone from the table and punched in a number. "Hey, I need to ask you something."

"You calling to make sure I locked up when I left?" Grace West asked. "Relax. I did."

"Not calling about that. I need some information regarding Morgan Ballard."

"Are you forgetting the rules, Jack? Even though we have shared quality sack time together, you know I cannot discuss a client with you."

"Okay, then let's forget about Morgan and talk about someone else."

"Who?"

"During the time you spent with Morgan, did you ever

meet a friend of hers named Suzanne Worley?"

"I did meet a woman named Suzanne, but I don't recall ever hearing her last name. Why are you interested in her?"

"What can you tell me about her?"

"Nothing much, really. I only saw her two or three times, but it was obvious that she and Morgan were very close. Once, when I was prepping Morgan for the trial, Suzanne showed up and said they needed to talk. Now I consider getting a client ready to take the stand to be of the utmost importance, especially one facing a possible murder conviction. But Morgan blew me off, said she needed to get with Suzanne, and that she would get back with me later on. I can't begin to tell you how pissed off I was."

"Did Morgan ever talk about Suzanne? Maybe say whether or not Suzanne was a practicing attorney?"

"She never once mentioned her to me," Grace said. "Why? Is she an attorney?"

"She passed the bar, that's all I can tell you. What was your take on Suzanne?"

"Very beautiful, very polished, elegant, confident. Lot of style, lot of class. Come to think of it, she's much like the Morgan Ballard I had a drink with last night. What does this Suzanne have to do with any of this?"

"Maybe nothing. Right now she's more of a mystery than anything. But thanks for your input, Grace. Every little bit helps."

When Dantzler closed his phone and looked up, Eric was smiling from ear to ear. "How is it that you have Grace West's number programmed into your cell phone? That was her, wasn't it?"

"Yes, Eric, it was Grace West. And so what if I have her number? It's no big deal."

"Ah, Jack, I sense that you are consorting with the enemy. That's never a smart plan."

"I'm not consorting with anyone," Dantzler protested. "She's just an acquaintance. Now, do you mind if we move on to more important matters?"

Eric nodded, the smile still firmly in place.

Dantzler said, "What about the phone records? You said

Jake pointed out something interesting."

"Jake found that Carl Banks called this number fifty-four times in the past three months. That computes to about four and a half calls per week."

"Did he find out whose number it is?"

"Cynthia Purcell."

"Jake speak with her?"

"Said he called her a couple of times and never got an answer."

"What about her address?"

"Park Plaza."

"That's right down the street." Dantzler stood and stretched. "Think I'll drop by and see if she's home."

"Want me to go with you?"

"No. See if Jake needs any help. If he doesn't, then start trying to locate some of Sahid Hassaine's friends. See if one of them can give you more info concerning his finances. I really want to know how he had enough money to play in that poker game."

"As Jake would say, 'roger that'."

"Isn't it illegal for someone who wasn't a Marine to say that?"

"How about I call Grace West and get her legal opinion on the matter?"

"How about you don't?"

Dantzler could still hear Eric cackling when he walked out of the building.

*****

If the world only had room for ten beautiful women, Cynthia Purcell would be on the list. She was tall and statuesque, with raven hair that touched her shoulders, an ample bosom, full lips, high cheekbones and a body any modeling agency would be quick to take advantage of. She had a smile that would warm the cold-hearted and entice a man of the cloth. In every respect Cynthia Purcell was a winner.

She welcomed Dantzler into her penthouse apartment as

though she had been expecting him. After closing the door, she moved with athletic grace to the expensive sofa, sat, crossed her legs at the ankles and patted the seat next to her, indicating that Dantzler should join her.

"Homicide, you say," Cynthia said, in a voice Lauren Bacall would have appreciated. "I can promise you, Detective, that I have not murdered a single individual, male or female."

"Never thought you did." Dantzler sat in the seat she had offered. "I just have a few questions for you, then I'll be on my way. You up for it?"

"You bet. I'm just relieved to be questioned by someone from Homicide and not Vice. That would've been a real bummer."

"Why would Vice want to speak with you?"

Cynthia smiled, said, "What questions do you have for me, Detective?"

Dantzler led his eyes scope out the room for several seconds before turning his attention back to Cynthia. "If you're concerned about Vice, that can only mean you're a hooker. Am I right?"

"Hooker is a cheap, vulgar word, wouldn't you agree, Detective? It creates such a negative image of scraggly women standing on dark street corners. Look around—do you see anything in this place that is even remotely cheap? You don't get luxury like this by giving blow jobs for twenty dollars a pop in the backseat of a car."

"How would you describe your occupation?"

"What about those questions you had for me, Detective?"

"Look, Cynthia, I don't give a rat's ass how you earn the money to pay for this place. I'm with Homicide, remember? Not Vice. All I ask is that you be honest and upfront with me."

"Fair enough, Detective. But a girl can never be too careful, can she? It's not above the cops to play dirty tricks."

"Like I said, Cynthia, I'm a homicide detective. You have my word on that."

"I believe you."

"Just to quell my own curiosity, how do you describe what you do?"

"Professional escort."

"Records show that Carl Banks phoned you fifty-four times in the past three months. What can you tell me about him?"

"Cunnilingus Carl?"

"Why do you call him that?"

Cynthia laughed. "Well, isn't it obvious? That was his thing. And like most men, he thought he was the absolute best at doing it. But like most men, he vastly overrated his abilities."

"Carl had Viagra in his system at the time of his death, so he was doing more than just the oral thing."

"Not with me he wasn't," Cynthia said. "He did his thing, then I would get him off by hand. We never once had intercourse."

"What did Carl pay for your services?"

"I charge five-hundred dollars an hour, Detective. Carl was normally with me for an hour, sometimes two, depending on how worked up he was."

"How often did you see him?"

"Usually twice a week. There were weeks when he came in more often, but that was rare."

"That calculates to one or two grand a week. Pretty steep price just to go down on a woman and get a hand job."

"That's what Carl wanted, and that's what he was willing to pay. Free enterprise at its best, Detective. It's the American way."

"How much did you make last year, Cynthia?"

"Why should I divulge that, Detective? How can I be sure you won't run back to the office and make a phone call to the IRS?"

"Homicide, remember?"

"Seven figures."

"Wow. Cash only, I presume."

"Absolutely. No checks or credit cards accepted here."

"Who's your pimp?"

"Please, Detective. That's an even more cheap, vulgar and vile word than hooker. I do not have a pimp."

"You don't keep it all. That's not how it works. There's got to be someone upstairs that you kick money to."

"In case you haven't noticed, Detective, I live in the penthouse. There is no upstairs. Now, aren't we getting off course here? I thought you wanted to talk about Carl Banks."

"You're an intelligent lady, Cynthia. I'll give you that."

"Thank you."

"Was Carl seeing other women?"

"I can't say for sure, but I would imagine that he was. He was a lonely guy. Sad, in a way. His wife had some health issue, so he wasn't finding much joy at home. I doubt that his hour a week with me fulfilled his needs."

"You can't be the only woman in Lexington providing these services. Got names of others that I might speak with?"

"I don't, but even if I did I wouldn't tell you."

"Sisterhood, and all that, right?"

"Something like that, yeah."

"When you were with Carl, did he ever mention having trouble with anyone? Did he talk about someone wanting to harm him?"

"At long last, Detective, you have finally asked a question related to homicide. Hallelujah. The answer is no, he never mentioned anything about his private life other than the business about his wife being unable to satisfy his needs. That's it."

Dantzler closed his notepad and put it in his coat pocket. Standing, he extended his hand, said, "Thanks for your time, Cynthia. You haven't been much help, but it has been interesting."

When they got to the door, she opened it and gave him a big smile. "Tell you what. If you ever put away that badge, come see me. I'll give you my retired detective's discount."

"Cynthia, I couldn't afford you at any price."

CHAPTER THIRTEEN

The sky was the color of burnt wood, the wind had gotten angry, and the rain was biding its time until deciding to come down, which could happen at any moment. Weather forecasters had been predicting a deluge, and for once it appeared they called it right. Lexington was about to get drenched.

So was Dantzler if he didn't hurry. Moving at a clip somewhere between a quick-walk and a jog, he made it to the building on East Main just as the first drops of rain began to fall. By the time he was inside those first drops had become a torrential downpour.

Dantzler was starved—he left his house this morning without eating breakfast—but going out now to grab a bite during this rainstorm would be an act of lunacy. Instead, he settled for a Diet Pepsi and a bag of chips purchased from the vending machine in the break room. Not exactly a nutritious meal, nor filling, but it would have to do. Sometimes pragmatism is the best route to take.

Back in his office, Dantzler phoned Sean Montgomery. Sean's secretary said he was currently with a client, but she would have him call Dantzler when the meeting had concluded. Dantzler thanked her and hung up.

He went into the War Room and began leafing through the stack of phone records Jake had assembled. He wasn't sure what he was looking for—or even *if* he was looking for anything specific—but deep in his gut he felt something of importance was in there waiting to be uncovered. Only one way to find out and that was to keep searching.

For no particular reason, he went through the pages until he found the list of calls made to and from Judge Kurtz. Although Dantzler was far from convinced that the Judge was the primary target, he was, based on his occupation, the most obvious choice. Judges make enemies, and it's not unheard of for one of those enemies to come back and exact a measure of revenge. Perhaps that's what happened in this instance.

But Dantzler was having a difficult time believing this to be the case. It simply didn't compute that a revenge-minded individual intent on killing Judge Kurtz would also take out four innocent bystanders. That made no sense. In addition to that roadblock standing in Dantzler's way, there was a second factor— a thorough review of Judge Kurtz's cases going back fifteen years failed to uncover a single individual considered to be a high-risk threat.

But . . . it was the Judge's poker game, and everything revolved around him, so he couldn't be dismissed outright as the main target.

Dantzler scooped up the stack of papers and went back to his office. Checking his watch, he wondered how much longer Sean's meeting was going to last. It had been thirty-five minutes since he spoke with Sean's secretary. Apparently her notion of soon didn't jibe with Dantzler's.

He gave some thought to phoning Grace but decided not to. With so much already on his plate, his love life was not a high priority. Calling Grace would have to wait.

His phone rang and he answered, relieved that Sean was finally getting back with him.

"Heard you called," Sean said. "What's on your mind? Suzanne Worley?"

"When you worked Vice, did you ever run across a woman named Cynthia Purcell?"

"Not that I recall. Why?"

"I just met her. She calls herself a professional escort, but you and I both know how that translates."

"High-priced call girl," Sean said. "How high-priced?"

"Five-hundred per hour."

"Well, hell, that rules both of us out as potential customers. Where does she live?"

"Penthouse in Park Plaza."

"Of course."

"Did you Vice guys ever run across any high-priced prostitutes?"

"Jesus, Jack, that was a long time ago. I only worked Vice for two years before joining the Homicide unit, so I'm not sure how much help I can be. Sure, there was no shortage of hookers, but I don't recall pinching any that charged five-hundred an hour."

"Well, Cynthia Purcell does. Said she made seven figures last year. All in cash."

Sean whistled, said, "Think she might be in the market for a husband? I could stand to marry a woman who made that kind of dough."

"But would you be willing to share her with the masses, Sean?"

"Yeah, as long as she shares her earnings with me. I'm a flexible guy."

"Here's what I think, Sean. This is much bigger than a one-woman operation. My money says Cynthia Purcell is part of a larger group."

"If you're right, that means someone is at the top, running things," Sean said. "You ask Cynthia about it?"

"Sure. But she was quick to change the subject. She's a very intelligent lady."

"You have seven homicides hanging over your ass, Jack. Why the sudden interest in something that clearly belongs to Vice? Talk to Tony Allen, let him deal with it."

"Because I have a feeling it's all tied together."

"Why would you make that connection?"

"Carl Banks was one of Cynthia Purcell's regular customers."

"That's awfully damn thin, Jack. A lot of dudes pay for sex. Just because one of your murder victims falls into that category doesn't really mean anything. There are coincidences in this life we live."

"Like I said, Sean, it's just a feeling I have. It may lead to something, it may not. But it is a path I'm going to follow."

"Check with Tony. He might be able to help."

"One last question, Sean. Any chance Suzanne Worley could be involved?"

"You mean a high-price call girl? Like the Purcell woman?"

"That's exactly what I mean."

"I think you've officially arrived on Fantasy Island, Jack," Sean said, laughing. "No, I don't think there's a chance in hell that Suzanne Worley is a prostitute. I'd bet my last dime on that one."

"Be careful, Sean. I would hate to see you lose that much money."

*****

The man known as Max was at a crossroad. He wanted to act—*needed* to act—but to make a play simply for the sake of overcoming his inertia could prove to be disastrous. Mistakes are made when there is action without thought. Regardless of this almost-overwhelming desire to take a step forward, the smart move might be to stand pat until more information could be gathered.

Why the inertia? That was the question he kept asking himself. Things were going well. He had more money now than he'd ever had in his life. Fifty grand and more on the way. Another twenty-five thousand due at any time for his most recent job. Seventy-five thousand was a nice bankroll. He could survive a long time with that much cash.

But the money was only good if he stayed alive. Maybe that was what was gnawing at his stomach, the idea that the man calling the shots just might send an assassin rather than cash. Send a bullet instead of dollars. You can't spend money when you're six feet underground.

Staying alive—why was he so concerned about that? There was no realistic reason for him to feel threatened. He had been contracted to do three jobs and he had done them well. Promises of future jobs had been given. Everything seemed kosher. The people he was working for were professionals who knew how to avoid mistakes. They were clear, efficient and precise.

The *people*. That's what was nagging at him. He had only spoken to one man, the one who gave the orders, but Max was convinced there was someone else involved. Maybe *that* person would be the one to give the order to put him down. No Max, no witness.

No worries.

Max was jarred out of his trance by his buzzing cell phone. He didn't recognize the number—the call obviously came from a burner phone—but he knew without any doubt who the caller was.

"I was wondering when I would hear from you," Max said.

"Outside, to your left, you'll see a black Escalade. That's where we'll meet."

"You alone?"

"Yes."

Max paid for his coffee and walked outside. Looking left, he saw the Escalade. Right hand on his pistol, he moved quickly toward the vehicle. He opened the door and peered inside. A lone man was sitting behind the steering wheel. Max climbed inside, keeping a firm grip on his weapon.

"You can take your hand off that pistol," the man said. "You're among friends."

Max hesitated for a few seconds, then raised his right hand for the man to see. "A guy can never be too sure who his friends are. Better safe than sorry."

"I take care of those who take care of me," the man said. "You've done good work, and I appreciate it. If you continue to do that, we'll get along just fine."

"Like I told you, I'm a guy who gets the job done properly."

"That's good to hear. Otherwise, we wouldn't be talking."

"Whatever."

The man, who was wiry and several inches taller than Max, reached into the glove box and took out an envelope. Handing it to Max, he said, "There's a little something extra in there—ten grand—just to show my appreciation. Thirty-five large—not exactly small potatoes. And there's more where that came from."

"Similar jobs?"

"Not unless difficulties arise. No, what I have in mind for you will be less complicated, less dangerous. Won't pay as much per job, but you'll have enough work to make plenty of money."

"What kind of jobs are you talking about?"

"You'll know when you hear from me."

"Any idea when that might be?"

"Think of it like the Rapture . . . it could happen anytime."

The man started the engine, sending a clear signal to Max that the conversation was finished.

"I want to know who your partner is," Max said, as he opened the door. "I like to know who I'm risking my ass for."

"What makes you think I have a partner?"

"Call it a hunch."

"Your job is to do what I pay you to do, not to ask questions. Don't let your hunches keep you from making a lot of money. Go. Wait for my next call."

Despite holding the thick envelope stuffed with cash, Max was not smiling as the Escalade drove away.

CHAPTER FOURTEEN

The rain had passed through Lexington yet the sky remained dark and threatening. More showers were expected, probably sooner rather than later. The weather folks were warning that the next band of storms would likely bring with them the threat of tornadoes. Never a good thing.

Sitting in the War Room, Dantzler's mood was in perfect synch with the outside gloom. With seven unsolved murders hanging over his head, and not a single solid lead to follow, how could his mood be anything but dark and gloomy? What he needed was something—anything—that would shake him out of his funk. And it happened the moment Jake walked into the room.

Seeing Jake, Dantzler immediately burst out laughing. "With those dark circles around your eyes you look like a raccoon, Jake. How long has it been since you slept?"

"Been so long I can't remember. Two days at least."

"Get out of here and get some rest. I need alert detectives, not zombies."

"If I went to bed now, all I would do is toss and turn thinking about what's going on and what needs to be done. I'm way too wired to sleep. I'm sure you've felt this way before."

"Way too many times. But when you do crash, and you will, get home and into bed."

Jake waved a piece of paper, said, "Got a bit of good news for us. Ballistics confirmed the weapon used to kill those two kids this morning is the same one used in the Kurtz murders. That means there's only one shooter."

"That is good news." Dantzler felt a sudden burst of adrenaline. "It narrows things down, which is a break for us. And right now we need a break."

"You didn't ask me to, but I had ballistics check to see if the forty-five used in these two cases was a match to the one the Ballard woman used to kill her husband. It didn't match."

"That would've been too good to be true. Did you find anything at the crime scene this morning that stands out?"

"Just the senselessness of it. I mean, they were just a couple of kids who had nothing but each other. Everybody we spoke with had kind things to say about them. They are all stunned that something like this would happen. It's just sad, that's all."

"Yeah, senseless is a perfect word, Jake."

"Hard for me to believe the murder of those two kids is linked to the Kurtz killings."

"There's a connection, Jake. We just have to find it." Dantzler pointed at the stack of papers on the table. "Great work on the phone records. I spoke with Cynthia Purcell, found her to be an interesting lady."

"Was she Carl Banks's mistress?"

"Mistress? No. Miss Purcell charges by the hour."

"Oh, I get it," Jake said, grinning. "By the way, did you check out the other phone numbers I highlighted?"

"No, I didn't. What numbers?"

"The ones on Judge Kurtz's page."

Jake picked up the papers and began going through them. When he found what he was looking for, he plucked it out, laid it on the table, then pointed at three numbers near the middle of the last page.

"These three calls—two Kurtz received, one he made—are the last times he spoke on the phone," Jake said. "The final call, one he received, came at six-twenty Saturday night. That's forty minutes before the poker game began. The calls that came later are either from his son or from Devon McIntyre. As you can see, they only lasted a few seconds. A gentleman named Adrian White made that final call Saturday evening. He may be the last person, other than the poker players, to speak with Judge Kurtz."

"Did you contact him?"

"Called several times, got no answer. I left messages, asking him to get in touch with me at his earliest convenience. So far, he hasn't responded."

"Got an address?"

"He lives on Chinoe."

Dantzler stood. "You up for paying Mr. White a visit?"

"I'm all in," Jake answered. "Want me to drive?"

"And risk you falling asleep at the wheel? No, I'll handle the driving."

*****

Adrian White's house was a moderate-size Ranch with a connecting garage and a nice front yard in need of some work. As thunder boomed overhead, Dantzler turned on Chinoe, pulled into the driveway and shut off the engine. After exiting the car, Dantzler went up on the porch, while Jake looked through the garage door window.

"Car's in there," Jake said, moving onto the porch as the rain began to come down. "Guy should be home."

Dantzler rang the doorbell and waited. Getting no response, he rang the bell a second time, punctuating it with a couple of loud knocks on the door. Again, no response. He turned the knob; the door was unlocked. Peeking inside, he called out Adrian White's name. Nothing. He called again, this time louder. More silence.

"Let's take a look inside," Dantzler whispered. "Something feels off about this."

"Do we have cause to go in?"

"Probably not. But we're going in anyway."

"Roger that."

Dantzler went into the small foyer, Jake close behind. "Go through that door, Jake," he said. "I'll go through this one."

Only seconds later, Jake yelled, "Think I've got blood here, Jack. In the kitchen."

Dantzler took out his Glock, left the den and went into the kitchen, careful to watch where he stepped. Jake, weapon in one hand, was pointing with his free hand at several small, dark stains on the wooden floor. Kneeling, Dantzler inspected the drops more closely.

"Can't say for certain, but I think you're right. Looks like blood to me."

"This is the kitchen," Jake said. "People cut themselves all the time in the kitchen area. Could have resulted from a harmless accident."

"True, but people also get murdered in the kitchen. You check upstairs, I'll see what I can find down here."

Dantzler went into the den, looked around but found nothing of real consequence. No more blood, no sign of a struggle, no disarray of any type. He then looked through a window at the back yard, which, like its counterpart in the front, needed work. Dantzler wondered why the yards were so neglected when everything inside the house was so neat and tidy.

Jake came down the stairs, a leather-bound book in his left hand. When he saw Dantzler heading for the garage, he laid the book on the kitchen table and followed his boss out of the main house. Inside the garage sat a late-model white Lexus.

"Nice ride." Dantzler placed his palm on the hood. "Cold. This car hasn't been driven for a while."

"The car is not the only thing that's cold," Jake was standing next to a large floor freezer, holding the top open. "This poor bastard is an icicle."

Dantzler looked inside. "Adrian White, I presume."

"Looks like plenty of blood at the bottom. What do you want to bet he was killed by a forty-five?"

"Call this in," Dantzler said, reaching down to touch the victim's arm. "Man, he is frozen solid. It'll take a while to thaw him out. That could make it difficult for Arnie to nail a TOD."

"If this is Adrian White, then we know he was alive at six-twenty on Saturday evening. That's when he spoke with Judge Kurtz. This had to happen sometime after that."

After Jake made the necessary calls, Dantzler asked, "Did you find anything interesting upstairs?"

"I did. Seems Adrian White kept a journal of some kind. Or

maybe it's a diary. I thumbed through it, saw some things you'll want to see."

"Any names?"

"No names, only initials. But I can tell you for certain that he was the missing poker player Saturday night."

"How do you know that?"

In the kitchen, Jake picked up the journal and opened it to a page he had dog-eared. "Read this," he said, handing the journal to Dantzler.

Dantzler took the journal and read aloud, "Migraine was brutal today, worse than it has been in years. Had to phone L.K. and let him know that I was in no shape to play tonight. Might need to visit the emergency room. Certainly will if this doesn't subside soon. Brutal, brutal, brutal. If this pain persists, I'll have to cancel with S.W. tomorrow night."

Jake pointed at the page. "S.W. is mentioned frequently in the few pages I scanned. Wonder who S.W. is?"

"I have a pretty good idea who S.W. is." Dantzler handed the journal back to Jake. "And if I'm right, I also have a pretty good idea what she does for a living."

*****

Dantzler stayed at Adrian White's house until Eric, Arnie and the crime scene gang showed up. Once they had everything under control, he and Jake drove back to the office. As they were getting out of the car, Dantzler ordered Jake to go home and catch a few hours of sleep. Jake protested, as Dantzler knew he would, but finally relented when he realized it was an argument he couldn't win.

Bruce Rawlinson called to Dantzler just as he was heading up the steps. "Got a guy on the line says he needs to speak with you, Ace," Bruce said, holding up the phone. "Says it might have something to do with the Kurtz murders. Want me to take a message or put him through?"

"Does he sound legit?"

"Says he's a prison warden. Says you two have met."

"Give me time to get settled, then put him through."

"You got it, Ace."

Dantzler hurried up the steps, stopped in the break room to grab a bottle of water, and then went into his office. Bruce's timing was perfect; the phone rang just as Dantzler dropped into his chair.

Picking up the phone, he said, "This is Jack Dantzler. How can I help you?"

"Well, I'm hoping I can help you, Detective Dantzler. I'm Warden Thad Curtis. You and I met a few years ago when you came to see Eli Whitehouse."

"Yes, I remember you, Warden. If I recall correctly, you mentioned that we once played a tennis match in the state tournament."

"I was hoping you wouldn't remind me of that debacle. You beat me love and love."

"Like I told you, Warden, I had a good day."

"And like I told you, Detective, you were way out of my league, which you proved by easily winning the championship."

"My desk sergeant says you might have some information relating to a multiple homicide we had here last Saturday. What can you tell me?"

"Don't know if what I'm going to say will be of any help to you or not," Curtis said. "But I do feel like it is something you should know."

"I'm listening."

"One of your victims was a man named Carl Banks, right?"

Dantzler's interest level instantly shot up about ten notches. "That's correct. What about Carl Banks?"

"His nephew, Mark Banks, was recently released after serving twelve years of a twenty-year sentence. During his exit processing, he informed me that he was relocating to Lexington. Yesterday, I put in a call to his PO, and was told that Banks had checked in with him when he arrived in Lexington three weeks ago. That doesn't necessarily mean he's still there, but it's something you should know."

"What was Mark Banks in for?" Dantzler asked.

"Voluntary manslaughter. Got into a scrap with a guy in a

bar, pulled out a gun and shot him."

"Do you know the caliber of the weapon he used?"

"Forty-five."

"Same as our shooter Saturday night," Dantzler remarked. "Who is his PO?"

"Bobby Franklin. Want his phone number?"

"Yeah, give it to me." Dantzler wrote down the parole officer's name and number. "I really appreciate this, Warden Curtis. We haven't been able to come up with much of anything. This might be the break we need."

"Well, there's more, Detective."

"I'm all ears."

"For the past two years, Mark Banks's cellmate has been a young man I think you are quite familiar with—Oscar Young."

Oscar Young was a three-time murderer Dantzler helped put away almost two years ago. "I know Oscar very well. How is he doing?"

"Heck, he's too stupid to cause much trouble. Has to be one of the dumbest offenders I've ever run across. Has a motor mouth, dishes out a lot of bold talk, but if push comes to shove, I can't see him as someone who can back it up. But if you want to pay him a visit, let me know and I'll arrange it."

"I may need to do that sometime down the road, but for the time being I'd prefer to focus on Mark Banks. He has quickly moved to the top of my person-of-interest list."

"Well, Detective, if you do need anything, don't hesitate to let me know. Mark Banks is, was and always will be a hard case. He's one of those guys who will never back down from a confrontation. My advice: If you run into him, keep your eyes open and your hand close to your weapon."

"Always," Dantzler said. "And thanks again for your help, Warden Curtis."

"Come on, Detective Dantzler. You crushed me love and love . . . the least you can do is call me Thad."

"Okay, thanks, Thad."

CHAPTER FIFTEEN

Having Mark Banks's name was a huge development in the case. How, or in what way, Dantzler didn't know. But it was important, that much he was certain of. Why? Because Mark Banks wasn't afraid to look a man in the eye, aim a gun at him and pull the trigger.

Mark Banks was a killer. That fact alone distinguished him from approximately ninety-nine percent of his fellow human beings on this planet.

Warden Curtis had been kind enough to fax over much of Mark Banks's file, keying on the more important points. Reading the file confirmed what Curtis had said about Banks—he was not a man to be taken lightly.

According to the records, Mark Banks was born in Sikeston, Missouri, in nineteen seventy-seven, making him thirty-eight years old. His father abandoned the family a few months after Mark's birth, and his mother died of a drug overdose two years later. Mark then moved to Paducah to live with grandparents. That proved to be a disaster; the aging grandparents couldn't control the youngster, who was never far from trouble. He was hauled in by the authorities on numerous occasions before finally being sent to a boys' home for juvenile delinquents. He remained there from ages nine to thirteen, when he was released into the custody of his uncle Carl Banks. Less than a year later, now living with his uncle in Lexington, Mark had his first serious brush with the law. He and a fellow teen broke into a liquor store, emptied the cash register and set fire to the place. They were arrested, charged and convicted.

Both were sent to juvie, where they were to remain until they turned eighteen.

Following his release, Mark continued to have run-ins with the law. Theft and assault and battery were the big two on his list of offenses. He spent time behind bars for those crimes, but he wasn't sent to prison until he was convicted of the voluntary manslaughter charge twelve years ago. That incident happened in Henderson, Kentucky.

Looking at the photo of Mark Banks, Dantzler saw the face of a man who fit a certain profile. A stereotype, even. The eyes were the giveaway. They were eyes filled with hate and rage and bitterness. His physique was another giveaway. According to his file, Mark Banks was on the small side, standing five-eight and weighing maybe a buck-sixty soaking wet.

Dantzler had seen hundreds of guys like Mark Banks, who, because they were undersized, always had to prove themselves. They had a chip on their shoulder the size of a cannonball, and they could never allow anyone to see them as weak or ineffectual. So they lashed out at the slightest provocation. Mutts like Mark Banks would fight a grizzly bear and not quit until either they or the bear were dead. Giving up was seen as a sign of weakness.

As Dantzler was about to pick up his phone, Richard Bird came into the office and took a seat. "Hate to bring this up, Jack, but I think it's time to call in reinforcements. With eight unsolved homicides, you can imagine that some folks in higher places are getting a little antsy. They want results."

"No one wants results more than I do, Rich. But we're only looking for one shooter. Eric, Jake and I can handle it."

"Give me a solid reason why I shouldn't call in some help."

Dantzler held up the Mark Banks file. "Because we now have a legitimate person of interest. Mark Banks. He was recently paroled after serving a twelve-year stint for voluntary manslaughter. Is that solid enough?"

"Do you know his location?"

"Here, in town. His PO is a guy named Bobby Franklin. I was about to phone him when you came in."

"Banks? Any connection to Carl Banks?"

Dantzler nodded. "Nephew. And get this. His cellmate for the past two years was none other than our own Oscar Young."

"Okay, Jack, you won me over with those last two bits of info," Bird said, standing. "But you know the score as well as I do. I can't hold the hounds at bay forever. You need to solve this thing, and you need to do it pronto. Otherwise, a shit storm will land at our feet."

When Bird was gone, Dantzler opened his cell phone and punched in Bobby Franklin's number. He got a recorded message saying Bobby Franklin was currently with someone, followed by instructions to leave your name and number, and he would return your call when he was free.

Dantzler knew that "free" might mean five minutes, after Franklin finished with whomever he was now with, or it could mean six o'clock, after he was finished for the day. Giving more weight to six o'clock than the five-minute scenario, Dantzler decided to get out of the office and grab a bite to eat. Not wanting to dine alone, he phoned Grace West.

"You up for something to eat?" Dantzler asked. "I'm buying."

"What a gallant lad you are," Grace answered. "If I could wave a magic wand, I would send you to a different time, a different century. You belong in another era."

"Can you make it one where the murder rate isn't quite so high?"

"Doubtful. Unfortunately, the pages of our history books are soaked in blood."

"Darn. Guess I'd better stay put. What about my offer? Yes or no?"

"Sadly, no. You were beaten to the punch by Morgan Ballard. I'm meeting her in about an hour."

"Are you still her attorney?"

"Yes. And no one is more surprised than I am. Trust me, I had my bags packed and was ready to head back to Chicago."

"Why do you think Richard Chambers decided to keep you?"

"Richard Chambers might be the one with deep pockets,

but I'm not convinced anymore that he's calling the shots. I think we all underestimated Morgan Ballard. She's no pushover."

"Listen, if Suzanne Worley happens to show up, don't mention that I was asking about her," Dantzler said. "I need to speak with her, but I want it to be a surprise."

"How does Suzanne Worley figure into any of this?"

"Maybe she doesn't. Won't know until I ask her a few questions."

"You are being very evasive, Detective Dantzler."

"Comes with the territory, Counselor. Comes with the territory."

*****

While Dantzler was on the phone with Grace West, a man and a woman were kissing in the front seat of a car parked in a vacant lot located behind a huge shopping center. They were lovers, and had been for several years now, but no one could know that. Not now, at least. Maybe in the future they could be open about the strong feelings they shared for each other.

Maybe . . . but a lot of pieces had to fall into place before that could happen.

He had been the first one to develop romantic feelings, but circumstances forced him to keep them to himself. Only later, almost a year to be exact, had he told her how he felt, that he was madly in love with her. To his great surprise, she said she was in love with him as well. With those declarations their affair began.

Mostly, they met at his two places, a small house located on Pepperhill, or the bigger house out in the county. Sometimes, late at night, they got together in his place of business. Then there were the occasional out-of-town excursions, when they drove to a nearby city and spent time in a motel room. Being single, he had freedom. She was married, so she had to be more secretive. But they made it work, and now, after nearly seven years of clandestine meetings, their love for each other, and their bond, was stronger than it had ever been.

"We can't," she said, pulling his hand away from her thigh.

"It's still too light outside. Someone might see us."

"Who fucking cares? Let 'em watch. They might learn something."

"We're too close now to take unnecessary risks." She swatted at his roving hand. "Stop it before you make me angry."

"Ah, babe, you could never get angry with me."

"Never believe that." She sat up and straightened her skirt. "Where do we stand with you-know-who?"

"We're cool."

"I know *we* are, but what about him? Can he be trusted?"

"Yes. He either does what he's told, or he suffers the consequences. And he knows what those consequences would be."

"You had better be certain about that," she said. "Right now, he's the only one standing between us and a lethal injection."

"You mean standing between *me* and a lethal injection, don't you? He has no clue you even exist, much less that you are a part of this. You're in the clear."

"Good. Let's keep it that way. Now get out. I have to be somewhere, and I don't want to be late."

"One last kiss for the road."

"God, you're so pitiful. Yes, one last kiss for the road."

"I love you," he said, before closing the car door.

"Love you more." She blew him a kiss and drove away.

*****

Bobby Franklin's call came just moments after Dantzler had polished off a plate of chicken parmesan at Paisano's on Nicholasville Road. He opened his cell phone, told Franklin to hold on for a second, then handed the waitress his credit card.

"Thanks for getting back with me, Bobby."

"Sounds like I caught you at a bad time. Do I need to call back in a few minutes?"

"Actually, you caught me at a perfect time. I just finished eating. Let me pay the bill, then we can talk." Dantzler signed the receipt, thanked the waitress and stepped outside. "What I need from you, Bobby, is information relating to one of your parolees."

"Which one?"

"Mark Banks."

"Banks? Well, I've only met with him twice, maybe thirty minutes total, so there's really not much I can tell you about him. I'll be happy to send a copy of his file for you to look at."

"I've already seen his file," Dantzler said. "What I want is your read on the guy. What you think, how you size him up."

"Well, if you've read his file, then you know what he was locked up for. Right off the bat that tells you a lot about him. He ain't afraid to put someone down. That means he's dangerous."

"I get that. But what's he like?"

"For starters, he has the shiftiest eyes I've ever seen on someone. They are constantly in motion, like he's always on the lookout for danger. He's been pleasant with me, but he can't run away from his true self. I'd say that underneath he's an extremely angry individual. Not someone I'd turn my back on."

"Are you aware that Carl Banks, one of the five men murdered last Saturday, was Mark's uncle?"

"No, I wasn't aware of that. Is that in his file?"

"Yes."

"I must have missed it. And Mark never brought it up during our conversations. Why? You think it's important?"

"The timing intrigues me."

"I can see why it would," Franklin said. "Mark showing up a couple of weeks before the murders. But why would he kill his uncle?"

"Maybe he harbored some long-held hatred for the man. Maybe he perceived an injustice. Maybe he blamed Carl Banks for all the bad shit that's happened to him during his life. When you're dealing with families, there can be a million issues at play."

"But why murder four innocent people if Carl was the primary target?" Franklin asked.

"That's the problem we're having with this case—finding out who the primary target was."

"Maybe there wasn't one."

"No, one of those five men was the reason for the killings." Dantzler thought for a moment, then said, "Did you ever have any dealings with Oscar Young?"

"No. But I've known Oscar since we were kids. We went to school together. Well, until he dropped out. Why are you asking about him?"

"He was Mark Banks's cellmate for the past two years."

"Really? Man, you're telling me things I didn't know."

"So Banks never mentioned Oscar to you?"

"Never. But like I said, I've only met with him twice."

"Do you have an address for Banks?" Dantzler asked. "And is he employed?"

"He's renting a room on Alexandria. At least, that's what he says. With guys like him, who knows if he's telling the truth or not. As for employment, he claims to have a couple of interviews lined up, but, again, who knows?"

After writing down Banks's address, Dantzler said, "When are you scheduled to meet him again?"

"Ten days. But he's supposed to call me on Sunday."

"Either way, don't mention that I was asking about him. If he hears that, he might take off. And once he's in the wind we may never locate him."

"When you do hook up with him, Detective, keep in mind what I said—don't turn your back on him."

"You don't have to worry about that."

CHAPTER SIXTEEN

At three-fifteen in the morning, Dantzler was at the Tennis Center exchanging a series of difficult shots with David Bloom. Grace West was perched in the umpire's chair, watching the action, more than a little impressed by their skill and athleticism. Although neither Dantzler nor Bloom were spring chickens, they performed with the ease of players many years their junior.

After thirty minutes of volleying, Dantzler asked, "You up for a set?"

"You want to show off for your lady friend, don't you?" Bloom answered. "I am many things my goyish comrade, but glutton for punishment isn't one of them. I have little interest in letting you defeat me for the five-thousandth time."

"Then let's go upstairs and have a soft drink." Dantzler walked over to a chair, grabbed his towel and began drying his face. "You need help getting down?"

"I'm as agile as a leopard," Grace said. "And after observing the show you two old guys put on, I would be embarrassed to ask for assistance."

"There's only one *old* guy here tonight and it's the esteemed psychiatrist," Dantzler said, pointing at Bloom. "He's gotta have at least ten years on me."

"Once again the celebrated detective can't get his facts straight," Bloom responded, wiping his face with a towel. "I am only five years older."

Grace did some math in her head, then asked, "If there's a five-year age difference, how could you have been teammates in college? That doesn't compute."

Bloom draped an arm around Grace, said, "Let's adjourn to the comfort of the lounge. There, I will detail for you the facts behind the unlikely coming together of John David Dantzler and Michael David Bloom."

Dantzler picked up his tennis bag. "Take everything he says with a pound of salt, Grace. Bloom is notorious for telling tales that stray many miles from the actual truth."

"As a member of the Hebrew tribe I have only a nodding acquaintance with the New Testament, but your friend here is the modern-day equivalent of Doubting Thomas," Bloom said, as they headed up the stairs. "Contrary to what he claims, I'm as honest as the great prophet Isaiah."

"Isaiah and Doubting Thomas?" Grace laughed. "More like Abbott and Costello, I'd say."

"Damn, Jack, I like this lady. She's every bit the wise ass we are."

*****

Upstairs in the lounge area, while Bloom was turning on the lights, Dantzler went behind the bar, scooped ice into three plastic cups and filled them with Coke. Grace grabbed a chair at one of the tables, scooted it back and took a seat.

"Must be nice owning the place, being able to come here at all hours of the night," she said.

Bloom sat in a chair next to her. "It's great to be the king, there's no denying that."

"You guys are really good." Grace took a cup from Dantzler. "I'm very impressed."

"I'm good." Bloom nodded at Dantzler. "He's exceptional. Has been from the first day I laid eyes on him."

"Which was about a million years ago," Dantzler said, sitting across from Grace. "If you don't believe it, just ask my knees."

"Do you come here often this late at night?" Grace asked.

"Not as much anymore," Bloom said. "There was a time

when we'd play practically until the sun came up. Did that three, four times a week. We're too old to do that anymore."

"Speak for yourself, Bloom."

Grace tapped Bloom on the shoulder. "Okay, tell me how the two of you came to be college teammates."

"I was a sophomore at the University of Kentucky, a member of the tennis squad. Your friend, the boychick boy wonder, graduated from high school at fourteen, enrolled at UK, and was playing number two as a fifteen-year-old freshman. The next year he was our number-one guy. Made all-conference and all-American in singles his last three years. He and I were an all-American doubles team my final two years. Like I said, he was something special."

"Wow, now I'm more than impressed," Grace said, looking at Dantzler. "But to graduate from high school that young you had to be more than a terrific tennis player. You also had to be really smart in the classroom."

"I enjoyed learning. And because of some things that happened in my life, I was highly motivated. I went to school pretty much all year round, took a lot of advanced classes, and was able to finish early. It really wasn't that big a deal."

"Your parents must have been very proud of their son," Grace said.

"My father was killed in Laos when I was six years old. Eight years later my mother was murdered. They weren't alive when I finished school, or when I went to college. But, yeah, I like to think they would have been proud of me."

Grace put a hand on Dantzler's, said, "That had to be extremely difficult for you. I'm not sure many people would have handled it as well as you did."

"I really had no choice. To fail would have felt like I was letting them down. I wasn't about to let that happen."

"Who raised you?"

"My uncle helped some . . . when he was sober. Mostly, it was Bloom and my tennis teammates. They became my family."

"I deny any and all responsibility," Bloom said. "My dear, what you're looking at is a self-made man."

Dantzler said, "Changing the subject, tell me about your meeting with Morgan Ballard. Did your new BFF share anything of importance with you?"

"She did not, but even if she had I couldn't talk to you about it. You know that."

After taking a drink of Coke, Dantzler asked, "Which Morgan showed up?"

"I've concluded that there is really only one Morgan Ballard—the strong, tough one. What you see when she's with her father is purely an act. It's a role she's been playing since she was a child. Gets her what she wants, so why do anything different?"

"Was Suzanne Worley there?"

"No. And her name never came up."

"I know Suzanne Worley," Bloom said to Dantzler. "Why did you inquire about her?"

"How do you know Suzanne Worley?"

"Hell, Jack, *you* know her. She was Suzanne Dunning before she married Tommy Worley. Obviously, she kept his name after he died."

"He was killed in a hunting accident, if I remember correctly. Somewhere in Scott County, right?"

Bloom nodded, said, "Shot in the head. It was ruled an accident, but the hunter who fired the shot never came forward. Probably wasn't aware of what he'd done."

"Was there an investigation?"

"You'd have to ask the Scott County authorities about that."

"I vaguely remember Tommy, but not Suzanne. Where would I know her from?"

"From here. She and Morgan Ballard—she was Morgan Chambers then—played tennis together. They were in a doubles league for a while."

"I must've been working, because I don't remember her at all."

"When you see her you will. She's a knockout. Or at least she was back then."

Dantzler looked at Grace and shrugged.

"She's beyond a knockout," Grace agreed. "Suzanne Worley is stunningly beautiful."

"I think it's time I met Suzanne Worley," Dantzler said. "In fact, I think it's past time that I met her."

*****

"Now you're the one with bags under your eyes," Jake said, as he came into Dantzler's office. "You look like you haven't slept in days."

Dantzler had been at work since six-thirty, sleepy but wired to the max. "I need to locate Suzanne Worley, but I can't seem to find her number anywhere."

"Well, this is your lucky day. I have it right here. That's why I came to see you."

"Where did you get it?"

"From Dustin Ridley's phone records. He called her twenty-nine times in the two months prior to his death. That's what I came to tell you."

"Now I *really* need to speak with her." Dantzler wrote down Suzanne's number. "Have you been able to get Morgan Ballard's phone records yet?"

"Still working on it."

"Make it a high priority, Jake. I have a feeling it's going to be revealing."

"You want to know who she was talking to on the night those five men were killed, right?"

"That, among other things." Dantzler stood. "Do you have Suzanne Worley's address?"

"She owns a loft on Angliana."

"Then that's where I'm heading."

"Not gonna call her first, make sure she's home?"

"No. If she's not home, I'll wait for her."

"Think you can stay awake, sitting in the car?"

"I'll be awake, don't worry about that." Dantzler went to the door. "Do your best to get Morgan Ballard's phone records. If someone is stalling you, don't be shy about letting them know their ass is on the line if they don't come through."

"Roger that."

*****

Prior to leaving his office, Dantzler put in a call to the Georgetown Police Department for the purpose of speaking with the lead investigator in the Thomas Worley case. He spoke with the Chief, who informed Dantzler that the investigation had been conducted by the Kentucky State Police. Two phone calls later, he had the name and phone number he was looking for.

Dantzler punched in the number and waited. His call was answered after a half-dozen rings.

"Damn straight I remember the Worley case," Kendall Langley said, after introductions were made. "Happened about a year before I retired. A bullshit case from day one."

"Why was it a bullshit case?"

"For starters, it weren't no damn accident. That poor man was deliberately gunned down just as sure as my hair is whiter than snow in Iceland. It was a damn murder that was ruled accidental. I'd bet my pension on it."

"How thorough was your investigation?" Dantzler asked.

"Son, when I bite into something, I bite in hard and with all the teeth I have left. On that case, I journeyed down every road I thought might take me somewhere. But none of them did. You see, I had a couple of things working against me from the start. First, Worley was hunting on private property, just him and the guy who owned the land. They were alone. Second, no one came forward to take claim for firing the shot, and we couldn't locate another soul who was in the immediate vicinity. So you see, I had very little to work with."

"What about the guy who was with Worley? The land owner? Did you look at him as the possible shooter?"

"He didn't do it. Hell, he was standing within a few feet of Worley when the bullet hit. Was covered in blood."

"Could he have been the intended target?"

"I looked into it from that angle, but nothing popped up to

cause me to think that way. No, he just had the bad luck to be standing next to a guy who had half his head blown off."

"Did you fight the accidental shooting ruling?"

"Damn straight I did. I begged them to at least call it suspicious or unknown. Told them to call it whatever, just so long as they kept the case open. They didn't listen to me. Instead, they went with accidental. But that's not how I saw it."

"Did you talk to Worley's wife?" Dantzler asked.

"Of course I spoke with her. She was out of state when it happened. Somewhere in Florida, if memory serves."

"I'm on my way to meet her. What can I expect?"

"Well, she's damn easy on the eyes, that much I can tell you."

"I've heard that, but looks aside, how did she react to her husband's death?"

"Shock, dismay, plenty of tears . . . a fairly standard reaction, I'd say. What's your reason for seeing her, if you don't mind my asking?"

"She was familiar with one of the five homicide victims we had here last week. I need to know what she can tell me about their relationship."

"Well, good luck, son. I hope you have a better outcome with your case than I had with her husband's, because justice was not served for Thomas Worley."

When Dantzler ended the call, Eric came into the office and took a seat. "Jake told me you were going to see Suzanne Worley," he said. "I just learned something you need to know."

"Enlighten me."

"Suzanne Worley is now a very wealthy lady. According to Dustin Ridley's will, everything he had went to her, including those five McDonald's franchises."

"Can he even do that?" Dantzler said.

"He owned them free and clear. Now they are hers."

"Any money involved?"

"About fifty-thousand in savings, another two-hundred grand in stocks, and an insurance policy worth two-million. Dustin Ridley set her up for life."

"Makes me wonder what kind of a relationship Dustin had with her."

"Can't answer that one for you, Jack. But if you're in the mood for a Big Mac, you're going to the right place."

CHAPTER SEVENTEEN

Dantzler wasn't at all surprised to find Suzanne Worley home at ten-thirty in the morning. If his suspicions about her were anywhere close to accurate, she was a classic night creature. For Suzanne, the day didn't begin until after the sun went down and the city lights came on.

Suzanne answered the door wearing blue silk pajamas and holding a mug filled with steaming coffee. Dantzler's initial thought was that the scouting report on her tended to be on the conservative side. Even without makeup, and her hair in slight disarray, Suzanne Worley was incredibly beautiful. She had dark black hair, black eyes, smooth, tanned skin and a body that made an impression in all the right places in those PJs. Although Dantzler would never have thought it possible, Suzanne Worley made Cynthia Purcell look almost ordinary.

"Detective Jack Dantzler, to what do I owe this early morning visit?" Taking a sip from the mug, she opened the door wider, said, "While I'm obviously not dressed to entertain guests, please, come on in."

Suzanne closed the door, followed Dantzler into the living room, and then pointed toward a chair. "Have a seat, make yourself comfortable. Would you like a cup of coffee?"

"No, thanks. I'm good."

Taking a seat in the chair next to his, she said, "I'm curious as to why you are here."

"Dustin Ridley. I have a few questions regarding your relationship with him."

"Poor Dusty," Suzanne sighed. "What happened to him was tragic. I was truly shocked when I heard about it. What kind of person would do something that horrible?"

"Can you think of anyone who had it in for Dustin?"

"No. He was sweet, kind young man. I can't imagine him having any enemies."

"What was your relationship with Dustin Ridley?" Dantzler asked.

"Relationship . . . that's a word that can have several different meanings, can it not, Detective? I have a sneaking suspicion that you are asking if I had a *relationship* with him. The romantic type relationship, right?"

"Was it a romantic relationship?"

"No, it most certainly was not. We were friends, that's all."

"You sure about that? He called you twenty-nine times in the past two months. That's a lot of phone time for just a friend."

"No, Detective, it's not all that unusual," Suzanne said, setting the mug on an end table. "Are you aware that I'm an attorney?"

"I'm aware that you passed the bar. I'm not aware of you actively working anywhere."

"That's because I don't. But I did help Dusty with some legal matters."

"How did you meet Dustin?"

"We were introduced by a mutual friend."

"How long ago was this? And who was the mutual friend?"

"I met Dusty six years ago. I can't recall who introduced us."

"So you met Dustin after your husband was killed, correct?"

Suzanne nodded, said, "Yes. Tommy died almost eight years ago."

"He died from a gunshot while hunting, didn't he?"

"Yes."

"Do you agree with the ruling that your husband's death was an accident?"

"Well, nothing has come up to contradict that ruling. So,

yes, I agree that it was an accident."

"Back to your relationship with Dustin Ridley. Was . . ."

"Once again, Detective, I must object to your use of the word relationship. There was no relationship. We were friends, that's all. Don't try to make it into something it wasn't."

"Suzanne, the man left you everything he had, including five McDonald's franchises. That has to make me stop and wonder. If you were *only* friends, it would have to rank as the closest friendship in recorded history."

"Have you done a thorough background check on Dusty, Detective? If you have, then you know he had no family. He also had no will, nothing set up in the event something tragic happened to him. I encouraged him to get his affairs in order, which he did. I even helped him do it. And in case you are wondering if I'm some ruthless gold digger, rest assured that I'm not. He made me the beneficiary over my stern objections. But his argument was that he had no one else to leave it to."

"So now you're in the hamburger business."

"Get real, Detective. What do I know about running a fast-food joint? No, I'll sell them. In fact, I've already had offers on all five franchises. Barring unforeseen problems, they'll be off my hands in less than a month."

"That should bring you a nice chunk of change. Add that on top of Dustin's savings, his stocks and his life insurance policy, and you move up to a whole different tax bracket."

"What are you insinuating, Detective Dantzler?"

"I'm not insinuating anything. Just saying that you are a rich lady."

"I had plenty of money before I met Dusty. While I agree that having money is a nice luxury, it's not the only thing that matters. There are many things more important than money."

"Funny how it's always rich folks who say that."

"Is there anything else, Detective? I don't mean to rush you, but there are errands I need to run."

"Just a couple more things I'd like to clear up, if you don't mind."

"No, I don't mind at all. What do you want to clear up?"

"Do you know Cynthia Purcell?"

"No."

A lie.

"You sure about that?"

"I'm sure."

A second lie.

Dantzler pressed on. "What about Morgan Ballard? You know her?"

"Morgan and I have been friends since we were kids." Suzanne grinned, said, "You knew the answer to that question before you asked it, didn't you?"

"What's your relationship with Morgan?"

"There's that word relationship again. What's with you, Detective? Morgan and I are longtime pals, that's all. We see or speak to each other virtually every day. We're friends, get it, *close* friends. I don't know what else to tell you."

"Are you in business together?"

"Business? What business? No, absolutely not."

A third lie.

Dantzler stood. "Thank you for your time, Suzanne. You've been very helpful. I appreciate it."

"Promise me one thing, Detective," Suzanne said, opening the door. "Please find the person who murdered Dusty. That's my one request."

"We'll find him. You can rest assured of that."

After closing the door, Suzanne rushed into the bedroom and picked up her cell phone. This was a call that had to be made.

Now.

*****

As Suzanne was making her call, Dantzler was on the phone with Tony Allen, head of the Vice squad. Tony was a veteran on the force, one of those grizzled pros who had been there, done everything and seen it all. He answered immediately, and listened quietly as Dantzler posed his question.

"A ring of high-priced call girls?" Tony said, after thinking about it for a few moments. "How high priced are you talking about?"

"Five-hundred per hour, maybe more."

"Jesus, Ace, who can afford snatch at those prices? Neither one of us, that's for sure."

"Have you heard of anything like that going on?"

"You know me, Ace. If I did know about it, I'd bring them in regardless of how much they charge. But I haven't heard. Why? Do you know something I don't?"

"I met a lady, Cynthia Purcell, who freely admitted that she charged one of the shooting victims at the Kurtz house five-hundred per hour for what she termed her 'escort services.'"

"Hell, Ace, one high-priced whore doesn't exactly make a ring," Tony countered. "Could be she's the only one."

"I don't think so."

"I'll bring her in, pose the right questions, and find out. Then we'll go from there."

"Hold off on bringing her in, Tony. Down the road I may need her help solving these murders. If you bring her in she'll get an attorney, he'll tell her to clam up, and that will kill any chance I have of learning anything. I want her feeling free and easy."

"You got it, Ace. But sooner or later I'll want to have a chat with her."

"With her, Tony, a chat is about all you could afford."

"I heard that."

*****

The man known as Max stood at his window, a can of Budweiser in his hand, and watched as the dark blue Subaru Forester parked on the street in front of his building. His initial thought was that an assassin had been dispatched to take him out. But when he saw two men exit the vehicle, he realized this wasn't the case. These weren't assassins; they were law enforcement officials, probably sent by his PO to check up on him. He could recognize a cop from a mile away.

Moving quickly, he grabbed his two pistols, went into the

bedroom, removed a section of the baseboard and hid the weapons inside a large hole in the lower wall. After stashing the guns, he slid a small wooden cabinet in front of the damaged section, then went back into the living room. He was at the front door when he heard the loud knock.

Opening the door, he said, "What can I do for you?"

Dantzler held up his shield, said, "I'm Detective Jack Dantzler and this is Detective Eric Gamble. We're with Lexington Homicide."

"So you're with Homicide. Is that supposed to scare me?"

"No, it's meant to inform you."

"Well, hell, you can consider me informed."

"Are you Mark Banks?" Eric asked.

"That's the name on my birth certificate."

Dantzler said, "We'd like to ask you a few questions, Mark. What do you say we step inside and talk?"

"Don't you need a warrant to come inside?"

"Nah, we don't need a warrant. See, Mark, you're a convicted felon out on parole. That gives us the right to come in and look around anytime we get curious." Dantzler wasn't positive if this was true or not, but he said it with enough conviction that it *sounded* true. "But if you invite us inside, it gives us the impression you have nothing to hide. It sells us on the idea that you might be a solid citizen."

Banks opened the door wider and stepped aside. Dantzler entered first, followed by Eric.

"Carl Banks was your uncle, wasn't he?" Dantzler asked, after the trio squeezed into the tiny living room.

"Yeah."

"When was the last time you saw or spoke with Carl?"

"Long time ago. Before I went to the joint."

"You didn't see or speak with him after you moved to Lexington?"

"That's what I just told you."

"Did he ever visit you in prison?" Eric asked.

"Nobody visited me while I was locked up." Banks looked from Eric to Dantzler. "Why are you guys hassling me? I ain't done nothing wrong. Check with my PO. He'll tell you I've followed all the rules since I've been here."

"We did check with him," Dantzler said.

"Yeah, and what did he tell you?"

"That you're practically a saint."

"There you go."

"Have you found a job yet?" Eric said.

"Still working on that," Banks answered. "Ain't many employers willing to hire an ex-con."

"How can you afford the rent for this place?"

Banks shrugged, said, "I won some money shooting pool."

"Oh, yeah, where'd you play?" Dantzler asked.

"Different places."

"Name one."

"Hell, I don't know the name of the damn place. It's a pool hall off Richmond Road."

"When you were playing pool, did you ever run into a guy everyone called Stick?"

"No."

"Tell me, Mark, did you have anything to do with your uncle's death?"

"Why the fuck would you ask me that? Hell, no, I didn't have nothing to do with it. Like I told you, I barely knew the man. Hadn't seen him in years. Why would I kill a man I hardly knew? If you're looking for his killer, you need to look somewhere else, 'cause it ain't me."

Eric said, "Do you own any weapons, Mark?"

"I'm a convicted felon. You know I ain't allowed to have a gun."

"So if we search the place, we won't find any weapons?" Dantzler said.

"Search, if it'll give you a hard-on. You won't find nothing."

"Tell you what, Mark. We're gonna give you a pass today." Dantzler went to the front door and opened it. "But that doesn't mean we won't be back sometime in the future."

"Want to know something, Detective? I don't give a fuck

what you do, or when you do it. You don't scare me."

Eric moved to within inches of Banks, bent down until the two men were at eye level and said, "Sometimes it pays to be scared, Mark. This just might be one of those times."

After watching Dantzler and Eric drive away, Banks hurried to the kitchen table, picked up his cell phone and punched in a number. His call was answered after four rings.

"We need to talk," Mark told the listener. "Immediately."

CHAPTER EIGHTEEN

Rachel White made two things clear at the start: Everyone calls her Shelley, and she had absolutely zero interest in discussing the late Adrian White. Only after some serious special pleading was Dantzler finally able to break down the barrier. She relented, agreeing to give him "no more than five minutes" of her valuable time talking about a man she likened to a "snake in the grass." She gave Dantzler her address on Bellefonte, adding that if he wasn't there within the hour, then their meeting was off. She didn't want to be late for her weekly bridge game.

Listening to her speak, Dantzler couldn't decide if it was bitterness or hate that dripped from her every word. Probably an equal measure of each one, he finally concluded. He doubted that this was going to be a pleasant conversation.

Dantzler made it to her house in twenty minutes. She met him at the door, said nothing as she let him in, then silently pointed at a chair next to the fireplace. Like a general telling a subordinate where to sit. Being a gentleman, he remained standing, waiting until she took a seat. He quickly realized that she wasn't about to move, and that hell would be blanketed in snow before she did. Manners be damned, he thought, as he sat in the chair.

"I am unclear why you wish to speak to me about that snake," Shelley White said, after sitting on the sofa. "We were divorced fourteen years ago. I have seen him maybe four times since we split up. While I am saddened by the manner of his death, I doubt I have any information that will shed light on who killed him."

"I'm looking for background information, Miss White. You might be able to help me with that."

"Doubtful, but proceed."

"How long were you and Adrian married?"

"Thirteen years, which was about twelve and a half too many," Shelley answered. "We didn't exactly have a blissful marriage."

"Who filed for divorce?"

"I did. The reason I gave was the standard irreconcilable differences. But that wasn't the real reason. Adultery was why I left the snake. He couldn't keep his dick in his pants. And he certainly had little interest in keeping it in me. After your husband comes home smelling of ladies' perfume a certain number of times, you finally say enough is enough. You want your freedom, pal? Well, you got it. So I filed for divorce."

Lucky for Adrian, given this woman's level of anger. "Our records show that you have a daughter," Dantzler said.

"Emily, yes. A lovely young woman. She's married and lives in Cincinnati. Her husband is a surgeon."

"What was her relationship with Adrian?"

"Believe it or not, they had a good rapport. One nice thing I can say about the snake is that he did treat Emily very well. They didn't see each other often, but when they did, things went very smoothly. I suppose even a cold-blooded reptile is capable of some kindness."

"You do know where your husband died . . ."

"*Ex*-husband," Shelley quickly corrected.

"You do know where Adrian was when he died, don't you?"

"At that damn poker game he loved so much. That was another bone of contention for me when we were still married. Anything I wanted to do on Saturday night, go to a movie, see a play, have dinner with friends, whatever, I either couldn't do, or had to do with someone other than my husband, because nothing was going to keep him from that poker game. He even missed several events Emily was involved in when she was young. That Saturday night poker game trumped everything, trust me."

"Sounds like Adrian had been a member for a long time."

"He was accepted into the group a few weeks after we got married. You should have seen the man, Detective. Jubilant beyond all measure. You would've thought he won the Lottery."

"Did you know any of the men who were members of the group?"

"No. All I knew for sure was that the game was played at Judge Kurtz's house. I only knew that because I once followed the snake when he left the house one Saturday night. He always left sometime around six-fifteen. That night I parked down the street, then I followed him when he drove away. I was certain he had a regular Saturday night tryst with some hot, young woman. But I was wrong. He went to the Judge's house, arriving at the same time as another man. Judge Kurtz was standing on the porch when they got there. I recognized him from pictures I'd seen in the newspaper."

"Back to the adultery issue. Did you know any of the women?"

"No. And I didn't want to know their names. Why would I? They were getting the love and affection I should have been getting from the man."

"What makes you so certain he was seeing other women?"

"Come on, Detective. A wife knows. That might sound like a worn-out cliché, but it happens to be true. I confronted the snake very early in our marriage and he freely admitted that he was seeing another woman. I demanded that he end it immediately. He looked me straight in the eyes and told me he would. Like the serpent in the Garden of Eden, he lied. That affair continued, and there were many more in the years that followed."

"Do you suspect your ex-husband of seeing prostitutes?"

"I would bet on it, especially as he got older," Shelley said. "When a man reaches a certain age, finding those hot, young babes becomes increasingly hard to do. If he was still interested in sex, and I have no doubt that he was, then he almost certainly had to visit whores to have his needs taken care of."

"One final thing—money. Did you know that each player in the poker game your ex-husband participated in had to show up with ten-thousand dollars in cash before being allowed to play? Ten grand, fifty times a year adds up to quite a bundle."

"Money wasn't a problem for my ex-husband; he had plenty of it, even after I took him to the cleaners." She almost laughed. "I should have been even greedier, taken him for twice what I got. He had money to spare."

"According to his will, he left everything to Emily," Dantzler said. "Except for his house and everything in it, which he left to you."

"And I will sell it lock, stock and barrel to the first person who makes a reasonable offer. I have nothing but bad memories about that damn place."

"Back to the money. Adrian was a retired high school teacher. Not many teachers I know make big bucks."

"First off, your facts are all wrong. Adrian didn't retire, he *quit* teaching after ten or eleven years. Said he got bored with it and wanted to do something else. He had the luxury of coming from a wealthy family, so he could take a risk most of us couldn't take."

"Where did his family's wealth come from?" Dantzler asked.

"It went back several generations, to a great-great-great grandfather who did business with the Rockefellers, the Vanderbilts and the Carnegies. I'm not sure what he did, other than become very, very rich.

"But, Detective, the story doesn't end there," she continued. "Not by a longshot. You see, even though I detested the man, I have to admit that he was extraordinarily intelligent. That's especially true when it came to the stock market. He had some kind of genius for spotting which low-selling stocks were about to go sky high. He'd buy when they looked like crappy losers, then sell a week later when they had shot up through the roof. He made millions doing that. People called him all the time seeking advice. So you see, Detective, my ex had no trouble coming up with ten grand for a poker game."

"One last question, Miss White. Are you familiar with a woman named Monica Plemmons?"

"I am not. Why do you ask?"

"Adrian called her number several times over the past few months. I thought maybe you might know her."

"One of his whores, no doubt. Just one of many, I'm sure."

Dantzler stood, said, "Thank you for taking the time to speak with me, Miss White. You've helped to fill in some important blanks for us. I know you and your ex-husband weren't close, but I would be remiss if I didn't tell you how sorry I am for your loss."

"It's Emily's loss, Detective, not mine. She feels far more pain than I do. That said, despite my dislike for my ex-husband, I was truly sorry to hear that he died in such a violent manner. No one, regardless of how despicable, deserves that."

Driving away, Dantzler toyed with the notion that perhaps Shelley White was the shooter. She certainly held enough hatred for the man. Or the *snake*, as she constantly labeled her ex-husband. She wasn't the shooter, of course; that would've been too easy. But she was definitely among the angriest, bitterest women Dantzler had ever encountered.

*****

Eric and Jake took a seat in the back row of the Opera House and watched two actors on stage rehearsing a scene from the Tennessee Williams play *The Glass Menagerie*. In the scene, Laura was showing the Gentleman Caller her collection of small animal figurines. Occasionally, Martin Conley, the director, and the man Eric and Jake were here to see, would interrupt the actors, offer instructions, and then tell them to proceed. After thirty minutes Martin said time was up, thanked his actors for doing fine work, and told them to be here tomorrow at ten a.m.

Martin waited until everyone had departed before making his way to the rear of the theatre. He was a small man with delicate features and a youthful face. Sitting in a chair one row in front of the two detectives, he shifted his body in order to face them.

"Thank you so much for your patience," he said. "I hope you weren't bored to death."

"On the contrary, I thought it was very good," Eric said. "Your two actors were excellent."

"At this stage they are about halfway to where I hope to get them. They both need to work on their body language. In this scene the body language speaks volumes, and they just haven't quite mastered it. But they are hard workers, and they listen, so I'm confident they'll eventually get there."

"Why did you become a director?" Jake asked.

"Because I was a mediocre actor, that's why," Martin answered, chuckling. "In college my dream was to become a professional actor. Like all aspiring thespians I wanted to be like Brando or Montgomery Clift or Bobby De Niro. You know, one of the truly great ones. But I quickly learned that I simply wasn't that talented. So, I became a teacher instead. The classroom became my stage and the students were my audience."

"But you taught history, not theatre, right?" Eric said.

Martin nodded. "That's correct. I figured that if I lacked the talent to be an actor, then I had no business trying to train young men and women who did have serious talent. That would be akin to a high school baseball player trying to tell a Major League player how to hit. I would have felt like a fraud. Besides, I love history, and always have."

Eric said, "As you know, we're looking into the death of those five men murdered at Judge Kurtz's house last Saturday night. According to people we've interviewed, including Amelie Hassaine, you were perhaps Sahid's closest friend. We'd like to ask you a few questions about him."

"Yes, Sahid and I were very close. We saw each other all the time, and we spoke on the phone at least once a day. His death has left a big empty hole in my life. I can't begin to imagine how poor Amelie is handling this."

"How long have you been friends?" Jake asked.

"We joined the faculty at the same time. We were tenured the same year. It was almost as though fate meant for us to become good friends. I never tired of being in his company. Sahid was perhaps the most intelligent man I've ever been around. He was extremely bright."

Eric asked, "How would you characterize the Hassaine marriage?"

"Perfectly normal. He and Amelie got along quite well." Martin paused a second, then continued, "If you've met Amelie, then I'm sure you are aware of the age difference between her and Sahid. That never seemed to be a problem in their marriage. I would say they were very happy."

"Are you married, Martin?"

"Well, my partner and I were finally married four months ago. At long last we were allowed to tie a knot as tight as our straight friends."

"I'm sure you know why Sahid was at the Kurtz house that night."

"Yes, to participate in a poker game."

"A very expensive poker game."

"Well, I wouldn't know about that. See, Sahid never shared any details about that game. Oddly enough, that's one subject we never discussed."

"To sit down at that game each Saturday night, every player was required to have ten-thousand dollars in cash. When we told this to Amelie, she expressed surprise and disbelief. She said there was no way Sahid could have had that kind of money. Obviously, he did. Can you shed any light on how a college professor might come up with that kind of cash?"

Martin's pause told Eric and Jake that he was thinking how best to formulate an answer to what was clearly a delicate subject. He sighed heavily and lowered his head.

"We need the truth, Martin," Eric said.

"Back in the nineties a man named Adrian White told Sahid about a couple of stocks that were about to go through the roof. He promised Sahid that if he invested a certain amount of money he would be filthy rich in a short while. Sahid was reluctant; he was skeptical of the stock market. Plus, he didn't have the amount of money Adrian White wanted him to invest. But Adrian kept dogging Sahid until he finally relented. Sahid had about half the amount Adrian said he needed. I loaned Sahid the rest of it. Well, Adrian White's prediction came true. When Sahid sold his stocks, he made just over five-hundred thousand dollars. He paid me back, with interest."

"How much did you loan him?"

"Thirty-five thousand."

"Would you say Amelie was lying to us, that she does know about the money, or is she truly in the dark?" Jake asked.

"She didn't know."

"Where did Sahid keep the money?"

"He has an account with Chase Bank."

"Why would he keep that secret from his wife?" Eric said.

"I can't answer that."

"Can't or won't?"

"All I can tell you is that Sahid asked me to keep it from Amelie. Why? I don't know."

"Did you know Adrian White?"

"I met him a few times over the years, but I didn't really know him."

"Are you aware that he was murdered in his home earlier this week?"

"No, I hadn't heard. I've been so wrapped up with this play that I haven't watched TV, or read a newspaper in several days. Jesus. Do you think his death is connected to Sahid's?"

Eric stood, said, "They both participated in that poker game. So, yeah, I'd say they are connected."

"Obviously, everything we discussed here is confidential," Jake said, handing a business card to Martin. "That includes talking to Amelie Hassaine about her husband's secret money. That task is best left to us."

"No, no I won't say anything to her about it. That would only add to her suffering." He hesitated, then continued, "You know, Detective Gamble, I saw you testify at the recent trial. You were excellent."

"The Morgan Ballard trial?"

"Yes. Sahid and I followed that trial with great interest."

"What was it about the Morgan Ballard trial that interested you guys so much?"

"We both had Morgan in class when she attended UK."

"You and Sahid Hassaine knew Morgan Ballard?" Eric asked.

"Well, she was still Morgan Chambers back then. I didn't know her nearly as well as Sahid did. In my case, she was just another student in a large freshman history class. Sahid had her in two classes, if I remember correctly. And I think she also worked in his office for a couple of years."

"What can you tell me about her?"

"Not much, really. Like I said, she was just another student in a big class. Sorry. Wish I could be of more help."

"Thank you for your time, Martin." Eric extended his hand. "We can see our way out."

*****

The individual Mark Banks phoned and demanded to meet immediately had an alternative plan: Meet in Shillito Park at two a.m. Being a naturally suspicious man, Mark wasn't happy with this new arrangement. But what could he do? He had information that needed to be delivered. And if the man wasn't willing to meet until the middle of the night, then his only option was to follow orders.

Shillito Park at this time of night was a dark, deserted place. Gone were the daylight walkers, joggers, tennis players, Frisbee throwers, kids in the playground area and families at the picnic tables. At two a.m., not another soul was in sight. Mark was sitting in his car, certain he was alone, when he saw a figure emerge from the shadows. Where did the man come from, and where had he parked his vehicle? Mark had no answer for either question.

The man stopped at one of the picnic areas. Mark got out of his car and walked quickly in the man's direction. As always, he kept his right hand on the .45 he had tucked into the waistband of his pants.

"Kinda spooky here at this time of night, wouldn't you agree?" Mark said, sitting on the picnic table.

"Depends on how easily spooked you are," the man

answered. "Me, I don't find it spooky at all."

"Well, I do."

"That's your problem."

"Not really. I can handle myself in spooky places, if I have to."

"The gun you used in those two situations. Do you have it with you now?"

"*Three* situations," Mark corrected. "And, yes, I have it with me. I always do."

"Let me have it."

"Why the hell would I do that?"

"Don't be stupid, Mark. That gun ties you directly to eight homicides. If the cops get it you'll go down. And I'll go with you. Know why? Because you'll start begging for a deal, and the only thing you have to offer is me."

"I'm no rat."

"You say that now, Mark, but when you're looking at the death penalty or life behind bars, you'll squawk. Guys like you always do. So hand over the gun. And those gloves you're wearing? Did you have them on at any of those places?"

"Yes, I did. Why? You want them too?"

"No. You can keep them. But don't forget, they have gunshot residue on them. Cops get their hands on those gloves, you're a goner. If I were you I'd burn them."

Mark took the .45 from his waist band and handed it to the man. "What are you going to do with my gun?"

"Dump it in the lake at Jacobson Park." The man placed the gun on the table next to Mark. "Now, what was so urgent that you needed to speak with me?"

"Two cops came to see me today," Mark answered quickly. "From Homicide. They asked a bunch of questions."

"About?"

"My uncle Carl, for starters."

"What did you tell them?"

"That I hadn't seen Carl since before I was sent to prison."

"Is that true?"

"Yeah, except for the night it all went down."

"Okay, so you're in the clear on that one," the man said. "What else did they ask you?"

"Was I employed, and where did I get the money to pay my rent. I said I was still looking for work, and that I won some money shooting pool. They wanted to know if I knew Stick. I told them I didn't."

"Sounds like legitimate answers to me. Think they believed you?"

"Yeah. They also asked me if I had any weapons. I told them no, that being a convicted felon I wasn't allowed to own a weapon."

"Did they search your place?"

"No."

"Did they ask you about Oscar?"

"Oscar? No. Why would they ask about him?"

"Here's how I see it, Mark. You have no reason to be so concerned. The cops asked questions, you answered, they left. They have no cause to suspect you of anything. Relax, stay cool, and everything will be all right."

Mark pointed at the .45. "And you'll get rid of this?"

"I'll get rid of everything," the man said, as he quickly picked up the pistol, placed the barrel against Mark's temple and pulled the trigger. "Including you, dumb ass."

Mark's body tumbled to his left and fell across the picnic table. The man eased behind the table, careful to avoid the blood spurting from Mark's head, and placed the gun in the dead man's right hand. He then lifted the man's right arm and let it drop naturally. Next, he reached into Mark's shirt pocket and took out his cell phone. No way was he about to leave that behind. Stepping back, surveying the scene, the man concluded that the cops would have a difficult time coming to any result other than suicide.

The gun used in a slew of homicides, the gloves with GSR on them, Mark's stint in the slammer—it all pointed to an eight-time murderer who, either from guilt or the fear of being caught and sent back to prison, decided to end his own life.

Perfect.

The man walked through a small wooded area until he

reached the parking lot. He got in his car and drove away, keeping his headlights off. The road was winding but he had been here many times in the past. In fact, Mark Banks was not the first person he had killed in Shillito Park.

When the man reached Reynolds Road, he turned on his headlights, made a right and headed for home. He smiled, knowing the woman he loved would be pleased when he told her what had just happened. And pleasing her meant everything in the world to him.

CHAPTER NINETEEN

Dantzler was in deep sleep when his cell phone buzzed at six-fifteen in the morning. Carefully moving Grace West's arm, he slipped out of the bed, picked up his phone and went quietly into the bathroom. Grace stirred briefly, mumbled something incomprehensible and then fell back asleep.

Dantzler closed the bathroom door and answered the call. The caller was Harold Embry, the night shift desk sergeant. Dantzler listened for a few seconds, then said, "You sure about the identification? And the body is in Shillito Park? Go ahead, give Eric and Jake a call, tell them to get there as soon as they can. What about Arnie Edwards? Has he been informed? Good. Tell him I'm on my way."

Forty-five minutes later, his body still a victim of late-night love-making and an early wake-up call, Dantzler arrived at Shillito Park. This was one of those times he envied the millions of coffee drinkers who, after a cup or two in the morning, somehow seemed to magically spring to life, regardless of how weary and beaten down they were. But he hated the taste and smell of coffee, so he was consigned to exhaustion.

Arnie Edwards stood off to the left of the picnic table where Mark Banks had taken his final breath. Banks was lying on his left side, eyes open, as though he had been given a big surprise. No doubt he had. A bullet to the head usually is.

"And good morning to you, Detective Dantzler," Arnie said, closing the pad he was writing in. "For once I feel safe in telling you that this man's demise contains no hidden mysteries.

Unless I am badly mistaken, this poor gentleman died as the result of a self-inflicted gunshot to the temple."

"Well, Arnie, I've got some bad news for you. This 'gentleman' did not commit suicide."

"Take a close look, Detective Dantzler. The gun is still in his hand, there are powder burns around the wound, indicating the barrel was in close contact with his head at the time he squeezed the trigger, and I'll bet a year's salary that we'll find GSR on his gloves. If those aren't the classic earmarks of a suicide, I don't know what is. Of course, I'll wait until after the autopsy before issuing my final report, but I will be surprised if my preliminary hunch is incorrect."

"Let me save you some time, Arnie: Your preliminary hunch is incorrect."

"My wager of a year's salary still stands, Detective," Arnie said, smiling. "While I disagree with you, being a man of science I will keep an open mind until all the facts are in."

Although Dantzler had no doubt that this was a homicide he spent a few minutes closely studying Mark Banks's lifeless body, looking for any sign that might cause him to alter his opinion. While the death did appear to result from the classic gun-to-the-head-pull-the-trigger formula, he couldn't see Mark Banks as someone with the courage to take that route to the afterlife.

Dantzler walked back to his car just as Eric was getting out of his. After greeting Dantzler, Eric trudged down to the picnic table, exchanged a few words with Arnie, made a quick inspection of Mark Banks and then came back to the parking area.

"Did this guy just solve eight homicides for us, Jack?" he asked. "Can we be that lucky?"

"Tell me this, Eric. Did Mark Banks strike you as a guy who could have such a crisis of conscience that he would put a gun to his head and check himself out?"

"Truthfully, he didn't strike me as someone with any conscience at all."

"Precisely. This was no suicide, no matter what conclusion Arnie comes to. Mark Banks was murdered."

"Or as Jake would say—*executed*." Eric corrected. "If

you're right, if this was a murder, it means Mark was following someone else's orders."

"Where is Jake? Has he been informed about this?"

"Yeah, I spoke with him as I was leaving the house. He was going by the office before coming here."

"Call him, give him directions to Mark Banks's place, then tell him to meet you there. Toss the place from top to bottom, see if you can find anything that might tell us who was giving Banks his orders. I'll see if Arnie found a cell phone on Banks. If he did, I'll go through it, see if any interesting numbers pop up."

"Will do," Eric said, as he began punching in Jake's number.

Dantzler was disappointed but not surprised when Arnie told him no cell phone had been discovered at the scene. Whoever committed this murder was too smart to leave the victim's phone behind, most likely because the killer knew his number was among those listed. He'd sooner leave behind a pristine fingerprint than forget a cell phone for the cops to find. Either one was more than a loose end; it was the noose.

Dantzler didn't know who the killer was, but he did know this much—the person was not lacking for brains. He was intelligent, cautious and cagey. He was also an experienced professional—this was not his first kill. No, this person had danced this dance many times before.

Eric had been right on the money about one thing, though—eight homicide cases had been closed. The weapon used in the presumed suicide of Mark Banks would almost certainly prove to be the same .45 that murdered the six poker players, Stick and his girlfriend, Darlene. Knowing this, Dantzler almost wished that Banks had ended his own life. With one pull of the trigger, Mark Banks would have made everyone's life a lot easier. The books could now be cleared.

But Mark Banks didn't commit suicide . . . he was murdered. Someone had eliminated an eight-time killer, and that someone was, Dantzler knew, a far more cunning and a far more dangerous animal.

*****

"Tell me again, Jack, why you are so intent on challenging Arnie if he rules this as a suicide?" Richard Bird asked. He was standing by his office window, stretching, trying to get the kinks out of his six-foot-six, fifty-three-year-old body. "From what he described, it looks like a no-brainer. Why don't you agree with him?"

"Because he's wrong, Rich, that's why. Mark Banks was murdered in cold blood. And if I'm not mistaken, you pay me to catch to killers, not to blindly go along with a medical examiner's findings. There is a killer walking free out there, and if I'm intent on anything it's putting that person behind bars."

"Fair enough, Jack." Bird took a seat at his desk. "But will you at least agree that eight murder cases have been closed? That the late Mark Banks was responsible for those homicides?"

"No, I won't make that conclusion until ballistics confirm that his forty-five was used to kill all eight victims. Do I think that's what we'll find? Yes, I do. But until then, I'm still a skeptic."

"For the sake of argument, let's say Banks didn't take his own life. Any thoughts on who killed him?"

"No. But I plan to find out."

Dantzler went back to his office and spent the next two hours deep in thought. Past experience had taught him that every homicide investigation was a puzzle with important pieces missing. Normally, those pieces were linked in some manner. Find one piece, study and analyze it, and it will bring you closer to the next missing piece. Ultimately, when all pieces are found and the puzzle is solved, those individual links make sense.

But in this case—so far at least—the various links go off in all directions. There was no cohesion. What he said to Eric earlier in the week still held true—there were many individual stars but no galaxy. Aligning those stars was mission number one at this stage. But . . . where were the links?

Dantzler's thoughts kept drifting back to Sahid Hassaine. His hidden money and the fact that he knew Morgan Ballard somehow played a big role in all this. Dantzler could feel it in his gut—Hassaine was the piece of the puzzle that could link them all together. But how? And in what way? Those were questions yet to be answered.

Dantzler picked up his cell phone and was about to call Grace when he remembered that she was scheduled to meet Richard Chambers sometime this afternoon. Out of the blue, Chambers had phoned her, asking that they get together. He had matters they needed to discuss. Grace was surprised to hear from him, but agreed to meet. When Dantzler asked her if she thought the ax was about to fall on her role as Morgan's attorney, she said no. That decision, she felt, would be made by the 'new' Morgan Ballard, not by her father.

Instead, Dantzler went to the break room, bought a can of Diet Pepsi and a bag of pretzels, then went back to his office. He gave some thought to phoning Amelie Hassaine but decided against it. When the time came to ask her about Sahid's secret bank account, he needed to do it in person and not over the phone. Although he was fairly sure that she wasn't aware of her husband's hidden money, seeing her reaction when she learned about it could be very telling. Giving the information in a phone call would rob him of the opportunity to see how she responded to the news.

After finishing off his makeshift meal, Dantzler combed through the pile of phone records until he found the one containing calls to and from Adrian White. Next to one of the highlighted numbers, Jake had scribbled Monica Plemmons's name and home address. Dantzler wrote them in his notepad, grabbed his cell phone and left the office.

*****

Monica Plemmons lived in large brick house on Richmond Road, one of those older houses that had been completely redone. Dantzler had no clue as to square footage, but he had no doubt that the price tag for the place was well above a million dollars. Whatever line of work Monica Plemmons was in, she certainly was successful.

Dantzler parked in the small driveway, got out his car and

went up to the front door. After ringing the doorbell, he stepped back, waited, and was somewhat surprised when a man opened the door. The man was in his late-thirties, of medium height, dressed in jeans, a Polo shirt and a pair of well-worn boat shoes. A big smile creased his tanned face.

"Whatever you're selling, I'm not interested," he announced, his smile growing wider. "Nah, just fooling with you. I know who you are. You're a cop, right? I've seen your picture in the paper many times. Can't quite put a finger on the name, though. Sorry."

"Jack Dantzler. I'm with Homicide."

"Yeah, sure, Jack Dantzler. You also play tennis, don't you?"

"I do."

"How can I help you, Detective?" the man asked, making no move to invite Dantzler inside.

"You can start by telling me your name."

"Mickey Plemmons."

"Is Monica Plemmons your wife?"

"Well, she was when she left the house this morning. But in today's world, who can ever know for sure? She very well might have a new beau at her side when she gets back home. Heck, she might even pull a reverse Bruce Jenner and come home a man."

Dantzler quickly judged Mickey Plemmons to be one of those guys who thinks every word out of his mouth is either funny or clever. One of those wannabe comedians who would never in a million years see themselves as obnoxious, which they usually are.

"Do you know when your wife will be home?"

"Haven't the foggiest, Detective. She and a friend went to the mall to do what they do best—shopping. If there was a professional league for shoppers, Monica would be an all-star. The LeBron James of shoppers."

"What time did she leave?"

"About an hour ago. Take my word, Detective, they are just getting started."

Dantzler took a card from his coat pocket and handed it to Mickey. "When she does get home, have her give me a call. At either of those numbers."

"Out of curiosity, why would a homicide detective want to speak with my wife?" Mickey asked, the smile now gone. "What could you possibly want from her?"

"Do you know a man named Adrian White?"

"No."

"Well, your wife does. He was recently murdered, and I need to ask your wife how she knew him."

"Monica owns a flower shop. He probably bought flowers from her."

Based on the number of phone calls, he must've bought a garden's worth of flowers. "You're probably right, Mr. Plemmons, but I need to hear it from her. So have her give me a call."

"I'll tell her as soon as she gets home."

"I would appreciate it if you would."

"Do we need to contact our attorney?"

"No need to do that. Your wife is not under arrest, nor is she a suspect in Adrian White's death. In fact, Mr. White's killer is now deceased. I'm simply trying to tie up some loose ends, and I believe your wife can help me. That's all."

"I can't begin to imagine how she can help you, but I will tell her to contact you."

"Thanks." Dantzler started to walk away, hesitated, turned and said, "What do you do for a living, Mr. Plemmons?"

"I'm a professional editor. I contract with several publishing houses. They send me manuscripts to edit and polish. I'm in the middle of editing a book for an author who has had several books on the best-seller lists."

"So you work mostly at home, right?"

"Exclusively at home."

"Do you work much at night?"

"That's when I do most of my work. I lock myself in my office. That's my method for shutting out the rest of the world. It's impossible for me to do my best work when I'm distracted."

"You and Monica have a very nice home," Dantzler said, surveying the house and grounds. "I couldn't afford this place if they tripled my salary."

"Thank you for the compliment, Detective. Monica deserves all the credit for making the place look so good."

And all the credit for paying the bills, Dantzler thought as he walked back to his car.

Dantzler had just pulled out of the driveway and turned left onto Richmond Road when his cell phone buzzed.

"Jack Dantzler."

"My husband said you needed to speak with me."

That was quick. "At your earliest convenience, Monica," Dantzler said.

"Speak with me about what, exactly?"

"Adrian White."

"I would prefer that our conversation be in private."

"I'm sure you would."

"What does that mean?" Monica snapped.

"Where and when do you want to meet?"

"O'Neill's on Richmond Road. Four-thirty. Will that work for you?"

"I'll see you at four-thirty, Monica," Dantzler said, closing his phone.

CHAPTER TWENTY

Dantzler had expected O'Neill's to be busy at four-thirty on a Friday and it was. The horseshoe-shaped bar was populated by those looking to get an early start on their weekend revelries, while the dining area was home to those hoping to beat the evening rush. Most everyone, diners and drinkers, were ignoring the many big-screen TV sets situated around the premises.

Despite the crowd of unfamiliar faces, Dantzler had no trouble locating Monica Plemmons. He recognized her immediately; not because she was sitting alone at a corner table, but rather because she was yet another incredibly beautiful woman. With her dirty blonde hair, her dark eyebrows and golden-brown skin, she reminded Dantzler of Sharon Stone in her prime. Approaching the table, he couldn't help but think that if someone put a gun to his head and ordered him to say who was more beautiful—Suzanne Worley, Cynthia Purcell or Monica Plemmons—he would have to take the bullet.

"Monica?" he said, arriving at her table. "I'm Detective Jack Dantzler. Mind if I join you?"

Monica motioned to the chair across from her. "Please, have a seat. Would you care for something to drink?"

"Coke, Pepsi, whatever they have."

Monica beckoned the waitress, then ordered a soft drink for him and a glass of merlot for herself. They said nothing until their drinks were served.

"Adrian White, huh?" Monica said, after taking a drink. "What makes him so interesting?"

"He's dead. I want to know who killed him, and why."

"I heard on the news that the murderer of those poker players was found dead in Shillito Park. Isn't he the one you were looking for?"

"I'm convinced there are others involved."

"Sorry, but I can't provide the answers to either of your questions."

"I didn't come here thinking you could," Dantzler said. "But I would like to know about your relationship with him."

"*Relationship*? You make it sound like we were lovers. That's ludicrous."

"Something was going on between the two of you. His phone records prove that. So let's go back to my question: What was your relationship with Adrian White?"

"We were friends, that's all."

"Good friends, based on the number of phone calls."

Monica took a drink, carefully weighing her words before answering. "Adrian was divorced, he was lonely, so he often called me late at night. We'd talk for a while, until he was feeling better, then he would hang up. That's about the extent of our *relationship*."

"Why call you?"

"I have a sympathetic ear, I suppose."

"And how much does your sympathetic ear charge?"

"What are you insinuating, Detective Dantzler? Please, speak your piece and stop beating around the bush."

Dantzler smiled. "You're a smart lady. You know exactly what I'm insinuating."

"No, Detective, I don't."

"How did you meet Adrian White?"

"I can't remember. Probably when he came in to buy some flowers. As my husband told you, I'm a florist."

"Did you ever spend time alone with Adrian White?"

"Absolutely not."

A lie.

"Not once?"

"Never."

A second lie.

"If I check your phone records, will I find that you made calls to him?"

Monica shoved her cell phone across the table. "Check to your heart's content, Detective. You won't find Adrian White's name in my Contacts list, nor will you find that I ever phoned the man."

Dantzler pushed the phone back to her. "Okay, I believe you on that one. But I don't believe you never spent time alone with him."

"Do you really think I was having an affair with Adrian White? Come on, Detective. The man was more than twice my age. If I were going to have an affair, wouldn't you agree that I could do better than him?"

"I've never once mentioned the word affair," Dantzler pointed out. "You weren't having an affair, but you did see him. We both know that's true."

"If it's true, where's your evidence?"

"Do you know Suzanne Worley or Cynthia Purcell?" Dantzler asked, shifting gears.

"No."

A third lie.

"You sure about that?"

"Yes, I'm sure."

"What about Morgan Ballard? Know her?"

"Yes, I have known Morgan for a long time. What's that got to do with anything?"

"Do you consider her a friend?"

"Who? Morgan? Yes, Detective, she and I are good friends."

"But not Suzanne Worley or Cynthia Purcell, right?"

"Tell me please, Detective, what are you driving at?"

"That house you live in had to cost more than a million bucks, Monica. Now, I don't care how many best-selling books your husband works on, or how many roses you sell, you guys couldn't afford that place based strictly on the income from those professions. So what I'm saying is, you have money—big money—coming in for another source."

"And what might that source be, Detective?"

"Prostitution."

Monica laughed out loud. "You're joking, right? Do I look like a prostitute to you? Really? That's beyond humorous; it's utterly ridiculous."

"All right, then let's use Cynthia Purcell's terminology— professional escort."

"You should be a stand-up comedian, Detective Dantzler. You're certainly a funny guy."

"So you deny that you belong to a group of women who are high-priced hookers?"

"You know, Detective, right now I don't know whether to laugh out loud or slap your face for making an insulting remark like that. Calling me a prostitute, a hooker, a professional escort— those are cheap and cruel things to say. And I resent it. If I were a man I would punch you, badge or no badge."

"Ease up, Monica. We're only talking here. No need for threats of violence."

"Answer this, Detective. If I'm guilty of these things you're accusing me of, don't you think my husband would know about it? And if it was true, and he did know about it, wouldn't it be safe to assume that he would divorce me?"

"Monica, I've met your husband. Now I've met you. I estimate that you are about fifty times more intelligent than he is. He doesn't have a clue what you're doing."

"How could he possibly *not* know? After all, we do live together."

"He works nights. So do you. He locks himself in his office to do his editing. Never knows when you come and go."

"You're in the wrong profession, Detective. With your imagination you should write fiction."

"Yeah, but then I would miss the chance to meet beautiful ladies like you and Suzanne Worley and Cynthia Purcell. Those women you *don't* know."

"When we began this little chat, Detective, you wanted to ask me about Adrian White. We have since strayed far off course.

If you have no more questions about him, then I think this conversation has reached its conclusion."

"No, we're done," Dantzler said, standing. He took out a twenty-dollar bill and laid it on the table. "You've been a real sport, Monica. Drinks are on me. And I do thank you for taking the time to meet with me."

"You really should write fiction, Detective."

"Nah. Reality is much more interesting," he answered, walking away.

Sitting in his car, Dantzler took out his cell phone and called Eric. "Where are you and Jake?"

"I'm at the office," Eric answered. "Jake left to have dinner with his parents. Why? What's up?"

"Nothing, really. Did you guys find anything worthwhile at Mark Banks's place?"

"Only if you consider eighty-five grand in cash worthwhile."

"A big payoff for a lowlife like him. That tells us how much he got for murdering eight people. Now we need to find out who paid him." Dantzler thought for a second, then said, "If you have everything cleared, take off. I'll see you on Monday."

"An entire weekend off? That's hard to believe."

"That should give you enough time to finish your novel."

"Yeah, right. I'm not even halfway through it."

"Keep plugging away. You'll get there. See you Monday."

"Wait, Jack, there's something I forgot to tell you. Been so busy it slipped my mind."

"Tell me what?"

"Remember Martin Conley, Sahid Hassaine's friend that Jake and I interviewed? He told us that he and Sahid both had Morgan Ballard in class when she attended the University of Kentucky. She was still Morgan Chambers back in those days."

"So they both knew her."

"According to Martin, he really didn't know her at all. But Sahid Hassaine did. In fact, Martin told us that Morgan worked in Hassaine's office for a couple of years. He knew her outside the classroom."

"I keep thinking Hassaine is the key to all this. In some way it all revolves around him. Where and how did he get the money to sit at that poker table? That's what we have to find out."

"Do we go back to his wife?"

"No. She can't help us."

"If she can't, who can?"

"I'm not sure, but I know where to start looking."

*****

Dantzler drove straight from O'Neill's to his house. He quickly undressed, hopped in the shower and let the hot water blast away at his weariness for fifteen minutes. Then he dressed in Levis, a T-shirt and sandals, went into the kitchen and mixed a Pernod and orange juice. After taking a drink, he stepped out onto the deck, opened his cell phone and made a call he had no desire to make.

Grace West answered after three rings. "I was wondering when I might hear from you. Long day, huh?"

"You could say that. Listen, how did your meeting with Richard Chambers turn out?"

"Much better than I expected, to be honest with you. He was very pleasant."

"Are you still on his payroll?"

"Surprisingly, yes."

"I hate to hear that."

"Why?"

Dantzler grimaced, bracing for the explosion he knew was only seconds away from happening. "Because I need to speak with Morgan Ballard."

"Under no circumstances will I let that happen, Jack. As her attorney of record, I *can't* allow it. You know that."

"You can sit in with us, Grace. And I give you my word that I won't ask one question regarding her husband or her trial. I have no interest in any of that. I need to ask her about matters totally unrelated to what went down in her house the morning she shot Deke Ballard."

"What *unrelated* matters?"

"Unfortunately, I'm not at liberty to discuss that with you."

"Listen to you, sounding all lawyer-like."

"It's no fun when the tables are turned, is it? Now you know how the non-lawyers of the world feel."

After an extended silence, Grace finally said, "Can't allow it, Jack. Sorry. Until her case is adjudicated, Morgan is off-limits to any and all law enforcement interrogation. That's just how it has to be."

"I'm gonna talk to that woman, Grace, even if it means I have to arrest her."

"Arrest her? For what?"

"Again, I'm not at liberty to share any details at the present time. I will when I can."

"Boy, this conversation sure went off the rails in a hurry. Or maybe I just forgot that you and I are essentially adversaries, and that butting heads is a natural part of the process. But adversaries or not, what I haven't forgotten is that I represent Morgan Ballard, and that I cannot allow you to interview her."

"Think about it, Grace. That's all I ask. Bring her in and I'll have her out of there in fifteen minutes. That's a promise. And you can be right by her side. If I ask a question you deem inappropriate, tell her she doesn't have to answer. I just need some information from her."

"Does it have to do with your murder investigation?"

"Possibly."

"I will discuss this with Morgan tomorrow. If she gives it the green light I won't stop her. But know this—I will be arguing forcefully against her doing it."

"Fair enough. Now, how about dinner?"

"Not tonight," Grace said, hanging up.

*****

He sat in his office at midnight, alone, his thoughts vacillating between love for his woman and the events of the past week. Thinking about the woman he truly loved held the top spot by a wide margin. How could it be any other way? His feelings for her were unlike any he had ever experienced. People were always talking about someone being "the love of my life"—hell, his late parents were forever making that claim about each other—but he had never bought into that romantic idea. Now, he wasn't quite the doubter he had once been. There had been many women in his past, including a few he genuinely cared for, but none of them owned his heart so completely as this lady.

If a "love of my life" truly existed, she was it.

But just as quickly, his thoughts shifted to the events of the past week. Thinking about the shit storm he had unleashed caused him to laugh out loud. Since last Saturday night, a mere six days ago, he had orchestrated the killing of seven men and one woman, and had committed one murder himself. And the outcome of it all far exceeded his wildest expectations.

The eight deaths, the ones he ordered, were all a necessary part of the plan. Those eight had to die in order to keep the enterprise from crumbling. Had that occurred, it would mean an end to the cash flow and sure prison sentences for the ones driving the train. Silencing those eight kept the money train from derailing.

Without question, though, it was the murder by his own hand that had him feeling so relieved and upbeat. The presence of Mark Banks had always been a potential boil needing to be lanced. The man knew this when he dispatched Banks to kill those six poker players. Giving that task to Banks meant bringing a total stranger into the game. That was always a dangerous thing to do, especially with someone like Mark Banks. Men like him are never satisfied; they always let greed get the best of them. Eventually, Banks would have demanded more money, using the threat of tipping off the authorities to squeeze extra cash from those running the show. In effect, Banks would have blackmailed them.

Thanks to fate, or good fortune, or plain old good luck, Banks was no longer a threat. A bullet to the side of his head ended any chance of him causing problems. With Banks out of the way everyone could now breathe a little easier.

The man looked at his watch and realized he had been in his office for almost an hour. He thought about giving her a call, but knew that wasn't a good idea. They still needed to limit their conversations and their meetings. It hurt not being able to be with her, to make love to her, to hold her, to be her guy. That would happen sometime in the future, maybe a year from now if things went smoothly. However, being together at this stage posed too many risks.

And he wasn't a man who took unnecessary risks, not even for the love of his life.

CHAPTER TWENTY-ONE

At a few minutes past nine on Saturday morning Dantzler entered the Chase Bank branch on Tates Creek Road. The branch manager, a lady named Eve Randolph, was initially reluctant to grant Dantzler's request to look at Sahid Hassaine's bank records, but when he informed her that it pertained to a murder investigation, she finally relented. Firing up her computer, she tapped on some keys and waited.

"Presently, Mr. Hassaine has in his checking account a little more than six-hundred thousand dollars," Eve said, after scrolling through several screens. "He opened his account with an original deposit of two-hundred thousand dollars."

"How long has he had the account?" Dantzler asked.

"Let me see. He has been with us for almost seventeen years."

"Was anyone else's name on the account?"

"No. Only Sahid Hassaine."

"Can you tell how he grew the amount from the original figure to the six-hundred thousand?"

"It appears as though Mr. Hassaine regularly deposited ten-thousand dollars during the first week of each month. There are also a scattering of withdrawals, but they seem to occur on a more random basis."

"What happens to this money now that Sahid Hassaine is dead?"

"I would assume that his wife gets it."

"His wife knows nothing about this account."

"Really? Well, I'm sure Mr. Hassaine left a will. If he did, and if he left everything to his wife, then she has a right to claim the money."

Dantzler stood, said, "Thank you for giving me this information, Eve. You've been very helpful."

"Will you inform his wife about the account?"

"That's my next stop."

"Strange, a husband hiding that much money from his wife. That has to tell you he was up to no good."

Dantzler could only nod in agreement with Eve's statement.

*****

Amelie Hassaine was in the front yard pulling weeds when Dantzler drove up. She stood, shielded her eyes from the rising sun, and offered a half-smile when she recognized Dantzler. Removing her gloves, she extended a hand, which he accepted.

"Let's go inside where it's more comfortable," Amelie said. "It's already hot, and it's only going to get hotter. Plus, I need a break."

Once they were inside she asked Dantzler if he wanted something to drink. He declined. She went to the kitchen and came back a few minutes later with a tall glass of water.

"What prompted this visit, Detective Dantzler?" She took a seat on the sofa. "Good news or bad news?"

"Both, I'm afraid."

"Begin with the good. I've had enough bad news lately, so tell me something positive."

"The man who murdered your husband is dead. His name was Mark Banks. There is no doubt that he was the shooter. Ballistics proved it was his weapon used that night in Judge Kurtz's house. So at least that will spare surviving family members from having to go through the ordeal of a trial."

"How did Mark Banks die?"

"His body was found two days ago in Shillito Park. Cause of death was a gunshot to the head. The coroner is likely to rule it a suicide but it wasn't. Someone murdered Mark Banks."

"Which means the person who hired him is still unaccounted for, right?"

"Right."

"So the good news is my husband's killer is dead, the bad news is the person behind the murders remains a free man? Does that about sum it up, Detective Dantzler?"

Dantzler paused briefly, then said, "Amelie, what I'm about to share with you now is going to be difficult for you to hear. But you need to know."

Amelie set her glass on the floor. "Does this have to do with money?"

"Yes. Your husband had a checking account at Chase Bank. I went there this morning and spoke with the branch manager. She pulled up his file, and it showed that he has a shade above six-hundred thousand dollars in his account. He opened the account almost seventeen years ago."

Amelie Hassaine's face went white, her hands began to tremble, and for a second Dantzler was certain she was about to faint. But after closing her eyes and taking several slow, deep breaths, she regained some measure of composure.

"I hope you're not thinking that I knew anything about this, Detective, because I most certainly did not."

"No, I don't think that at all."

"Do you have a theory as to how he accumulated that much money?"

"No."

A lie.

Amelie said, "For him to keep it a secret tells me he was into something illegal. Or maybe he was the great poker player he always claimed to be and he won it in those games at the Judge's house. Think that's a possibility?"

"Sure."

A second lie.

"Did your husband leave a will?"

"Of course."

"What did he leave to you?"

"Everything."

"According to the bank manager, you have the right to claim that six-hundred thousand dollars. You'll need to meet with someone from the bank and fill out the required paperwork. Then the money is yours."

"Detective Dantzler, I wouldn't touch that money under any circumstances, not even if I was a beggar on the street. Who knows how dirty it might be? If the money is mine I'll donate every last penny to charity. That way, what is most likely bad money can do something good."

"That's your call, Amelie." Dantzler stood and went to the front door. "If I hear anything else about your husband, I'll let you know."

"No, Detective Dantzler, if you learn anything else please keep it to yourself. I have zero interest in learning more about his secret life."

*****

Dantzler spent most of Saturday afternoon at the Tennis Center giving lessons to a set of female twins whose parents held fast to the belief that the girls were destined to be the reincarnation of Venus and Serena Williams. What Dantzler knew, and the parents didn't, or refused to acknowledge, was that the girls had little if any desire to succeed as tennis players. They played to please mom and dad. It was the classic example of parents trying to vicariously live their dreams through their children. As someone who had been around tennis all his life, he had witnessed this misplaced desire far too many times.

After finishing his work with the twins, Dantzler showered, dressed and went up to the lounge area hoping to run into Sean Montgomery. He was in luck; Sean was sitting in a booth drinking lemonade.

"Those twins on the fast-track to Wimbledon glory yet?" Sean joked.

"Should win it within the next five years." Dantzler took a seat across from Sean. "If they don't, their parents will be mighty disappointed."

"Are the girls any good?"

"Good, yes. But for what the parents are hoping for, you have to be much better than simply good. You have to be extraordinary, which they aren't."

"Oh well, parents can dream, can't they, Jack?"

"Yes, but those dreams need to be within reason."

Sean grinned, and said, "Where is your lawyer lady friend? Bloom tells me you two are tighter than the spin on Clayton Kershaw's curveball."

"We both know Bloom talks too much."

"True, but is what he says accurate, or is it bullshit?"

"To be honest with you, Sean, I don't know. All I can say is she seems to be a little pissed off at me."

"What transgression did you commit to earn her wrath?"

"I told her I needed to interview Morgan Ballard."

"And she vetoed that proposal?"

"Faster than a Clayton Kershaw fastball."

"And what, you're surprised? Jesus, Jack, she's Morgan's attorney. There is no way she'll let you interview Morgan. I wouldn't either if I represented the woman."

"I have no interest in asking Morgan anything about the death of her husband," Dantzler pointed out. "What happened that night is of no concern to me. My questions will take her down an entirely different road."

"Where are you going with this, Jack?"

"I'm not sure. But whatever it is, Morgan Ballard is somehow involved."

"As what? A high-priced hooker?"

"That's only a part of it. And that's not the part I care about. Look, Sean, Sahid Hassaine was one of those six poker players who were murdered. He had six-hundred grand in a checking account his wife knew nothing about. Morgan Ballard was in his class when she was a student at UK. She also worked in Hassaine's office for two years. Then the man who committed eight murders is found dead. You want me to believe none of this is connected?"

"You don't suspect Morgan Ballard of killing the Banks

dude, do you?"

"No. She shoots men when they are asleep, not when they are looking her in the eyes. Plus, there is no way Banks would have handed his weapon to her. Morgan didn't kill him."

"Richard Chambers?"

"He's a man who could do it, but I don't think he did. Whoever took out Mark Banks is the person running the show. That's who I'm after, and I'm certain Morgan Ballard has the answer I'm looking for."

"Grace West isn't going to let you anywhere near Morgan. You can forget about that. So you had better look for another source of information."

"In the final set of a close match against a strong opponent, it's no longer about tennis, Sean. It's about will. The player who can break his opponent, bend his will, usually wins. Being mentally tough was my strongest attribute. I beat many players who had more talent that I did simply because my will was unbreakable. And that's what I'm counting on now, that my will is stronger than Grace West's."

"That's a marvelous speech worthy of Vince Lombardi," Sean said, laughing. "Just keep in mind that she's already kicked your ass once. I wouldn't put her in the win column just yet, regardless of how good you are in the sack. She's every bit as tough as you are."

"And people say I'm a negative prick."

*****

Dantzler spent Saturday night and all day Sunday sitting on his deck doing nothing but watching baseball and golf on television. The Cincinnati Reds, not his favorite team but one he closely followed, beat the San Francisco Giants, a team he had always hated. On a pristine golf course located somewhere in sunny Florida, Adam Scott, a handsome Aussie, overcame a two-shot deficit on the final three holes to capture the title. Other than staring at the tube, Dantzler did little else Sunday but drink Pernod and orange juice.

He thought about calling Grace but decided not to. No point in continuing the disagreement. She could call him once she calmed down. If that didn't happen, well, then it wasn't meant to be.

At nine-thirty Sunday night Grace did call. Dantzler answered, unsure what her mood was going to be.

"Sorry for not calling earlier," Grace said, in a most-pleasant tone. "I had business in Chicago. Just got back to Lexington about an hour ago."

"I had begun to think I might never hear from you again."

"Because of a petty squabble? Where's your faith, man?"

"If I remember correctly, you were the one who labeled us as adversaries."

"That's business, not life. Never confuse the two."

"Got it. So . . . back to business. Are you gonna let me speak with Morgan?"

"Is the pope a Muslim?"

"I take that as a no."

Grace laughed. "See, you are quick to catch on. No, you will not be speaking with her. Sorry."

"Did you inform Morgan that I wanted to meet with her?"

"No."

"But you will, right? Isn't that what you said you would do?"

"I'll tell her, but I will also strongly advise her against it."

"Fair enough. Do you want to come over for a while?"

"Goodnight, Jack," Grace said, closing her phone.

Damn, Dantzler thought, business was still beating the crap out of life.

CHAPTER TWENTY-TWO

Dantzler, Eric, Jake and Richard Bird were assembled in the War Room waiting patiently as Arnie Edwards opened a folder and withdrew papers relating to the Mark Banks case. Eric and Jake were bright-eyed and ready to tackle the day, looking like a pair of well-rested men who spent two full days away from work, while Dantzler displayed all the signs of a man who had slept little while consuming far too much alcohol. Captain Bird, clearly unimpressed with Dantzler's Monday-morning appearance, scowled, but kept his thoughts to himself.

Arnie spread some papers on the table, looked up at Dantzler and said, "Jack, I realize you are going to fight me on this, but given all the facts as I see them, I have no other alternative but to declare the death of Mark Banks to be a suicide. I have studied this case until my eyes bled, looked at it from every possible angle, and the only conclusion I can come up with is the man took his own life."

Everyone waited for Dantzler to protest but he remained silent. Finally, Arnie said, "There's a part of me that wanted to call it a suspicious death, but I couldn't bring myself to do it. The evidence for suicide is just too compelling."

"Well, Jack?" Bird said, after another extended silence. "What do you think?"

"I don't give a shit how compelling the evidence is for suicide," Dantzler replied. "This was a homicide, pure and simple."

Arnie said, "Read my final report, Jack, and look at the

photos. Then you tell me how I could have arrived at a different conclusion."

Dantzler shook his head but didn't answer.

Arnie scooped up the papers, returned them to the folder and stood. "Detectives, if there is nothing else, I'll be on my way. As always, if you have questions you know where to find me."

After Arnie was gone, Bird eyed Dantzler and said, "Okay, Jack, since you are so quick to torpedo Arnie's suicide ruling, give us your theory on who murdered Mark Banks, and why."

"I don't know who, Rich, but the why is easy. To silence him."

Bird stood and went to the door. Turning, he said, "If you believe that, then go find the killer."

"You can count on it, Rich."

When Bird left, Eric spoke up. "Where do we start looking?"

Dantzler rubbed his temples, trying to shake off the last remnants of his morning hangover, while Eric's question hung in the air like a bad odor. Jake, patient as always, drank from a bottle of water and waited quietly for Dantzler to answer.

Dantzler ignored Eric's question, choosing instead to share with the two detectives what he had learned about Sahid Hassaine's secret checking account. He remained convinced that Hassaine was central to whatever was going on, and that how he got the money was a critical issue. For Dantzler, this meant Hassaine had to be the focus of the investigation.

This was especially true if Grace West kept Morgan Ballard off-limits.

"Six-hundred grand. Damn, that's a shitload of bucks," Eric said. "Where do you think he got it?"

"Not from playing poker, that much is clear. The key for us is finding out where the initial two-hundred thousand came from. How many college professors have that much cash at any given moment? My guess would be none."

"Are you convinced his wife was in the dark on this? I find it hard to believe she didn't know."

"She was genuinely shocked when I told her," Dantzler

said. "Amelie Hassaine played no part in whatever her husband was into."

"Maybe Hassaine wasn't into anything criminal," Jake offered. "After all, he did make a bundle on the stock market right off the bat. Could be he continued to play the market with success."

"It was about fifteen years ago that we went to war in Iraq, Jake. The way I remember it, the stock market tanked. So I think we can safely rule that out as a possibility. Besides, the stock market wouldn't account for those regular deposits of ten grand a month." Dantzler thought for a few moments, then said, "What was the name of Hassaine's pal that you guys spoke with?"

"Martin Conley," Eric answered.

"Talk to him again. See if he can offer more insight into how Hassaine came by his money. Also, get names of other friends of Hassaine. Surely this Conley fellow wasn't Hassaine's only close buddy."

Jake said, "Are we making a mistake by focusing so much attention on Sahid Hassaine? I mean, there were five other poker players who were murdered. Isn't it possible that one of them was the primary target?"

"That's an excellent question, Jake," Dantzler answered. "And yes, anything is possible. But ask yourself this: Who murdered their murderer? That's the individual we're after. And since Sahid Hassaine was the only financially challenged player in the group, where and how he came up with the resources to participate in the game makes him the one most worthy of our interest. I could be dead wrong about all of this, but I don't think so. His source of income and those murders are connected."

"What's your next step?" Eric asked.

"Speak with Cynthia Purcell again. Of the three ladies I've spoken with, she's the friendliest and the most forthcoming about what she does for a living. I'm hoping she can give us something more to work with."

"Sure you don't want me to handle that assignment?" Jake said.

"You're too young and innocent, Jake. I don't want your

mom blaming me for you getting corrupted." Dantzler stood. "Get going, guys. We'll meet back here at four-thirty."

*****

Martin Conley appeared to be more nervous and ill at ease than he was the first time Eric and Jake met with him. His hands kept fidgeting, and his eyes wandered off in all directions. He forced a smile, giving a supreme effort to be cordial and polite. Despite his best acting, he couldn't hide his discomfort.

"Are you all right, Mr. Conley?" Eric asked. "You seem a little stressed."

"I'm fine, really. It's just the play is only a few days away and we're nowhere close to being ready. I'm always nervous at this point. But . . . what questions do you have for me?"

"Since we spoke with you we've learned more about Sahid Hassaine's finances," Eric said. "You told us he made close to five-hundred thousand dollars after selling off some stocks. Is that accurate?"

"Yes, it is. As I also told you, he paid me back for the money I loaned him. That was the only time I had any financial dealings with Sahid."

"At the time of his death he had six-hundred thousand in his checking account at Chase Bank."

"Well, I wouldn't know about that," Martin replied.

"His initial deposit was two-hundred grand," Jake told Martin. "Since then he regularly deposited ten-thousand into his account during the first week of each month. Any idea where that money came from?"

"I can only assume it came from his pension or his retirement money."

"He deposited the money in cash," Eric said.

"Then he must have taken the cash from his pension or retirement benefits and deposited it in the bank. That makes sense, doesn't it?"

"Not really. If he did that it's highly likely that his wife would have known about it. But she didn't know. And why have a secret account? That tells us he *didn't* want his wife to know."

"I don't know what you expect me to tell you. Sahid and I were close friends, but we didn't discuss business. I didn't tell him mine and he didn't tell me his."

"What about women?" Jake asked. "Did the two of you ever discuss them?"

"Women? I'm unclear as to what you're asking me."

"Did you and Sahid have conversations about the ladies?"

"I'm gay, Detective. *Ladies*, as I interpret the spirit of your question, hold no interest for me."

"What about Sahid? Did they interest him?" Eric said.

"Are you asking me if Sahid was unfaithful to Amelie, Detective?"

"That's exactly what I'm asking."

"I would have no way of knowing that," Martin said, now clearly flustered. "We did not discuss our sex lives."

"Come on, Martin, guys talk. We're not here to judge his morals, only to see if you can help us find a killer. If he was seeing other women, or one woman, tell us. I give my word that your name will never come up."

"Honestly, I don't know if he was unfaithful or not. But another friend of ours, a man named Nick Howard, might be able to help you."

"Who is Nick Howard?"

"He also taught at the University of Kentucky. In the Theatre Department."

"Is he retired?"

"Yes."

"Where does he live?"

"In Griffin Gate."

"Can you think of anything else that might be pertinent to our investigation?"

"No."

"You have our card, Martin," Jake said. "If you think of anything else, give us a call."

CHAPTER TWENTY-THREE

Nick Howard was one of those guys that come off as effortlessly cool. There was no other way to assess him. You could see it in the way he dressed, how he acted, and the ease in which language rolled off his tongue. And part of his coolness was that he seemed to be unaware of it. Or if not unaware, then indifferent.

"Tragic how the final curtain came down on Sahid," Nick said, after taking a drink of wine. "No one's life should end in such horrible circumstances."

"How well did you know Sahid?" Eric asked, taking out his notepad.

"We were good friends. I'm several years younger than he was, but we got along well together. Sahid, Martin Conley and I were brothers in some strange way."

"Are you still teaching?"

"No, I retired three years ago. Playing golf is how I stay busy these days. Occasionally, I'll assist Martin with one of his productions. But that's rare."

Jake said, "Do you know Sahid's wife?"

"Amelie? Sure. A wonderful woman. She's from France, you know."

"How would you characterize their marriage?"

"Normal, I suppose. I've never heard either one complain about it. I'm certainly not aware of any major problems they were having."

"What would you say if I told you Sahid had six-hundred thousand dollars in a checking account, and that his wife didn't know about it?"

"I would say I'm shocked. Why? Is that true?"

Both Eric and Jake nodded.

"Where did he get that kind of money?"

"We were hoping you might tell us," Jake said.

"Sahid played in that big poker game every week, so I can only assume he won the money."

"Don't think so," Eric challenged. "You see, he deposited ten grand into his account at the beginning of each month. That leads us to believe the money was coming from another source. Do you have any idea what that source might be?"

"No, absolutely not. To be perfectly honest with you Detective Gamble, I'm having a hard time processing this. Sahid never once mentioned having a secret bank account, or that he had that kind of money. This is stunning news to me."

"What about women?" Jake asked. "Did Sahid have a mistress? Or see prostitutes?"

"I'd rather not answer that."

Eric said, "Mr. Howard, we are well beyond worrying about Sahid Hassaine's morals. We're looking for a murderer. You need to provide us with any information you have that might help us close this case."

Nick let out a long sigh before speaking. "A few years ago, maybe ten, I know he was seeing someone. He told me her name was Monica. I never got a last name."

"What did he say about their relationship?"

"He didn't get into intimate details, Detective. All he said was that they had been seeing each other for several months. I have no clue when the affair began, or how long it lasted."

"Do you know Morgan Ballard?" Jake said.

"I do. In fact, she was in one of my classes when she attended UK. She had me for theatre history. This was when she was still Morgan Chambers."

"Did you know that Sahid also had Morgan in class? And that she worked in his office for two years?"

"Yes, I am aware of that. What does Morgan Ballard have to do with anything?"

Eric wrote in his notebook, then looked up. "Do you know Suzanne Worley or Monica Plemmons?"

"Those names don't ring a bell."

"Never had either one in class?"

"I can't answer that without checking my records. I taught thousands of students; I can't remember them all."

"We would appreciate it if you would check your records." Eric handed one of his cards to Nick. "Get back with us when you do. And we thank you for taking time to speak with us. You've been a big help."

"No, what I've been is a gossip monger who dished out dirty laundry on a close friend. And that doesn't make me feel good about myself."

*****

Smiling broadly, Cynthia Purcell opened her apartment door and waved Dantzler in. She was elegantly dressed in white slacks, a black top and a pair of expensive black shoes. This time, however, she was not alone. Sitting on the sofa was another incredibly beautiful lady. She was also dressed elegantly in slacks, blouse and shoes that Dantzler guessed were just as pricey as the ones Cynthia was wearing.

Although it was early in the afternoon, both women were holding a glass of what appeared to be bourbon.

"Tell me, Detective, does this mean you have put away your badge, and have decided to take me up on my offer?" Cynthia said, smiling.

"Let it go, Cynthia. You're way out of my price range."

"Discount, remember?"

"Not today." Dantzler nodded toward the lady on the sofa. "Who's your friend? Don't think I've met her."

"Kelsey Williams." Kelsey stood and extended her hand. "And you are right. I don't think we've ever met, although I have read about your tennis exploits. You are quite exceptional, it seems."

"Thanks, but I'm not here to discuss tennis." To Cynthia: "I need to ask you a few follow-up questions, if you don't mind."

"Sure, Detective, feel free to ask me anything." Cynthia held up her glass. "Would you care for a drink? Four Roses Single Barrel. Mighty tasty."

Dantzler looked at his watch and shook his head. "Little early in the day for me."

"Come now, Detective. It's never too early for top-of-the-line bourbon. You're a Kentucky boy. You should know that."

"Some other time." Dantzler glanced at Kelsey, then looked at Cynthia. "Kelsey might not be interested in what we discuss. Perhaps she'd like to move to another room."

"Would you prefer that she moved, Detective?"

Hell, no. "She can stay, or she can leave. That's her call."

"Then Kelsey stays."

Great. "The reason I came back to see you is because I think you are an honest lady. I hope I'm right about that, because if I have any chance of catching a killer, you need to be totally honest with me again."

Cynthia looked at Kelsey, said, "The good Detective here thinks I am involved with a ring of what he calls 'high-priced hookers.' How he came to this conclusion is anyone's guess. I made it clear to him that I am an independent contractor, and that I work only for myself. I don't think he believes me."

"What about you, Kelsey? You in the same line of work as Cynthia?"

"What line might that be?" Kelsey asked.

"Professional escort."

"I'm an interior designer, Detective. If you ever need my services, let me know. I'll give you one of my business cards before you leave."

"And I'll give you one of mine." Dantzler turned toward Cynthia. "Tell me about Morgan Ballard."

"Morgan? Why on earth would you ask me about her?"

"Because I'm convinced she's in your line of work, along with Suzanne Worley and Monica Plemmons." Dantzler glanced back at Kelsey. "Am I leaving someone out?"

All he got from Kelsey was an enigmatic smile.

"Okay, Detective Dantzler, here are the facts," Cynthia said, after taking a drink. "Morgan and I are good friends. Have been for a long time. But I hardly know Suzanne and Monica. I've maybe met them four or five times, that's all. We are not a band of sisters who spend a lot of time hanging out together. Sorry to disappoint you."

"What about you, Kelsey?" Dantzler asked. "Do you know Morgan, Suzanne and Monica?"

"I know Morgan," Kelsey replied. "Suzanne and Monica, not so much."

"What does not so much mean?"

"That they are acquaintances."

"Clearly, Morgan is at the center of the wheel. Is . . .?"

"Here's what I think, Detective Dantzler," Cynthia interrupted. "You have it in your head that all the women you've named are high-priced call girls, and that Morgan is the person running the show. Does that about sum it up?"

"Couldn't have said it better myself."

"Please, Detective, disabuse yourself of that notion. It's simply not true."

"What you want me to believe is that you are the sole 'professional escort' in Lexington? Is that right?"

"Since I don't know what goes on in all of Lexington, I cannot answer that question. There certainly could be others . . . it's a big city, after all. But if there is one more, or fifty more, I don't know their names. And I most assuredly am not part of a group. That's really all I can tell you."

"Like I said before, you're an intelligent lady, Cynthia. I almost believe you."

"But you don't."

"No."

"Well, Detective, despite your belief that I'm a liar, just to prove how magnanimous I am, my offer of a discount still holds true. Lose the badge, then come pay me a visit."

Dantzler went to the door, turned back toward the two women, and said, "Thanks for your time, Cynthia. And it was a pleasure meeting you, Kelsey."

"You don't know what pleasure is, Detective," Kelsey answered, her enigmatic smile still in place.

*****

Eric and Jake were in the War Room when Dantzler showed up. He left the room, bought a can of Diet Pepsi, then rejoined his fellow detectives. Taking a seat, he opened the soft drink and said, "Learn anything good from Nick Howard?"

"Two things of interest," Eric answered. "Nick also had Morgan Ballard in class when she attended UK. Also, he told us that a few years ago Sahid Hassaine was having a relationship with a woman named Monica. No last name. Nick said Sahid had been seeing her for a few months."

"Monica has to be Monica Plemmons," Dantzler said. "Did he shed more light on how Sahid made his money?"

Eric shook his head. "No. He was shocked when we told him about Sahid's secret account."

Jake said, "What about you, Jack? Learn anything new from Cynthia?"

"All I got from her were stern denials that only reinforce what I already suspected. She did have a friend with her, a beautiful woman named Kelsey Williams. You need to dump her phone records, Jake. We need to see if she's been in touch with Morgan, Suzanne or Monica. I don't care what any of them say, they are all in this together."

"Aren't we getting way off-base here, Jack?" Eric said. "Aren't we supposed to be looking for a murderer, not hookers?"

"It's all connected, Eric. The eight murders are linked in some way with what these women do. I'm absolutely convinced of that."

"Where do we go from here?"

Dantzler looked across the table. "Jake, you really need to get Morgan Ballard's phone records."

"Got 'em earlier this morning. Don't know who Morgan was talking to that night at two-fifty, but it was with someone in a place called The Pit Stop."

"The Pit Stop? Where have I heard that before?" Dantzler wondered, his mind racing through a week's worth of interviews. After a few seconds, the answer came to him. "From Trudy Spears, Darlene Johnson's mother. She told me she tended bar there."

"That's correct," Jake agreed. "It's a bar located in the Woodhill Center."

"I've been to that shopping center, but I don't recall seeing a bar called The Pit Stop."

"That's because it was called The Long Branch Saloon until very recently."

Bang! Just like that everything linked up. The stars had formed a galaxy.

"Why are you smiling like that?" Eric asked.

"Because I now know who we're looking for. Jake, pack an overnight bag. You're taking a road trip."

"Where am I going?"

"To have a little chat with an old sparring partner of yours."

CHAPTER TWENTY-FOUR

Oscar Young's eyes grew wide when he saw Warden Curtis usher Jake into the prison's interview room. His surprise was rivaled in equal measure by his look of fear, no doubt brought about by memories of a rumble he had with Jake two years ago. A rumble Jake ended with a single punch. Getting decked tends to stick in the loser's memory for quite a while.

Twisting in his chair, Oscar looked at the guard who escorted him in, and growled, "I ain't talkin' to that bastard. Take me back to my cell."

When Oscar tried to get out of his chair, the guard, a massive black man named Henderson, pushed him back down. Oscar growled at Henderson but said nothing. Then he looked across at Jake and Warden Curtis, folded his arms and stared down at the floor like a petulant five-year-old.

After several seconds of silence, Oscar raised his head and looked at Jake. "That bastard hit me, Warden, for no good reason. I should have sued him for police brutality."

"Oscar, if he hit you I'm sure he had a perfectly good reason," Curtis replied.

"Yeah, right, you would take his side," Oscar countered. "Tell you one thing—you let me have a shot at him and it'll be a different story."

Jake said, "Warden Curtis, do you have a boxing ring in this facility?"

"No, we don't, but we can rig one up in a matter of minutes."

"How about it, Oscar?" Jake asked. "You and me in the ring? Gloves or no gloves, your call. You want another shot at me, here's your chance. What do you say?"

"I ain't scared of you, pretty boy."

"Good. Then let's get at it."

"I ain't fightin' you, and I ain't talkin' to you. And nobody can make me."

"You've got it all wrong, Oscar," Curtis corrected. "You don't have to get in the ring with Detective Thomas, but you are going to talk to him. And you will answer every question he asks. Got it?"

"And what if I don't?"

"You work in the laundry room, don't you?"

"Yeah, so what?"

"Just this: If you don't answer his questions, and answer them honestly, you'll be scrubbing pots and pans three times a day for the remainder of your time here. That means for the rest of your life."

"That ain't fair," Oscar yelled.

"Life's not fair, Oscar. Now stop griping and answer Detective Thomas's questions."

Jake sat across from Oscar and leaned forward. "What did you say to Mark Banks prior to his leaving the prison?"

"I didn't say nothin' to Banks."

"You didn't say anything to him about a bar called The Pit Stop?"

"Never."

"You know what a 'tell' is, Oscar?"

"Sure. It's a dude or a chick that works in a bank."

"No, Oscar, that's a *teller*. A 'tell' is a look, a gesture, a certain body language that lets people know when another person is lying. And you have a 'tell', Oscar. You always look down and to the left when you aren't telling the truth. I've asked you two questions, and you've looked down and to the left both times. Keep lying to me, or you'll be working in the kitchen tomorrow."

"Listen to what the man says, Oscar," Curtis ordered. "The truth or the kitchen. Your choice."

"I never heard of no bar called The Pit Stop," Oscar said, holding his hand over his heart. "Swear to God that's the truth."

"What did you say to Mark Banks?"

"When he told me he had relatives in Lexington, and that he was thinkin' about relocating there, I gave him the name of a man who might hook him up with some work. That's about the extent of it."

"This man, does he own a bar?"

"Yeah, but it ain't The Pit Stop."

"The Long Branch Saloon?"

"Yeah, that's the one."

"Did Banks tell you anything about the relative in Lexington?"

"Only that the guy wasn't hurtin' for money."

"Did Banks have any communication with this relative?"

"How the hell would I know that? I work in the laundry room, not the office."

"Did you talk to the man who owns the bar, maybe tell him about Banks?"

"Ain't heard a peep from him since I landed in this joint, and I don't expect I ever will."

"You looked down and away, Oscar. Sure you're telling me everything?"

"Yeah, I'm sure."

"Can you think of anything else you can tell me about Mark Banks?"

"I already told you everything I know. Don't know nothin' else."

"All things considered, you did pretty good, Oscar." Jake looked up at Warden Curtis. "I think Oscar can keep his current job."

"If you say so," Curtis said.

Jake stood and looked at his watch. "Thanks for your time, Oscar. Stay safe in here."

"Right, like you really care."

"Take it easy, Oscar," Jake said, walking away.

"Hey, ain't you gonna ask me the name of the guy who

owns The Long Branch?"

"No need, Oscar. We already know his name."

*****

Morgan Ballard and Suzanne Worley were standing in the Hyatt lobby when Grace West walked in. They met her seconds after she entered, walking side by side past a group of incoming guests, a look of deadly seriousness on their faces. Grace registered surprise when she saw the two ladies approaching.

"You're early, aren't you?" Grace asked. "Didn't think we were supposed to meet until sometime tomorrow."

"No, we need to meet right now," Morgan said, sharply. "Let's go to the bar. We can have a drink while we chat."

After they were seated and the drinks had been ordered, Grace said, "As you already know, a new judge has been assigned to your trial, a lady named Pamela Lipton. The fact that she's female and black works in our favor, I believe. I'm hoping she'll be more sympathetic toward you. That's a plus for our side. She asked the assistant D.A. to find a way to settle out of court, but his suggestion that you plead guilty to a lesser charge was totally unacceptable. So we shall proceed. Jury selection begins a week from Monday."

"That's all well and good, but I'm not concerned about my trial. I have every faith that you will get me acquitted. For the moment, however, I—we—are here to discuss other matters."

"What other matters?" Grace asked.

"Your new boyfriend."

"I wasn't aware that I had a boyfriend, new or otherwise," Grace answered. "Who are you referring to?"

"Jack Dantzler. He is the homicide detective you've been sleeping with, isn't he?"

"Do you really think I'm going to respond to that, Morgan? I certainly hope not. What I do with my time, and who I spend it with, is of no concern to you. You're my client, not my Mother Superior. I don't answer to you."

"Whatever. But your new 'friend' is asking a lot of

questions about matters that are unrelated to homicide. That needs to stop."

"Has Detective Dantzler spoken to you, Morgan?"

"No. But he has talked with Suzanne. And he's spoken with several other friends of ours."

Grace looked at Suzanne. "What questions did he ask?"

"I would prefer not to discuss it. What I will say is that he made some accusations I found to be offensive."

Grace said, "I can't tell Detective Dantzler how to do his job. And to be perfectly frank and honest, Suzanne, I couldn't care less that he spoke to you. Or to your other friends. None of you are clients of mine. Morgan is. And I will not allow Detective Dantzler to speak with her."

"Maybe you can't tell him how to do his job, but you can damn sure suggest that he stop asking questions in areas that hold no interest for him."

"Tell you what, Suzanne. Why don't you wait for Morgan out in the lobby? I need a few minutes alone with her."

"No, I think I'll stay right here," Suzanne snapped.

Grace turned to Morgan. "Either she leaves now, or I'm out as your attorney."

After a few seconds, Morgan said, "It's all cool, Suzanne. I won't be long."

Grace waited until Suzanne was gone before continuing. "Detective Dantzler has been insisting that I allow you to speak with him. He swears it has nothing to do with the death of your husband. What else could he possibly want to question you about?"

Morgan shrugged.

"What are you into, Morgan? Why is Dantzler so intent on speaking with you?"

"Ask him. That should make for interesting pillow talk."

Grace stood, said, "You know what, Morgan. I just might do that."

*****

"That lawyer of yours is a certified bitch," Suzanne announced. She was still steaming from having been dismissed by Grace West. They had just turned onto Vine Street and were heading out of town in Morgan's BMW. "Not too long ago, women like her were burned at the stake."

Morgan laughed. "Make up your mind, Suzanne. Is Grace a bitch or a witch?"

"Both, in my book."

"Don't trouble yourself with Grace. She's not our main concern."

"What are we going to do about Dantzler?"

"I'm not sure. It depends on how deep he digs."

"Any digging is too deep."

"Grace said he wanted to speak with me. Maybe I should let him."

"Are you insane? That would be a foolish thing to do."

"Not necessarily. I wouldn't give away anything important. But his questions might tell us the direction he's heading, and how much he knows. Or thinks he knows."

"It's too risky, Morgan. Cops are tricky. He'll figure out that you're dodging the serious questions, so he'll ask about other matters. That way he knows what you're hiding by what you aren't telling him. You cannot allow him to interview you."

"Then we have no alternative but to deal with him in other ways. And I know just the person to take care of it for us."

"That's more like it," Suzanne said, adding, "a dead man can't ask questions, can he?"

"No, a dead man cannot."

CHAPTER TWENTY-FIVE

In what can accurately be termed "The Age of Kardashian", where fame and celebrity seldom rub shoulders with talent and genuine accomplishment, it's easy to forget that there are still individuals who carve out reputations built on skill, expertise and hard work. Not everyone on the world stage is a fraud, a headline seeker, an empty-headed self-promoter, or an endless shooter of selfies. Yes, Paris Hilton exists, but so does Meryl Streep. Thankfully, as singer Leonard Cohen once sang, "there are heroes in the seaweed."

Jack Dantzler's reputation as a world-class homicide detective fits comfortably in the heroes category. His knack for nabbing the worst of the worst, those who took the lives of fellow citizens, was nothing short of extraordinary. His job, which he defined as a "righteous calling", was one he loved. It had been that way since he received his gold shield twenty-five years ago, the youngest detective in Lexington history to earn that distinction.

During his remarkable career Dantzler had never failed to solve a case. Every murderer he went after ended up either behind bars or deceased. Not one avoided some kind of reckoning, some form of justice. Each one answered for his or her crimes.

Dantzler's record, in the words of his late partner, Dan Matthews, was "flawless, like God's soul." While Dantzler often challenged Matthews's claim—"what about those babies that died in Noah's flood, or the little children living in Sodom and Gomorrah when those cities were destroyed? How can you say God's soul is flawless when he sanctioned those mass killings?"—

he would get no argument from anyone concerning his success on the job.

Everyone agreed that he had a perfect solve rate.

Everyone, that is, except Dantzler himself.

Technically, Dantzler did have an unblemished record. Those he apprehended had their day of reckoning, either in a court of law, or on a cold slab in the morgue. But Dantzler knew in his heart there was one killer who had managed to avoid capture. This was a stain that had to be removed, and now was the time to do it.

But it wouldn't be easy.

The man was smart and cagey. He was also very lucky. When the shit hit the fan two years ago, it flew in all directions but his. He somehow managed to avoid getting smeared. Here's where luck came into play: His victim, Rufus Young, was thought to have been killed by a guy named Paul Shelton, who was eventually gunned down by his girlfriend after she mistakenly thought Shelton had killed her brother. But Shelton, though a shady character, didn't murder anyone. With Shelton's death, along with Rufus Young's, and with Oscar Young admitting to three murders, the case was effectively closed. Justice had been served.

Though not in Dantzler's professional opinion. Not quite.

The man who killed Rufus Young benefited from all the chaos surrounding the complex case. He came out on the far side, free and clear, with absolutely no evidence tying him to any of the murders. Rufus Young and Paul Shelton were the only ones who could have pointed a finger at him, and they were dead. So the man who murdered Rufus, and in all probability blackmailed Shelton for two-million dollars, went about living his life as though nothing had happened.

That fact haunted Dantzler.

But now he felt the man's time was up. His luck had run out, his day of reckoning was drawing near. Dantzler could feel it deep in his gut. He was certain the man was involved with whatever Morgan Ballard had going on. How, or in what way, or to what degree, Dantzler couldn't say. What he did know was that the man was going down.

Buddy Raymond.

*****

Just as a loud blast of thunder disturbed the late afternoon quiet, Dantzler pulled into the Woodhill Center parking lot, cut the engine and got out of the Forester. Stretching, he looked up at the sign above the place he had come to visit. Above the main entrance, the plain white wooden sign with black letters that once advertised The Long Branch Saloon had been replaced by a gaudy yellow plastic monstrosity with red letters advertising The Pit Stop. In the lower left corner of the sign, there was a race car, in the upper right corner, a black flag. Dantzler wasn't a fan of NASCAR, and didn't know much about it, but he assumed the checkered flag was the one waved when the winning car crossed the finished line.

Back a long time ago the bar was known as The Library Club. But in 1972 it was purchased by Neil Raymond, a one-time bit actor whose only steady gig was as one of the townsfolk on the classic TV series *Gunsmoke*. As a tribute to his old pals, he quickly changed the name to The Long Branch Saloon.

Neil did manage to land a role in the George C. Scott caper film *The Flim-Flam Man*, which was filmed in Central Kentucky. While on location, Neil met a local girl named Betsy Gilbert, whom he wooed and married. The couple moved to Los Angeles, but when it became clear that Neil couldn't support his family as an actor, they moved back to Lexington. There, Neil borrowed some money from Betsy's father, purchased The Library Club, and christened it The Long Branch Saloon.

Stepping inside for the first time in two years, Dantzler felt like he was entering a different world. Everything about the interior had changed. All the old tables, chairs and booths had been replaced by newer, more modern-looking furnishings. The bar was either new, or the old wood had been polished to a shine, and the old four-legged wooden stools had been upgraded to chairs with soft cushions and high backs.

But the biggest difference was the bar's overall motif and character. When Neil owned the place, the walls were lined with framed pictures of him with *Gunsmoke* regulars. Some were stills of scenes in which he was in the Dodge City crowd, while others were photos of the many famous guest stars who frequently appeared on the show.

The biggest picture of all, one that had previously dominated the wall behind the bar, featured Neil standing between James Arness and John Wayne.

When Neil's health began to decline, he sold the bar to his son, Neil junior, whom everyone called Buddy. Unlike his father, who was a straight-laced law-abiding citizen, Buddy was a rebel and a troublemaker, one of those individuals born with a criminal's mentality and nerves of steel. Buddy had spent his life breaking the law in one way or another, mostly stealing high end automobiles and selling them to chop shops, or dealing drugs.

He was also, Dantzler knew, a killer.

Buddy had not only upgraded the furnishings, he had replaced all the *Gunsmoke* photos that once lined the wall with pictures of all the top race car drivers. Young studs like Jeff Gordon, Jimmie Johnson and Kevin Harvick, old legends like Bobby Allison, Darrell Waltrip and Cale Yarborough. Some were head shots signed by the drivers, while others showed them during the race, or celebrating a victory.

Behind the bar there were now two big pictures instead of a single photo. Gone was the one that featured Neil, Matt Dillon and the Duke; in its place were pictures of Richard Petty and Dale Earnhart. The cowboys had apparently ridden off into the sunset, removed in favor of the King and the Enforcer.

As Dantzler approached the bar, he wondered if Buddy had kept his father's tradition of calling all female bartenders Miss Kitty. Probably not, he guessed.

"Are you Miss Kitty?" Dantzler asked, as he sat in one of the soft cushioned chairs.

"The last one," she answered, smiling. She was a woman in her fifties, probably the lone holdover from the days when Neil still ran the place. "What's your poison?"

Dantzler thought for a few seconds, recalled Cynthia Purcell's thumbs-up review, and said, "You have Four Roses Single Barrel?"

"We do. The good stuff. Want it straight?"

"With Diet Coke." Dantzler looked toward the end of the bar where Buddy was sitting, head down, studying The Racing Form. After being served his drink, Dantzler took a sip, laid a ten-dollar bill on the bar, thanked Miss Kitty, and moved to the chair next to Buddy.

"Got time for a chat?"

"Not really," Buddy replied, not taking his eyes off The Racing Form. "It's hard enough picking winners when I'm concentrating, impossible when I'm distracted."

"Make time, Buddy."

"You know, I remember when you were in here before." Buddy finally looked at Dantzler, his eyes icy cold. "I recall that you talk tough, like to give orders. Well, I'm not one who takes orders very well. In fact, I don't take orders at all."

"I'm not here to give you orders, Buddy. I'm here to let you in on a little secret."

"I'm about to piss my pants in anticipation."

"You might just do that when you hear what I'm about to lay on you."

"If I piss, I'll make sure to aim it in your direction."

"You're going down for murder, Buddy. Just as sure as the sun will come up tomorrow morning. You skated on the Rufus Young killing, but not this time. Your luck is about to run out."

Buddy laughed and spoke in an easy, steady voice, "Who is it that I supposedly murdered?"

"You mean, other than Rufus Young?"

"I didn't kill Rufus. If you had even a shred of proof that I did, I'd be behind bars. But you don't have any proof, do you? So, tell me who it is that I murdered."

"Mark Banks."

"I don't even know Mark Banks."

"See, there's your first lie. We know for a fact that you knew Mark Banks. Your old friend, Oscar Young, told us he gave your name to Banks before he left prison, that you might help him find a job."

"Couple of things, Detective. First, Oscar Young isn't my

friend. He's an idiot and a loudmouth and a liar. If you believe anything he says, then you're a fool who has been duped. Second, if Banks got my name from Oscar, it doesn't mean he ever showed up here. And he didn't. I never met Mark Banks."

Buddy put his pencil behind his ear and closed The Racing Form. "If I'm not mistaken, the medical examiner ruled that Mark Banks committed suicide."

"Well, Buddy, that only means you and I know something the M.E. doesn't know."

"I wouldn't be too sure about that. I've always heard those dudes are pretty smart."

"They are. But even smart dudes make mistakes. Like you, for instance. You made a mistake that's going to cost you big-time."

"What mistake would that be?"

"A twenty-seven minute phone conversation with Morgan Ballard in the early morning hours after those five poker players were murdered. That little chat will be your downfall."

"Who's Morgan Ballard?" Buddy asked, his voice still calm and cool.

"Someone you obviously know."

"Detective, plenty of people call this number. If this Ballard chick called, she could have spoken to a dozen people or more."

"Buddy, the sign on the door says the bar closes at one p.m. Morgan's call lasted from two fifty-eight till three twenty-five. Who, other than you, would be here at that time? No one, that's who. Morgan talked with you."

"Did this Morgan tell you that?"

"Haven't asked her about it yet."

"When you do, I'm positive she'll tell you it wasn't me she was talking to."

"You're probably right, Buddy. But what she tells me really won't make much of a difference. The phone records are all I need. And they don't lie."

"Here's how I see it, Detective. You're trying to frame me for a death that was ruled a suicide, and you're trying to link me to a phone call that could have been answered by a dozen different people, which means you don't have shit. Seems to me you're a long way from bringing about my downfall."

"Your downfall is much closer than you think, Buddy." Dantzler stood and looked around the place. "Hate to tell you this, but I liked the bar the way it was before. It had more character."

"Then drink someplace else. There are plenty of bars in Lexington."

Dantzler grinned, said, "Get your affairs in order, Buddy. Life as you know it is about to end."

"I kinda doubt it," Buddy answered, as Dantzler turned and headed for the door.

*****

Dantzler concluded this: If Buddy Raymond had lived on the right side of the law, the two men could be friends. The guy was definitely cool under pressure, and that was a trait Dantzler ranked at the high end of the scale. As a tennis player, Dantzler's reputation was that of a competitor who rose to the occasion when things got tight and dicey. He could remain calm under intense pressure, and so could Buddy Raymond.

But Buddy worked the wrong side of the tracks so, cool or not, he had to be put away.

There was one moment during their conversation when Dantzler detected a possible crack in Buddy's armor. It was brief, just a fleeting second, but Buddy flinched slightly when told about the twenty-seven minute early morning conversation. Thinking back on it, Dantzler realized that at that split-second Buddy probably knew his ass was toast. He recovered well, put the cool look back on, and didn't give anything away. A pro's pro.

But . . . he had to know that it was close to game, set and match.

Dantzler had two stops to make before calling it a day. His first stop was the next hamburger joint he ran across. McDonald's, Wendy's, Five Guys, Smashburger . . . he didn't give a damn. He wanted something greasy, something nasty in a tasty way—burger, fries and a chocolate milk shake. Something to replenish his empty tank and raise his energy level.

His second stop was the one that mattered. It was of extreme importance. If all went well, and he was confident it would, he would go to bed tonight with many of his crucial questions answered. And that would make for a peaceful sleep.

CHAPTER TWENTY-SIX

Cynthia Purcell was clearly surprised when she opened the door and saw Dantzler standing there. She leaned to her right and looked over Dantzler's shoulder, half expecting someone to be following close on his heels. Looking back at Dantzler, she smiled and opened the door wider, inviting him inside with a gentle wave of the arm.

"Come in, please," she said.

"I take it you were expecting someone else."

Cynthia grinned and shrugged.

"A client?" Dantzler asked.

Cynthia nodded.

"Call him, tell him something has come up and you have to cancel."

"Come on, Detective, this guy is good for three hours, minimum," Cynthia pleaded. "That's fifteen-hundred bucks you're costing me."

"Then call, tell him to come back in two hours. We should be done by then."

"Can I assume from your request that the purpose of your visit isn't to arrest me?"

"Homicide, not Vice, remember?"

Cynthia went into the den, picked up her cell phone and made the call. A minute or so later, she came back to where Dantzler was standing, and said, "he wasn't pleased, but when I told him I would cut his rate in half, he was more than willing to delay our engagement."

"Engagement? Is that what you call it?"

"That's as good a word as any, I think." Cynthia pointed to the glass on the coffee table. "Would you care for something to drink before we get started?"

Dantzler glanced down at the glass. "More of the Four Roses Single Barrel, I presume?"

"What else? When you have the best, why change?"

"No, I think I had better pass. Thanks, though."

"Mind if I drink?

"Your place, your rules."

"Okay, Detective, why are you here?" Cynthia said, after taking a long drink.

"Cynthia, I like you. I think you are an honest person who will level with me. My hope is that I'm right about that. What I need from you now are honest answers to my questions. If you are straight with me, and if what you tell me implicates you in any way, I will make it known to those in power that you went out of your way to help me. I will make sure that you get every consideration, every possible break. That means, if there is any way I can keep you out of jail, I will."

"Are you here because I'm a prostitute?"

"Homicide, not Vice. That should answer your question."

"I don't deal in homicides, so I don't know how much help I can be."

"We'll see." Dantzler sat on the sofa, took out his notepad and pen. "I want you to tell me about Morgan Ballard, about this business she's running. I need you to take me all the way back to the very beginning. How it got started."

"I wasn't there at the beginning." Cynthia sipped her bourbon. "Kelsey and I didn't come along until several years later. But Morgan and Suzanne have both shared with me the details of how it all came about, so I have a pretty good idea of what went down in those early days."

Dantzler didn't like this at all. Although he had every confidence that Cynthia would be truthful with him, if this thing ever got into a court of law, even a second-rate defense attorney could get her testimony dismissed as hearsay evidence. But that was something to worry about at a later date. Now, the main objective was to get as much of the story as possible.

"Then tell me what you do know."

"Morgan had this professor in college, one of the men

murdered during the poker game," Cynthia began.

"Sahid Hassaine."

"Yes, that's the one. Anyway, he fell madly in love with Morgan, and pretty soon they were having an affair. For Morgan, it was little more than an adventure, probably a way for her to get better grades, but for Hassaine, it was love. The man must've been crazy about her; he apparently gave her anything she asked for. This went on for a couple of years. At some point, Morgan got tired of his being so goo-goo eyed over her, so she called it quits. He took the separation really hard. He even threatened her with violence on a couple of occasions. Morgan had her dad step in and tell Hassaine to back off or he'd have his skull crushed. Well, that ended the affair."

"Are you telling me Richard Chambers is involved in Morgan's business?" Dantzler asked.

"Oh, no, he's clueless. He thinks Morgan is pure as fresh snow."

"Okay, go ahead."

"As you know, Morgan is really tight with Suzanne. They are like flip sides of the same coin. Always have been, always will be. Their bond is unbreakable. However, there is one big difference between them—Suzanne is naturally more adventurous than Morgan. She was the one who came up with the idea to start the escort service. In college, she used sex to get just about anything she wanted—money, gifts, clothes, whatever. When Morgan saw what Suzanne was doing, she wanted in on it. For a while, they made it with guys who had money and influence. But things didn't really pick up until they recruited Monica Plemmons to join the group. Having Monica on board was the real game-changer."

"How so?" Dantzler asked.

Cynthia took a sip of bourbon. "Monica's father was a state senator, and she worked in his office from the time she was in college until she got married. That was about ten years. It was through Monica that Morgan and Suzanne began to hook up with men who had real money, power and prestige. That's when the big bucks began to flow in. Word about what was going on spread like wildfire. They had clients from Frankfort, Louisville, Washington D.C., just about every major city you can name."

Cynthia took a deep breath followed by another sip of bourbon. "It was seven years ago that Morgan approached me and asked if I would be interested. She said business was booming, and she needed another girl or two. Some fresh faces for the clients, you know? Kelsey Williams is a close friend of mine, so I tossed out the possibility to her. She quickly said yes. And that's how our little group came together."

"How close are you and Kelsey to the other three?" Dantzler inquired.

"We all get along, but Kelsey and I are outsiders. Even Monica was kept out of the loop on certain things. We're not privy to all the decision-making, or to many of the pertinent details of the operation. We're included, but only to a certain degree."

Dantzler was buying Cynthia's story up to now. She had given him no cause to doubt anything she had said. He could only hope the rest of her tale went as well.

"Even though Morgan had dismissed him, Sahid Hassaine figures in this story in some way, doesn't he?

"You're good, Detective. Yes, he most definitely does."

"How?"

"Hassaine never really got over his crush on Morgan. He continued to see her, even after being threatened by Richard Chambers. I think Morgan felt sorry for the guy, which turned out to be a big mistake on her part. No one seems to know how, but Hassaine got wind of what was going on. When he did, he got big dollar signs in his eyes. He told Morgan and Suzanne that he would go to the police and turn them in if they didn't meet certain demands."

"Money, correct?"

"Money, and free sex for himself and a few of his close friends."

"Why didn't Morgan go to her father, tell him what Hassaine was demanding?"

"Oh, Morgan would never do that. She wanted her dad to always see her as the virgin princess."

"According to bank records, Hassaine was depositing ten grand into a checking account at the first of each month," Dantzler said. "What do you know about that?"

"Every month we all gave Morgan two-thousand dollars, which, when added to hers, amounted to ten grand. That was to ensure Hassaine's silence. In effect, he blackmailed the hell out of us."

"Until he was murdered."

Cynthia nodded. "Until he was murdered."

"What do you know about that?"

"About what? The death of those poker players?"

"Yes. Do you think Morgan was involved?"

"Honestly, Detective, I don't know. If she was, Kelsey and I weren't aware of it. Monica, too, if I had to make a guess. She was never a true insider. But I can't say for sure if Morgan was involved. Although . . ."

"Although what?"

"Well, it's clear, isn't it? With Hassaine dead, no more paying out ten grand each month. A dead blackmailer has no need for money."

Cynthia's last bit of information sealed it for Dantzler: Sahid Hassaine was the primary target, something Dantzler suspected from the early stages of the investigation. The money had always troubled him. How did Hassaine accumulate that much money? Now Dantzler had his answer.

"What was your initial reaction when you heard those men had been murdered?" Dantzler asked.

Cynthia thought about the question for almost a minute, then finally said, "Suspicion, sadness, confusion."

"Explain that to me."

"Suspicion, because with Hassaine dead, no more payoff. Since Morgan is our leader, naturally, I wondered if she was behind it. I didn't want to believe it, but the thought was in my head. Sadness, because no one should die in such a violent, ugly and painful way, no matter how evil they are. And confusion, because if Hassaine was the one doing the blackmailing, then why did those other five men have to die?"

"Did you know those men?" Dantzler asked.

"Hassaine, Adrian White and Cunnilingus Carl were regulars. We all knew them. To the best of my knowledge, Judge Kurtz and the Dawkins guy were never involved with any of us. So I didn't know either of them."

"You didn't mention Dustin Ridley. What about him?"

"He was strictly Suzanne's boy. And she made it clear that he was off-limits to the rest of us, including Morgan."

"Was he a client or Suzanne's lover?"

"Don't know. Maybe both."

"Ever heard Mark Banks's name mentioned?"

"No, but I saw his name in the newspaper. Isn't he the one who killed those six men?"

"Yes, on someone else's orders."

"Morgan's?"

Dantzler shrugged, said, "Does the name Buddy Raymond mean anything to you?"

"You mean Morgan's secret paramour?" Cynthia said, snickering.

That was exactly the answer Dantzler was hoping for. "Are you saying Morgan and Buddy Raymond are lovers?"

"Have been for years, although it's supposed to be all hush-hush, which, of course, it isn't. We all knew about it. She's all ga-ga over the guy. Mention his name and her face lights up like the tallest building in Times Square on New Year's Eve."

"Based on your tone, I get the impression that you don't like him?"

"I've only met the man one time and that was at a bar he owns in Woodhill Center. He didn't say five words to anyone other than Morgan. It was like we didn't exist. But he gives off a certain vibe, you know? Danger, evil, those kinds of things." Cynthia took another sip of bourbon, said, "How do you know about Buddy Raymond?"

"Buddy and I have a history together," Dantzler replied. "Also, he spoke to Morgan on the night those murders went down at Judge Kurtz's house. A twenty-seven minute conversation at three in the morning. They don't know it yet, but that little chat is going to hang those two."

"To be honest with you, Detective Dantzler, I have a difficult time believing Morgan could be involved in something so cruel. But based on the vibe I got from Buddy Raymond, yes, I could see him doing it."

"Why are you being so kind to Morgan? She did shoot her husband in the head while he was sleeping. That's pretty damn cold-blooded."

"Well, yeah, you've got a point there."

"And did you ever see any evidence that he was abusing Morgan? No, you didn't. Nobody did. That's because he wasn't abusing her. She did it because she wanted him out of the way."

"Maybe you're right. I don't know."

"How did all this work vis-à-vis the husbands? How could they be so clueless to what was going on right under their noses?"

"For one thing, not all of us have a husband. Kelsey and I don't. Morgan and Monica did, so they had to be extra careful. In Monica's case, it was simple. Her husband works at night. Plus, he's not very smart. She could come and go without ever having to worry about him finding out what she was up to. But Deke Ballard was a different sort of animal. He was very intelligent, very observant. I think he had begun to get suspicious. Morgan told us a few months ago that he was beginning to ask a lot of questions. Maybe . . ."

"That's why he had to die," Dantzler said, finishing Cynthia's thought for her. Then: "Did you know Thomas Worley?"

"Suzanne's husband? No, he was killed a few weeks before I joined the group. Why are you asking about him?"

"The manner in which he died intrigues me."

"It was a hunting accident, wasn't it?"

"That's the official ruling, but I'm not buying it. I think he was murdered. And unless I'm badly mistaken, Suzanne had it done."

"She was in Florida when it happened," Cynthia pointed out.

"That only means she hired a shooter." Dantzler paused for a few seconds, then said, "How did Suzanne behave in the weeks after her husband's death?"

"She wasn't exactly a grieving widow."

"That ought to tell you something."

"Jeez, who would ever have thought Morgan and Suzanne could be so ruthless," Cynthia commented, genuine sadness in her voice. "I never would have, that's for sure."

"Okay, Cynthia, I'm going to give you a piece of friendly advice. Given what has gone down with the murders, and what is going to happen in the next few days, what you do for a living isn't going to be high on our list of priorities. You will be called in to repeat what you've told me today. We'll need to get it all down officially. But the 'escort service' thing will be on the back burner. For a while, anyway. However, sooner or later, Vice will get involved. What that means is that one day you'll have a client who will ask for sex, hand you money, then show you his badge. You'll be a dead duck. So, your best course would be to change professions."

"And do what, Detective? Become a secretary, a nurse, a teacher? I make more in one week than women in those professions make in a year." Cynthia held up her glass. "This is crystal, cost me three-hundred dollars. Teachers and secretaries can't afford this stuff. I've become accustomed to a certain lifestyle, Detective, one I'm not sure that I can give up."

"Then I would advise relocating. Move to Cincinnati, Louisville, Knoxville, one of those major cities you named. I'm sure there are plenty of clients in those places. But if you continue to work in Lexington, you will eventually get busted. You can take that to the bank."

"But you do believe me about not being involved in the murders, don't you?"

"Yes. Like I said, you'll have to come to the station and tell us what you know. So will Kelsey. But I will make it clear that you guys were not involved in the murders."

"Thank you." Cynthia walked Dantzler to the door. "What's going to happen to Morgan?"

"She's going down," Dantzler said, adding, "and you can also take *that* to the bank."

*****

On his way home Dantzler thought about calling Grace but decided against it. Instead, he stopped at the Liquor Barn on Richmond Road and purchased a bottle of Four Roses Single Barrel, which at some point he would give to Cynthia for being candid and upfront with him. The information she provided was not only truthful, it was also helpful. Plus, he simply liked the woman. A bottle of expensive bourbon was a small price to pay for her openness and candor. What Cynthia told him, he felt, would serve to drive another nail in Morgan Ballard's coffin.

And Buddy Raymond's, as well.

*****

While Dantzler was buying bourbon for Cynthia, Morgan Ballard was on her way to see Buddy Raymond. Only moments earlier, sitting alone at home, she received a text message from him, telling her to "meet me in the country house." She left her place immediately after getting the message.

Rendezvousing at the house in the country wasn't that unusual; they'd often met there since Buddy purchased the place two years ago. In fact, it was the safest place they could meet. Her house as a meeting place was out of the question. So was the bar or his house in town, which carried with them the potential for being seen. Out-of-town motels were safe but costly. When Buddy bought the house outside the city, all problems were solved, and it became their primary love nest.

But for some unexplained reason, as Morgan drove out of town, she felt acid in the pit of her stomach, like she was nervous and about to be sick. But why did she suddenly feel this way? She didn't know the answer to her question, but in the past few seconds a strange, unwanted feeling of dread flushed over her like water out of the shower. Thinking about it, she felt the bile rising in her throat. It took all her strength to fight off the urge to vomit.

As the lights from downtown Lexington gleamed in her

rearview mirror, she willed herself to calm down, to gain control of her emotions, her fear. There was nothing to worry about, no cause for concern. Everything would be all right.

Buddy would make sure of that.

He always did.

CHAPTER TWENTY-SEVEN

By nine o'clock the next morning, Dantzler had already been in his office three hours. Firing up his computer, he typed his notes from the interview with Cynthia Purcell. After finishing that task, he went into the squad room and grabbed a bottle of orange juice and a stale doughnut. At eight, when Eric and Jake sauntered in, he brought them up to speed on his talk with Cynthia. A half-hour later, when Captain Bird showed up, Dantzler filled him in, then told him what he needed before proceeding with the investigation. Bird listened intently, nodded, and told Dantzler to take whatever action he deemed appropriate.

What Dantzler needed were warrants to search The Pit Stop bar, the apartment above the bar, Buddy Raymond's house on Pepperhill, his Escalade and the house on Old Ironworks Pike he purchased fifteen months ago. News of Buddy owning that piece of property came as something of a surprise to Dantzler when Jake told him about it. Dantzler was familiar with the place—it had once belonged to the late Rufus Young.

Dantzler approached Judge Goodwin, explained what he needed and why, and the good judge signed off on it with the usual admonishment to "stick within the guidelines of what's on those warrants." Goodwin had once been a cop, so he was always friendly with the boys in blue. Given his druthers, Dantzler would never go to anyone other than Judge Goodwin.

With the proper papers in hand, Dantzler assembled his team at the bottom of the station house steps and gave out orders. He and Jake would go to The Pit Stop, while Eric and two uniformed officers would meet at Buddy's house on Pepperhill. Two more teams of uniformed officers were ordered to be on standby in case they all had to go to the house on Old Ironworks Pike. With assignments firmly established, the men quickly departed the station.

Twenty minutes after leaving, Dantzler and Jake walked into The Pit Stop, which was empty save for a pair of old-timers sitting at the bar. The two men were already well into their drinks. They peeked up and eyed the intruders with a look of curiosity, as though Dantzler and Jake might be aliens, then returned their focus to the booze. The bartender was a younger lady than the one Dantzler previously spoke with, and he seriously doubted that she was called Miss Kitty.

He guessed right. When asked about it she shook her head and informed him that her name was Brenda. She was a slender woman with auburn hair, green eyes and a slightly crooked smile. It was one of those smiles that, if seen on a movie character, would make you think the person was not to be trusted.

"Sorry, but Buddy's not here at the moment," Brenda said, responding to Dantzler's question. "Haven't seen or heard from him all morning. Don't expect I will until later in the day."

Dantzler pulled out two pieces of paper from his briefcase, then carefully laid them on the bar side by side. "These are warrants that give us the right to search the bar and the apartment up above," Dantzler told her. "You're welcome to read them, but I can assure you they are proper and legitimate."

"Tell me what you're looking for," Brenda said. "Maybe I can save you some time and effort."

"Thanks for the offer, but we can handle it." To Jake: "Check out upstairs. Give it a thorough going-over."

"Roger that," Jake responded, as he headed up the staircase.

The search yielded nothing of interest, nothing that would help make a case against Buddy Raymond. This didn't come as a surprise to Dantzler; he had Buddy pegged as a smart, cagey guy who would never leave incriminating evidence lying around for the police to find. Jake did come downstairs with one piece of news that caused Dantzler's heart to beat a little faster—there was a small safe in the apartment's bedroom.

The safe was locked, so Dantzler asked Brenda if she knew the combination. To his great surprise, she did. Brenda hustled up the stairs, went into the bedroom, and had the safe open even faster than Willie Sutton could have. With that done, Dantzler thanked Brenda, and then told her she could head back down to the bar.

Inside the safe Dantzler found a little more than one-hundred dollars in cash, a large jar filled to the brim with quarters, several Lottery tickets, and a stack of papers that turned out to be job applications, all filled out by women hoping to become the next Miss Kitty, or whatever name they went by in the bar's latest incarnation.

On his way downstairs, Dantzler's cell phone rang. The call was from Eric.

"No sign of Buddy at his house," Eric informed Dantzler. "Doesn't look like anyone's been here for a while."

"Here's what I want you to do, Eric. Tell one of the uniformed guys to stick around, see if Buddy shows up. I doubt that he will, but we need someone there in case he does. Who do you plan to leave at the house?"

"Kelvin."

Kelvin Richardson was a big guy, a former linebacker who went to high school with Eric.

Dantzler said, "Let Kelvin know that if Buddy does make an appearance, he should arrest him and transport him to the station. Also, make it clear to Kelvin that Buddy is a dangerous guy, to be ready for anything. Tell him to do what he has to do to stay safe."

"No need to do that. Kelvin could whip a gorilla," Eric said, adding, "What do you want me to do?"

"Who else is with you?

"Benny."

"Leave the cruiser with Kelvin. You and Benny take your car and head out Georgetown Road until you come to Old Ironworks Pike. Make a left and meet us there. Radio Bruce, have him dispatch two cruisers to that location. If you guys arrive before Jake and I do, make sure they know to wait for us."

"We're on our way."

As Dantzler and Jake were about to leave the bar, it hit Dantzler that he should have brought more personnel. There was no one to leave behind in case Buddy showed up. If Buddy did make an appearance, and no cop was there to detain him, Brenda would let him know what had gone down. With that, Buddy Raymond would disappear faster than a streak of lightning in the night sky.

Dantzler had no intention of leaving Jake behind, so all he could do was put in a call to Bruce, and direct him to dispatch another officer ASAP, then keep his fingers crossed that the patrolman would be here if and when Buddy did show up.

After making the call to Bruce, Dantzler and Jake left The Pit Stop and headed toward Old Ironworks Pike. They were silent for almost ten minutes before Jake spoke.

"You seem upset about something. Everything okay?"

"Yeah, everything is fine. I'm just a little pissed at myself for not taking an officer with us to the bar. I don't like making blunders, and that was a blunder."

"I'd say one of the guys is there by now."

"You're probably right, Jake. But, still, it was a screw up on my part, and that's not acceptable."

"Cut yourself some slack. We're only human. We all make mistakes. It goes with the territory."

Dantzler chuckled. "If you're trying to cheer me up, it ain't working."

"Well, I'm a cop, not a comedian, so there you have it."

"You're a helluva cop, Jake. In some ways the best we have."

"I'm not even in the same league with you and Eric," Jake protested. "And won't be for a long time."

"Don't kid yourself, Jake. You're already in our league."

When Dantzler and Jake turned onto Old Ironworks Pike, they saw six men standing in a semicircle, talking and sweating in the warm noon sunshine. Eric and Benny were to the left, with four uniformed officers completing the group. Their three vehicles, Eric's car and the two cruisers, were lined up head to tail.

Dantzler stopped, rolled down the passenger's side window, and told the six men to follow him. He waited until all six were inside their cars and buckled up before taking off. The convoy had traveled less than a mile when Dantzler hit his left turn signal. To the left, across the road, there was a wide enough space for the four cars to safely pull off. Once parked, all eight men exited their vehicles.

Buddy Raymond's house, the one formerly owned by Rufus Young, was about seventy-five yards farther down and on the opposite side of the road. The house was three stories high, a truly massive wooden place, which it had to be to have comfortably accommodated Rufus's brood of eleven children. The house was twenty-five yards or so off the road, and it was situated in the middle of a wide open field. To the right of the house was a large wooden garage, wide enough to easily handle four good-sized vehicles. A few feet to the left of the garage stood a smaller structure that was likely being used as a tool shed. Farther back in the yard there was a stack of hay bales fronted by a large target. Protruding from the target were several arrows, a reminder that Oscar Young had once been extremely proficient with a bow and arrow.

Dantzler took a pair of binoculars from his car and scanned the area. Buddy's black Escalade was nowhere in sight. There was one car parked in front of the house, a dark green BMW. Dantzler read the license plates to one of the patrolmen, who got on his computer, then came back a minute later, saying the vehicle was registered to Richard Douglas Chambers.

Dantzler continued looking through the binoculars, hoping to see movement inside the house, but he saw nothing. Had they been spotted by whoever was in the house? That was possible but Dantzler doubted it. They were far enough away from the house, and situated at a relatively severe angle from the front windows to make them difficult to spot. Still, though, with four cars parked together, including two patrol cars, not having been seen was far from a given.

"We going in?" Eric said, breaking a silence that had stretched into five minutes.

Dantzler didn't like this situation at all. Disaster was written all over it. What troubled him was that open space between the road and the house. When the convoy turned onto the gravel driveway, anyone in the house was going to hear them approaching. The element of surprise would be lost.

Those front windows on the top two floors were also worrisome. If someone, Buddy, or Richard Chambers, or both, were up there with rifles, when the men exited their vehicles, they would be easy targets. Even a mediocre shooter would have no trouble blowing them away.

"Is everyone wearing a vest?" Dantzler asked. Heads nodded all around. "Guys, we don't know who's in there, so be extra alert. Keep an eye on all windows. The last thing I want is for a shooter to start picking us off."

Dantzler turned and took a final look at the house through the binoculars. And saw movement. The front door opened and a woman stepped outside. It was Morgan Ballard. Buddy followed her a few steps, leaned down and gave her a long kiss. Then a second kiss, this one even longer. With that one, his right hand dropped down to her ass and pulled her closer.

"New plan," Dantzler announced, suddenly excited. To Darryl: "Wait until Morgan turns onto the road and is heading this way, then pull your cruiser across the road to block her. I'll handle her when she gets out."

"You want lights flashing?" Darryl asked.

Dantzler initial instinct was to say no but he told Darryl to light them up. More than likely, Buddy would watch her drive away, and if he did he would see her being stopped, whether or not the car's lights were flashing.

At this point Dantzler couldn't care less what Buddy Raymond saw or didn't see. Buddy was now a trapped animal with two basic choices—give up peacefully, or go down fighting.

Either way was fine with Dantzler. Dead or alive, Buddy Raymond's day of reckoning had arrived.

CHAPTER TWENTY-EIGHT

Morgan Ballard's eyes narrowed to slits, and a stream of profanity rushed past her lips when she saw the blue and white police cruiser pull across the road, lights flashing, blocking her way into town. Her first instinct was to do what she always did in times of crisis or uncertainty—take out her phone and call her father. He would be there within minutes, ready to confront and challenge anyone, cops included, who had the audacity to treat his daughter in such a shameful manner. That's what Morgan had always done in the past, and that's what she would do now. How dare these assholes stop her in the middle of the highway.

However, before she could dig into her purse and retrieve her cell phone, the driver's side door opened. When she looked up she saw Dantzler standing there, a slight grin creasing his handsome face. *God, I can't believe I'm thinking that.* Behind him was the black detective, Eric something, the one who testified against her at the trial. *Damn both of you.*

"What the hell is the meaning of this?" Morgan snapped, removing her sunglasses. "Why are you harassing me? I've done nothing wrong, broken no laws."

"Please step out of your vehicle," Dantzler ordered, his voice calm and steady. "We can discuss the situation once you do."

"Situation? What situation? You and I have nothing to discuss, Detective. Nothing."

"Please, Morgan, get out of the vehicle."

"And what if I don't?"

"Then things could get ugly."

Morgan complied, slowly getting out of the Beemer. Free of the vehicle, she smoothed her slacks and put her sunglasses back on. Dantzler could feel the heat of anger emanating from every pore of her body.

"I will have your badge for this, Detective," Morgan said, brushing hair out of her eyes. "My father won't rest until you have been fired. And then he'll sue the city and the police department for more money than you can imagine."

"Threats aren't going to work, Morgan," Dantzler answered, keeping his voice and temper under control. "And besides, I don't think you want your father to know about the side business you've got going."

"I don't know what you're referring to." Morgan smiled nonchalantly, trying to act cool and calm. "Like I told you, I have done nothing wrong, certainly nothing to warrant this shabby treatment."

"I'm happy to hear that, Morgan. If what you say is true, then you should have no objection to speaking with me at the station. There are some things I need to get cleared up."

"What *things*?"

"We'll discuss it once we're back at the station."

"Am I under arrest?" Morgan asked.

"I have no cause to arrest you," Dantzler lied. "I simply need to ask you a few questions, that's all."

"Should I have my attorney present?"

"That's your prerogative, Morgan. I can't advise you one way or the other. However, I will tell you that if you do have your attorney with you, then that changes things considerably."

"How long will I be there?"

"It shouldn't take too long. I have some business to finish up here, then I will get with you at the station."

"But I'm not under arrest?"

"No, absolutely not."

"All right, I'll go. But I don't want to spend a lot of time there."

"Not a problem," Dantzler said, lying a second time. To Darryl: "Drive Miss Ballard to the station and put her in my office.

Make sure she's comfortable. If she's thirsty or hungry, ask Bruce to order something for her."

"What about my car?" Morgan asked, pointing at the Beemer.

"I'll have one of the officers drive it into town."

"I would feel much better if I drove it in."

"Your car will be fine, Morgan. I promise."

"This way, ma'am," Darryl said, pointing toward his cruiser. "Here, I'll open that door for you."

"He's a lot nicer to her than I would be," Dantzler said, once Morgan and Darryl were in the cruiser.

"Driving Miss Daisy," Eric said, as the cruiser drove off. "Who knew Big Darryl was the next Morgan Freeman?"

"Yeah, Eric, only there's one huge difference. That Miss Daisy is in a world of deep shit."

*****

Buddy Raymond was watching from a first-floor window when the cop car pulled across the road, lights flashing, forcing Morgan to stop. He had no idea what was happening, but it couldn't be good. He knew right then that if the cops were stopping Morgan, they were also looking for him. They weren't in this area by accident. He also knew that any dream he had of living the rest of his life with Morgan had just vanished. The cops had nothing on him, but if they squeezed Morgan hard enough, what were the odds she wouldn't break? Slim to none. She was a tough broad, but not *that* tough. She would cave, sooner or later, and give him up in exchange for a better deal from the district attorney. Hell, he couldn't blame her if she did.

As he watched the scene unfold seventy-five yards away, Buddy's cool demeanor melted away when he recognized that it was Dantzler who was speaking to Morgan. *That asshole*, Buddy whispered to himself. *Should've taken you out two years ago.* Buddy continued watching until the big black officer helped Morgan get into the police cruiser, got behind the wheel and drove back toward town.

"So long, Morgan," Buddy mumbled. "I do love you."

Buddy remained at the window, waiting to see if Dantzler and the other cops would follow the cruiser into town or head toward him. Strangely enough, they did neither.

*****

Now that Dantzler knew for certain that Buddy was in the house, he decided against approaching from the front. It was simply too risky. He and his men would be in harm's way with virtually nowhere to take cover should they come under fire. That was a totally unacceptable situation. Better to call in the SWAT team—technically, the Emergency Response Unit—and have them enter the house. Those guys were pros . . . fearless, brave, tactically efficient and incredibly well-trained. If Buddy was insane enough to engage them in a firefight there would be no need to worry about a trial at a later date.

The dead rarely had to stand trial.

CHAPTER TWENTY-NINE

"What the fuck are you assholes doing?" Buddy muttered aloud, still peering out the window. "Either shit or get off the pot."

Buddy was stumped by the cops' actions. Or more specifically, their lack of action. After Morgan was driven away, Buddy expected the cops to either head for town or for him. But they remained by their vehicles, talking and laughing like a group of football fans at a tailgating party. Not one of them even looked toward the house, much less made a move in his direction. This could only mean one thing, Buddy realized. They had put in a call for reinforcements, probably a SWAT unit. If that was true, Buddy knew he had to get moving fast.

He sprinted up to a second-floor bedroom, grabbed his .44 Magnum and a flashlight from off the dresser, then bounded back down the stairs and into the kitchen. Opening the refrigerator, he pulled out six bottles of water, dropped them into a plastic bag and headed for the hallway.

It was there that Buddy would perform his own version of The Great Escape.

Standing in the middle of the hallway was an ancient grandfather clock. No one knew how old it was, but it had been in the house since the original owners built the place back in the thirties. It was a heavy sucker, solid as an oak tree, and it took quite a bit of effort to move. Behind the clock, two of the wooden wall panels had been transformed into a hidden door. It opened inward, so there was no handle on it. If you didn't know the door was there, you would never see it, even if you had enough muscle to move the clock.

Buddy laid a shoulder against the clock, and using every bit of his strength managed to nudge it away from the wall maybe twenty inches. It was a tight squeeze, but he was thin enough to make it past the clock. He pushed the door open, entered into the dark tunnel, put his gun and the bag of water bottles on a metal chair, turned back, and after a difficult struggle was able to get the clock back to its original position.

Inside, Buddy removed the flashlight from his hip pocket and turned it on. Pitch black was gone in a heartbeat. He aimed the light toward the end of the tunnel, which was twenty-five feet in length, nine feet wide, and its ceiling seven feet high. Plenty of room for Buddy to stretch out or move around comfortably. There were three metal chairs and a large steel safe. This was a place only two people in the world knew existed, and one of them, Rufus Young, was dead.

The tunnel was originally the opening to a huge bomb shelter the owners had constructed back when everyone feared the Russians were about to drop the big one on us. The shelter extended from the house all the way to the farthest section of the back yard. When Rufus and Buddy had discovered the shelter, they built a wooden wall twenty-five feet from the hallway entrance. Having no fear of a Russian attack, nor any need for all that extra space, they reasoned that it made no sense to keep the entire shelter open. The small tunnel was more than enough to suit their needs, which consisted mainly of hiding money, drugs and weapons. In fact, all but four-hundred-thousand dollars of the two-million Buddy had blackmailed from Paul Shelton was in the large steel safe.

Buddy sat in one of the chairs, opened a bottle of water, took a long swig and plotted his strategy. He really had but a single option—stay in the tunnel until the cops completed their search and departed. Even if they tore the house apart they would never find him. He was safer than the gold in Fort Knox.

But how long should he remain here? That was the question. Two days, three maybe? He had no food, but he did have the water, so staying put for two or three days wouldn't be a problem. True, his stomach might rebel at being neglected for that length of time, but he wasn't going to die of starvation. It only meant he had to be judicious in his use of the water.

After letting all this run through his mind, Buddy shone the flashlight on his wristwatch—it was now one-thirty—then made the decision to stay in the tunnel until midnight rather than wait two or three days. By midnight the cops would surely have completed their search. If they found nothing of interest, or any incriminating evidence, they would most likely leave before midnight. Looking at it from all angles, he doubted they would leave anyone behind to guard the big empty house. Of course, that was something he couldn't take for granted.

Buddy's plan was simple: At midnight he would open the door, ease the grandfather clock forward a few inches, then listen for any sounds that let him know the cops did leave someone behind. If he heard something, he'd head back into the safety of the tunnel. If the house remained silent, he would go back into the tunnel, fill a large duffel bag with as much of the money as possible, and then sneak away from the house using the darkness as a shield. No doubt the cops had impounded the Escalade, leaving him without an escape. This wasn't a problem. He'd simply call the last Miss Kitty—she was like a sister to him—and have her come pick him up a mile or so down the road from the house.

It was a solid plan, one Buddy felt good about. For now, though, there was nothing he could do but stretch out, get some rest, and let the clock tick toward midnight.

Then, when both hands pointed straight up at heaven, he would be off.

*****

The SWAT vehicles led the way to Buddy's house, followed by the four cars belonging to Dantzler's group. The SWAT guys—twenty plus their commander—arrived first, exited their vehicles, and without a word from anyone split into two teams of ten. One team went to the front door, while the second group circled around the house to enter from the rear. Their movements were quick, silent, performed with precision and in perfect harmony.

The team commander, Steve Todd, had earlier instructed Dantzler to have his men keep close tabs on those second- and third-floor windows until the SWAT team was inside the house. Dantzler, Eric, Jake and two unnies spread out, staying behind the SWAT vehicles, their eyes scanning those upper level-windows.

As Todd was about to give the Go command, the lead guy turned the knob and the front door opened. Buddy had neglected to lock it after Morgan left. In less than three seconds, ten fully-armed men were inside the house. From the rear Dantzler heard the sound of glass being shattered. This told him the back door had been locked and was just kicked open.

The next few moments would tell the story, and it was a story with only two possible endings. Buddy would either go quietly, or he'd choose to fight it out. If there was screaming, yelling, gunfire, the chaos of combat, then Buddy chose poorly. If he surrendered, he'd made the right choice. Buddy held his fate in his own hands.

After a minute, there had been no gunfire, no screaming and yelling, only the sounds of the SWAT guys' boots pounding those old wooden floors. Another minute passed, still nothing. As each second ticked away, Dantzler began to believe Buddy had given up peacefully. Wise decision on his part, if he did.

Dantzler tapped Eric on the shoulder, motioning him to go over and check out the garage. Dantzler pointed to his own chest, signaling that he would inspect the tool shed. Eric nodded his understanding, and they headed to the right of the house.

A thorough search of both structures yielded nothing of importance. The garage was home to a riding mower and a floor drenched in motor oil, while the shed was crammed full of every type of tool or lawn-care equipment imaginable.

Dantzler and Eric had just returned to the front when Commander Todd stepped outside. Todd removed his head gear, took out a bandana from his back pocket and wiped sweat from his face. Shaking his head, he said, "Not a damn soul in that place, Jack."

"He has to be in there. I saw him, Steve. He was standing right where you are now."

"Jack, we combed through that entire house, inch by inch, and I'm telling you, ain't nobody in there." Todd raised his arms in a what-can-I-tell-you gesture, said, "I don't believe people vanish into thin air, so my guess is he slipped out the back while you were waiting for us."

"And went where? There's nothing but an open field back there. Buddy Raymond is in that damn house."

"Well, good luck finding him, is all I can say, 'cause we sure didn't."

"Damn."

"Lots of clothes in there, Jack. Bring in a dog, turn it loose. If the guy did leave the house, the hound will sniff out his trail in a matter of minutes."

"Did you find anything worthwhile?"

"Yep, found a thirty-eight, a rifle and a hunting knife."

"What kind of rifle?"

"Thirty aught six with a powerful scope."

Dantzler called over Rick Preston, one of the uniformed guys who had remained on the scene. "Have Commander Todd get you the rifle," he said. "Take it to the station and tell Captain Bird I want ballistics to get me the results ASAP. Got it?"

"You bet," Preston answered.

Dantzler said, "Eric, here's what I want you to do. Go to Suzanne Worley's place and ask her—politely—to accompany you to the station. She'll bitch about it, but make it clear that I just want to talk with her a little more about Dustin Ridley. Once you get her to the station and situated, then go do the same thing with Monica Plemmons. Only tell her I need more information about Adrian White."

"I don't know where Monica lives," Eric said.

"In my briefcase there's a folder with her name on it. You'll find her address in the folder. And here's the key thing, Eric. When you get both of them to the station, put them in separate rooms. It's okay if they see each other—in fact, I'd prefer that they did—but don't let them communicate in any way. And under no circumstances is either of them to know that Morgan Ballard is there. That's critical. They cannot know she's in the house."

"Want Jake to go along with me?" Eric asked.

Dantzler shook his head. "No, I have a different job for Jake."

*****

After Eric was gone, Dantzler spent a few minutes conferring with Commander Todd. Dantzler persuaded Todd to have his men give the house one final search. Todd, always the pro, agreed, even though he knew it was a waste of time. Dantzler asked if they found keys to the Escalade; Todd told him they did. The Escalade had been searched, Todd continued, but nothing important turned up. Dantzler told Todd to have one of his guys drive it back to town, where the crime scene unit could give it an even more detailed inspection. Todd concluded by saying that would be no problem.

While Todd's men were swarming through the house a second time, Dantzler pulled Jake aside and gave him his instructions. Jake nodded and grinned, clearly pleased with his new assignment. Dantzler asked him if he wanted something to eat; he declined, saying with an assignment like this, he preferred working on an empty stomach.

Dantzler left Jake and walked over to his car. Taking out his cell phone, he looked up a number, punched it in, then waited. After three rings a female voice answered.

"This is Cynthia Purcell."

"Cynthia, Jack Dantzler."

"Oh, hello, Detective. What can I do for you?"

"I need your advice on something."

"*My* advice? On what?"

"Cynthia, if it was important for you to extract vital information from either Suzanne Worley or Monica Plemmons, which one would you go after the hardest?"

"Suzanne, definitely."

Cynthia's answer came as a surprise to Dantzler. He'd have bet his best tennis racket that she would have picked Monica. "Why Suzanne?" he asked. "I've met them both, and Suzanne struck me as being a much stronger individual."

"You're correct . . . Suzanne is much stronger, easily the strongest one in our group. Monica is strong, but she's no match for Suzanne."

"Why pick her, then? Why not go after Monica?"

"Because Suzanne's strength is also her weakness."

"You'll have to unravel that mystery for me."

"Suzanne is extremely vain and arrogant, thinks she's smarter than everyone. She could walk into a room where Einstein and Stephen Hawking were sitting together, and she would still be one-hundred percent convinced that she was the most intelligent person there. If you can challenge her vanity, question her intelligence, she will explode like a nuclear bomb. I've seen it happen on a couple of occasions."

"Tell you what, Cynthia. If this thing plays out like I hope it will, I'll buy you a case of Four Roses Single Barrel."

"Then by all means, don't fail."

CHAPTER THIRTY

Dantzler and Jake did a quick run-through of the house while the SWAT guys were finishing their second search of the big place. They checked out all three floors, looking for anything the SWAT guys might have overlooked, or thought to be of no importance. They found nothing but empty rooms on the third floor, a second-floor bedroom that had a walk-in closet lined with clothes, another room with a stationary bike and a treadmill, and a bathroom that had all the signs that this was the one Buddy used. The first floor was fairly standard—living room, hallway, den, kitchen, bathroom and a room that had been converted into a make-shift office.

In the office, Dantzler grabbed the laptop, a flash drive and a stack of CDs, and carried them out to his car. After placing them in the backseat, he walked over to where Commander Todd was standing. Todd took a drink from his canteen, then turned it upside down and poured the remainder of the water on his head and the back of his neck.

"Sorry we came up empty, Jack," Todd said, wiping water from his eyes. "Sometimes the bad guys get lucky, you know?"

"His luck will only take him so far. Eventually, we'll get him."

"Oh, yeah. In today's world, with cameras on every corner and in every store, it's damn near impossible to hide. And that's not even taking into consideration that almost everyone on the planet now has a cell phone or a smart phone they take pictures with. Everyone is a professional photographer these days."

"That's a fact. Technology all but sent privacy straight to hell."

"Are you going to keep someone here in case the guy decides to come back?" Todd asked.

"I'll have a cruiser come by periodically, but he's not coming back. He's a smart guy—he'll know that his only chance is to get out of town quick. I'm sure he has a network of friends he can reach out to. One of them will help him."

"Well, if you don't need us anymore, we're hauling ass outa here."

"Thanks, Steve. You guys are terrific. Take it easy, okay?"

"Always, Ace," Todd said, shaking Dantzler's hand.

When Todd and his team were gone, Dantzler went back inside the house. Jake was standing at the kitchen sink, filling a plastic cup with water. Hearing the running water triggered Dantzler's urge to pee. He found the bathroom, did his business, washed his hands, and then came back into the kitchen.

"See you back in the office, Jake."

"Roger that."

Dantzler went outside, climbed into his car, put on his sunglasses and fired up the engine. Slowly, he pulled away from the house, his tires crunching the gravel, until he hit the main road. He made a hard left and headed back toward town, certain in his belief that Buddy Raymond would be apprehended sooner rather than later.

*****

Buddy Raymond was getting antsy. He had no stomach for being cooped up and caged like a circus animal. As he paced around inside the tunnel, that's exactly what he felt like—a caged animal. A trapped tiger. Every time he checked his wristwatch he was certain an hour or so had passed. Turned out to only be ten or fifteen minutes. Time was dragging. He'd already finished off one bottle of water; if he kept up this pace he'd have none left by tomorrow. And that would be disastrous if the cops left someone behind and he had to stay in the tunnel for several days.

He willed himself to sit down and take some deep breaths. To think. To use his intelligence. He had spent a lifetime committing every crime in the books, yet he had never served one second behind bars. That cannot happen unless you're smart, and Buddy had always recognized his own high level of intelligence. Now was not the time to suddenly become dumb.

Getting away was a given. True, certain events had to take place, but he knew they would. Leave the house with the money, phone Miss Kitty, walk up the road a mile or so, and wait until she came to pick him up. Then she would take him to her house. There, he'd phone Chester Jackson, an old pal who owned an RV and would do anything for money, which he needed to support a serious drug habit. For five grand Chester wasn't about to say no to anything Buddy requested. Hell, he'd suck Buddy's dick for half that much. But Buddy didn't want a blowjob; he wanted Chester to drive him to Mexico. If he could get down there with the money he had, he'd be safe. Maybe he'd even buy a small place on the Gulf, live life free and easy, a prince in a foreign land.

Buddy checked the time again. It was now four-thirty. Based on what he'd heard while the cops were in the house, he was certain no one had stayed behind. About an hour ago, with his ear pressed against the wall, he heard a couple of guys talking. He couldn't be positive, but one of the men sounded like it could have been Dantzler. Whether it was or wasn't didn't matter. It was what one of the men said that was important. He'd said that since Buddy was obviously gone, it made no sense to leave anyone behind to guard the place.

Music to Buddy's ears.

Based on what the cop said, Buddy decided to move his departure time from midnight to six o'clock. That trimmed his wait time to ninety minutes. Then the caged animal would be free again.

Time for another bottle of water.

*****

Entering the station, Dantzler saw Eric and Captain Bird jabbering at the bottom of the stairs. At first, neither man noticed

Dantzler, but after a few moments both men turned and saw him heading in their direction. Dantzler could tell from the expression on Eric's face that bad news awaited him.

"Hate to tell you this, Jack, but . . ."

"Miss Daisy has driven away," Dantzler said, completing Eric's bit of news.

"Morgan left here faster than an Indy five-hundred driver on the final lap."

"Well, she'll eventually be making a return appearance."

"I especially liked her departing words as she stormed out," Bird chimed in. "She said, 'tell the detective that my time is as valuable to me as his is to him.' And then she added, and I quote, 'inform him that if he wants to see me in the future, contact my attorney, the one he's been sleeping with.' Unquote."

"And I thought Morgan had more class than that."

"Explain to me, Jack, what she meant by that last part," Bird said, eyes narrowing. "Have you been sleeping with Grace West?"

"The woman is delusional, Rich."

Behind Bird, Eric rolled his eyes and fought hard to suppress a laugh.

"What about Suzanne and Monica?" Dantzler asked, happy to change the subject. "Are they here?"

Eric nodded. "Suzanne is in the War Room, Monica is in Captain Bird's office."

"Did they see Morgan?"

"No."

"I'm assuming they are both royally pissed."

"Let me put it to you this way, Jack. If you were married to either one of them, you'd be sleeping on the sofa tonight."

"Eric, with what those two women charge, I couldn't even afford the sofa."

Dantzler went into his office and dug through a folder until he found Kendall Langley's name and phone number. Langley was the retired KSP trooper who had investigated Thomas Worley's death. Dantzler dialed the number, waited, and after a half-dozen rings, Langley picked up, identified himself, and asked how he could be of assistance.

"Trooper Langley, this is Jack Dantzler, from Lexington Homicide. We spoke a while back about the Thomas Worley case. Remember?"

"Sure, I do," Worley said, his voice ragged, most likely resulting from years of heavy smoking. "What can I do for you, Detective?"

"Were you able to ascertain the type of weapon used to kill Thomas Worley?"

"Yes, sir. A high-powered rifle."

"Any idea what caliber it was?" Dantzler asked, taking a deep breath. Langley's answer, if it was the right one, would go a long way toward possibly tying up some important loose ends.

"You betcha. The weapon was a thirty aught six. Winchester Supreme cartridges."

Dantzler exhaled. This was exactly the answer he was hoping for. "Were you able to locate the bullet?" he asked, again taking a deep breath.

"We did. Found it in a soft mound of dirt not fifteen feet from the victim's body. It was somewhat damaged, but not to the extent that our people couldn't tell that it was from a thirty aught six. The bullet actually went through the guy's jaw, then into that pile of dirt. Like I said, it sustained some damaged, but not nearly as much as if it had gone through his skull. Why are you asking about this?"

"We found a rifle, a thirty aught six that belongs to a suspect in the murders of those six poker players," Dantzler said. "I have a strong suspicion he was also involved in the death of Thomas Worley."

"Didn't I read in the newspaper that the guy who murdered those men committed suicide?"

"Trooper Langley, I have the same opinion about that ruling as you have in the Worley case. It's bullshit."

"I told everyone here, including the goddamn coroner, that Thomas Worley was murdered, but they wouldn't listen. Now you're about to prove I was right all along."

"Don't get ahead of yourself. Right now I can't prove a

damn thing." Dantzler hesitated for a second or two before continuing, "Does KSP still have the bullet that killed Thomas Worley?"

Once again, it was hold-your-breath time while waiting for Langley's answer.

"Yes, sir. It's stored away in the evidence locker," Langley replied.

Breathing again, Dantzler continued, "How do I go about getting my hands on it?"

"Hell, son, you don't have to do a damn thing. You just tell me when and where you want it, and I'll get it to you. No problem."

"Can you have it in two days?"

"Son, I can have it to you first thing in the morning."

"That would be better than good."

"Your office, say eleven o'clock?"

"I'll be here. And Trooper Langley, I know I don't have to remind you, but make sure you do what needs to be done to keep the evidence chain of custody in order."

"Don't you lose a minute of sleep over that, Detective Dantzler. Everything will be handled by the book. I'm not about to screw up now, not with the truth about to come to light. I want Thomas Worley to get the justice he deserves."

*****

Dantzler ended his call with Langley, and was about to leave his office when his cell phone buzzed. He checked the number and groaned.

"What's up, Grace?" he said, making an attempt to sound cheerful.

"I have just spoken to an irate client of mine who tells me you hijacked her, and that you took her to the police station for no apparent reason. Didn't I make it clear to you that she was not to be interviewed?"

"She wasn't interviewed. And it's nice to hear from you, Grace."

"The only reason she wasn't is because she left before you got to your office."

"That's true."

"Detective, this is my final warning. Stay away from Morgan Ballard, or I will rain down holy hell on your head. Do you understand what I'm saying?"

Dantzler was now officially pissed. He did not much care for being threatened, even from a woman he'd been sleeping with.

"Okay, *Counselor*, here's the deal," he said, sternly. "I'm going to interview Morgan Ballard tomorrow morning, and nothing you say, nor any threats you toss my way, is going to change that. Have her in my office by ten a.m., or I will come to her house with a warrant for her arrest. If you choose to go that route, no doubt it will mean a confrontation with Richard Chambers, which will very likely end in bloodshed. I don't want that. If you can persuade Morgan to come in with you, it will be better for everyone involved."

"Arrest her? On what charge?"

"I will not discuss that over the phone. Bring her in, we'll talk, and maybe, just maybe, she can walk out of here free and clear." This was a lie, one meant to ease the tension between him and Grace. "And as I've told you in the past, I will not ask her a single question relating to the death of her husband. That is not an area of interest for me."

"What, then, is your area of interest?"

"I will fill you in on everything tomorrow. Do you feel confident that you can get her to voluntarily come in with you?"

"I don't know."

"Well, for her sake, do what you can to see that she does."

CHAPTER THIRTY-ONE

Suzanne Worley's dark eyes were like hot coals when she saw Dantzler enter the War Room. She had been pacing the room, but stopped when he closed the door. Leaning forward, both palms flat on the long table, she started to say something but was so angry the words couldn't find their way out.

"Have a seat, Suzanne," Dantzler said, pointing at one of the chairs. "Make yourself comfortable."

"Comfortable? In this place? How is that even possible?"

"I agree that it's not nearly as swanky as your place, but come on, it's not that bad."

"It's worse than bad. It's filthy and it stinks."

"Ah, the dirt and stink tend to grow on you after a while. Pretty soon, you won't even notice it."

"You think this is funny, don't you, Detective?"

"Not in the least." Dantzler enthusiastically pointed at the chair. "Sit down, Suzanne."

Suzanne waited the appropriate time, long enough to make him think (or convince herself?) that she wasn't allowing him to boss her around. God forbid he should get the idea he's in control. When she felt enough time had passed, she slid the chair back, sat, and crossed her arms in front of her chest.

"There, that's better." Dantzler sat down across from her and turned on the small tape recorder lying on the table. "Now we can talk like grown-ups."

"We have nothing to talk about," Suzanne countered.

"That's where you're wrong. We have much to discuss."

"I certainly hope you don't intend to bring up the crazy notion that I'm a prostitute, because I most certainly am not."

"Yes, Suzanne, you are. But that's not what we're going to talk about."

"I have nothing to say to you, Detective."

"Good. Then you can listen to what I have to say."

Suzanne grunted and looked away, feigning indifference.

"You are going to be arrested and charged with conspiracy to commit murder. You . . ."

Suzanne nearly flew out of her chair, lips trembling, eyes bulging. "Conspiracy to commit murder?" she screamed. "Who do you think I murdered?"

"Thomas Worley," Dantzler quietly answered.

"You must be kidding. I was in Florida when Tommy was killed. The police in Scott County know this. Check with them, they'll confirm my story."

"That sunny alibi isn't going to hold up, Suzanne. I know you were in Florida when it happened. I also know you hired Buddy Raymond to kill Thomas."

"Who's Buddy Raymond? I don't know anyone named Buddy Raymond. You've gone off the deep end, Detective."

Now was the time to follow Cynthia Purcell's strategy.

"Suzanne, you've got it in your head that you're so much smarter than everyone else, that you reside on a mountain of IQ points high above the rest of us, that intellectually we're just not in your league. It must be nice to have such a lofty opinion of yourself. But the truth is, you're actually not nearly as intelligent as you think you are. In fact, you're kinda dumb."

With that, Suzanne did come out of her chair. "How dare you impugn my intelligence?" she said. "You don't know me."

"I know you were dumb enough to hire a weak man for the job. A smart lady would never have made a bone-head move like that."

"I never hired Buddy Raymond to do anything. I don't know the man."

"That's not what Buddy says," Dantzler lied. "He's given us a full statement detailing how you hired him to get rid of your husband, because, in Buddy's words, 'the dude was beginning to get a little too inquisitive about the business she and those other women had going on. She wanted the guy gone.' Can't get much plainer than that."

"I don't believe you. Buddy wouldn't roll over like that."

"How do you know, Suzanne? A minute ago you told me you didn't even know Buddy Raymond. Are you telling me now that you do know him? Which story are you gonna go with?"

"Yes, I have met him, okay. He's close with Morgan. But I don't believe he told you I hired him to murder Tommy."

"We have the murder weapon, Suzanne," Dantzler said, now back in truthful territory. "A thirty aught six rifle. Found it when we searched Buddy's house on Old Ironworks Pike. We also have the bullet that killed your husband. And guess what? It was fired from a thirty aught six. At this very moment our ballistics people are testing Buddy's rifle. Once they've done that, they'll compare the bullet they retrieve with the one that killed your husband. What do you want to bet they match? If they do, well, it's game over for you and Buddy."

"I had nothing to do with my husband's death, I don't care what anyone tells you," Suzanne said, but her words lacked conviction. "If Buddy Raymond says otherwise, he's a liar."

"Trouble is, Suzanne, the evidence doesn't lie."

"Why would I want to murder my husband?"

"Like Buddy said, he was beginning to ask too many questions. He was becoming a threat."

"That's insane."

"You want to know what else Buddy told us?" Dantzler asked, now back in liar's mode. "That he hired a guy named Mark Banks to murder those six poker players, and that you and Morgan were the ones who sanctioned it. If my math is correct, that ups your conspiracy-to-murder count to seven."

Suzanne shook her head and forced a smile.

"If I were in your shoes Suzanne, I would confess and say it was all Morgan's idea. The whole thing. That might earn you a few points with the D.A."

"I want a lawyer." Suzanne flung herself back in the chair.

"I will not say another word until I speak with my attorney."

Dantzler was surprised—and pleased—that she hadn't requested one at the start of the interview. Her failure to do so proved that she really *wasn't* all that intelligent. Whether she knew it or not, she'd practically made his case for him. He picked up the tape recorder and clicked it off.

"You can make the call from downstairs. Please stand up." When she did, he put the handcuffs on her, and said, "Suzanne Worley, you are under arrest for the murder of Thomas Worley. You have the right . . ."

When Dantzler finished reading Suzanne her rights, he motioned through the two-way glass for Eric to come into the War Room. "You get all that on video, Eric?"

"Every word and gesture," Eric answered.

"Take her downstairs and let her make the call to her lawyer. Then begin the booking process."

Eric took Suzanne by the arm and led her out of the room. She left quietly, head bowed, the earlier fire now all but extinguished. Dantzler always felt a brief twinge of sympathy for someone being arrested. It had to be a sad, lonesome feeling knowing your life will soon be altered forever. As she walked away Dantzler could see tears streaming down her face.

The dominant queen had been broken.

*****

Grace was angry at Dantzler but even angrier at herself for allowing her temper to hit the boiling point. That was uncalled for. Like her, he was simply doing his job. And the truth is, built into each of their jobs' DNA was one indisputable fact: they would invariably come out of opposite corners when the bell rang. She just had to accept that and deal with it.

But Grace hadn't dealt with it, and that was burning her more than the verbal exchange with Dantzler. She wasn't living up to her own words of wisdom. After all, she was the one who told Dantzler that they would always be adversaries. She's the one who warned him to never let the professional interfere with the personal. And now here she was, doing exactly that.

Get over yourself, Grace, she mumbled to herself. *There are more important things to do than sit around beating up on yourself, or on Dantzler.*

Important things like getting Morgan Ballard to Dantzler's office tomorrow morning. This was not going to be a simple task, that much Grace knew for sure. And Dantzler was correct—if Richard Chambers inserts himself into the situation, violence was not only possible, it was likely. The man was a grenade always but a second away from detonating.

Grace didn't know why Dantzler wanted to interview Morgan, but she did have a strong inkling. It had to do with the murder of those poker players. Dantzler had come to believe Morgan was somehow involved, and he must have some solid evidence to back up his belief. Arresting a person is serious business.

Until recently Grace would have laughed at the suggestion that Morgan was capable of murder. But now she wasn't so sure. Not after having been in the company of the "other" Morgan Ballard. That Morgan gave the impression she might be capable of doing just about anything, including murder.

None of this mattered at the moment. Dantzler was going to question Morgan regardless of Grace's feelings, and she needed to accept that inevitability. Fighting it wasn't going to do anyone any good. Better to play ball and do the wise thing, which was to get Morgan to the station without her father present. That was easier said than done, especially if Morgan had already contacted her father and filled him in on what had happened. If that were the case, getting through tomorrow morning without violence might be next to impossible.

Grace yanked her cell phone off the car seat, punched in Morgan's number, and waited. Four rings later the call was answered. A man's deep voice.

Richard Chambers.

Oh, shit, Grace said to herself.

CHAPTER THIRTY-TWO

A rush of adrenaline surged through Buddy's body when he realized his departing time had arrived. A check of his watch told him it was six o'clock. His energy level rose with each new blast of adrenaline. So did his feelings of anxiety, of trepidation, of worry. Hell, if he was being completely honest with himself, a nice dose of fear was also present, and fear was a virtual stranger to Buddy. He was known as one of those guys who had ice water in his veins, someone who was always cool under pressure. But today . . . his nerves were shaky.

The last thirty minutes seemed like two hours. It was easily the longest half-hour of his life. He'd spent the time alternating between sitting in one of the chairs, mindlessly flipping one of the empty water bottles into the air and catching it, and prowling around the tunnel. Once, more out of boredom than necessity, he'd walked to the back of the tunnel and relieved himself.

At long last those thirty minutes had passed. Now it was time to leave the tunnel, time to free the caged animal. Time to set his escape plan in motion.

Getting out of the tunnel was a much more difficult task than getting in. That heavy oak grandfather's clock was the problem. To move it Buddy had to first push the door panel about four inches forward, until it hit against the back of the clock. Then, using only his left hand, and summoning all the strength he could muster, he had to slide the heavy clock forward another fifteen inches or so. Possibly even more, given that he also had to create enough of an opening to allow for the money-filled duffel bag to make it through. This wasn't going to be an easy task.

Before any of this could happen, though, he had to make sure no one else was in the house. Placing his right ear against the door panel, he closed his eyes and listened hard. Nothing. Next, he carefully and silently eased the door open three inches. Standing perfectly still, he closed his eyes again and listened, both for movement and sounds. If someone was in the house, and if that person took two steps, those old wooden floors would creak, instantly letting Buddy know he wasn't alone. If he heard or felt anything, he would close the door, go back inside the tunnel, and wait.

Hearing only silence, he was confident the cops had left no one behind. He opened the door wider, until it was stopped by the clock, then he reached around with his left hand, got a good grip on the side of the clock, and gave a mighty heave. The clock slid forward about twelve inches, just enough to allow him to use both hands for the next shove. Having the extra strength provided by the use of two hands proved to be the difference. After a hard struggle he was able to create an opening wide enough to accommodate both him and the duffel bag.

Although moving the damn clock had required plenty of strength and energy, he had performed the difficult task with a minimum of noise. Still, he wasn't going to take any chances. Standing just inside the hallway, he closed his eyes and listened. The only thing he heard was his own beating heart.

More confident than ever that he was alone, Buddy went back inside, picked up the duffel bag off the floor, slung it over his left shoulder, then grabbed the .44 from the chair with his right hand and headed out of the tunnel. It was only then, once he was in the hallway, that he realized there were still two hours of daylight left. Accustomed to the tunnel's darkness, the outside light hit him like a slap to his face. Maybe he should have waited until midnight, when the cloak of darkness would have provided cover. Maybe leaving so quickly was a bad idea. But he had made his decision, and he wasn't turning back at this point. It only meant he had to be more careful.

Setting the duffel bag down, and sticking the .44 inside his waistband, he pulled out his cell phone to see if he could get a signal. Inside the tunnel he hadn't been able to get one. Now, in the hallway, he saw that he finally had service. He was good to go. First, a stop in the kitchen to see if he could scrounge something to eat, then a phone call to Miss Kitty.

After that, hang around until it was dark, leave with the money, walk a mile or so up the road, then wait for Miss Kitty to pick him up. Then she would take him to Chester Jackson's place, where he'd pay Chester a couple grand for a ride in his big RV.

Next stop, Mexico.

*****

Jake had once spent two full days sitting on a mountain ridge in Afghanistan waiting for a notorious Taliban leader to emerge from the cave below. Two days of searing heat, two nights of icy cold. No food, only the occasional drink of water from his canteen. On the morning of the third day, the Taliban chieftain stepped out of the cave, stretched, and cast his gaze to the East toward the rising sun. It was the last sunrise he would ever see. Jake blew the man's head off with a single shot from his rifle.

Two days and nights of misery spent waiting to take out a really bad dude.

Compared to that, four-and-a-half hours sitting in a kitchen waiting for Buddy Raymond to emerge was a piece of cake.

Jake felt Buddy several seconds before hearing him. There was a slight movement of the floor, like the house let slip one of those belches that are out before you know it, or you just experienced a sudden and unexpected shudder for no apparent reason. Only after the *feeling* did Jake hear the sound of soft footsteps on the wooden floor in the hallway.

His waiting was over.

Jake grinned, remembering what Dantzler had said after the SWAT guys departed: "I agree with Commander Todd about one thing—people don't vanish into thin air. Buddy Raymond is still in that damn house."

And as usual, Dantzler nailed it on the head.

In Jake's past combat experiences, time did seem to slow down considerably. He'd heard other veterans talk about it happening to them, but he never really bought into it. Sounded too dramatic, like movie-talk bullshit. Bogus, like that when-you're-about-to-die-your-life-flashes-before-your-eyes line people always hit you with, even though most of the people telling you this never once came close to losing their life. It was just more of the hand-me-down nonsense laid on us from the time we're old enough to understand English.

But for Jake, for whatever unexplained reason, it was true. Time had a way of slowing to a crawl when the bullets started flying. While he realized that time didn't actually slow down—if it did, that would really fuck with all the physical laws of the universe—he did have a unique ability to see events unfold in a slow, precise time.

In seconds.

For Buddy Raymond, five seconds; for Jake, only one.

It unfolded like this:

Second one: Buddy leaves the hallway and comes into the kitchen.

Second two: Buddy is startled to see a lone male standing by the kitchen table.

Second three: Buddy slings the duffel bag off his shoulder.

Second four: Buddy reaches into his waistband and takes out the .44 Magnum.

Second five: Buddy begins to raise his right arm.

Second five for Buddy was second one for Jake.

It was also Buddy's last second alive on this earth.

As Buddy was raising his weapon, Jake fired off two shots in rapid succession. The first bullet slammed into Buddy's chest, maybe a quarter-inch to the right of his heart. The impact drove Buddy to his right, so that the second bullet hit him a quarter-inch to the left of his heart, ripping Buddy's upper chest to shreds. Either bullet would have proved fatal.

Buddy tumbled to the floor, hitting it with a soft thud, like a big sack of grain had just been dropped. The .44 made a louder noise when it banged off a kitchen chair and fell to the floor.

Buddy made no noise at all. He was dead by the time second six had ticked away.

Jake moved quickly to the body and kicked the .44 farther away. Kneeling, he placed two fingers on Buddy's neck, checking for a pulse. There was none.

Buddy Raymond was dead.

Jake stood, took out his cell phone, and punched in Dantzler's number. Dantzler answered after the first ring. He'd been waiting for the call.

"The invisible man is down," Jake said.

*****

Standing in the kitchen, looking down at Buddy Raymond's lifeless body, Dantzler had decidedly mixed feelings about the way things unfolded. Yes, he fully expected events to play out the way they had. He was confident that if it came down to Jake versus Buddy, and if Buddy didn't surrender peacefully, Jake would come away the winner. In a contest between those two, that was a no-brainer. Jake was clearly the better man.

Still . . .

In a perfect world Jake would have wounded Buddy, not killed him. Of course, when the event was being played out in real time, Jake wasn't thinking about what might or might not happen down the road. He didn't give a shit about a perfect world. His only thought at that moment was killing Buddy before Buddy killed him. And, thank God, Jake walked away from the encounter, unharmed in any way.

However, with Buddy dead, there was no chance to question him. No opportunity to get his testimony regarding the murder of those six poker players. Of hiring Mark Banks to commit the actual killing. Of his involvement in the death of Thomas Worley. Or the death of Rufus Young.

Even more problematic, with Buddy dead, the evidence against Morgan Ballard and Suzanne Worley had all but died with him. Any hope of eliciting solid evidence against those two ladies lay on that bloody floor with Buddy. Now the case against them would revolve around circumstantial shit, which tended to almost always play in favor of the defense.

Sitting at the kitchen table, Jake seemed to read Dantzler's mind. "Sorry I had to take him out, Jack. But he really gave me no choice."

"Don't apologize, Jake. When I left you here, knowing Buddy like I did, this is the outcome I fully expected. I'm just relieved that it's him and not you lying on that floor."

Before Jake could respond Dantzler's cell phone rang. He checked the caller ID and immediately recognized the number. Grace West.

What does she want now? he wondered. *To rip my ass some more?*

"Grace," he said, ready to feel the full force of her anger.

But he was wrong.

"Jack, Richard Chambers is involved." Her words came out rapid-fire. "He's going to be a big problem for you."

"Calm down, Grace. What are you saying?"

"I called Morgan to let her know that she needed to get with me tomorrow at nine, that the two of us had to be in your office by ten. But . . ."

"But . . . what?"

"Richard Chambers answered."

"And what pearls of wisdom did he have for you?"

"That I was fired as Morgan's attorney. And that if you or any other cops show up to arrest Morgan, you will only get to her over his dead body."

"That can certainly be arranged."

"How are you going to handle this, Jack?"

"I won't. Where are they?"

"At Richard Chambers' house."

"Thanks for the heads-up, Grace. I owe you."

"What . . ." she asked, but Dantzler had ended the call.

While Grace was finishing her unanswered question, Dantzler was already punching in a different number. The call was answered almost immediately.

"Hey, Steve, you SWAT guys up for a new gig?" he asked.

CHAPTER THIRTY-THREE

It didn't take long for Richard Chambers to push aside the notion that this was going to be a *mano a mano* confrontation with that arrogant prick Dantzler. This was definitely not going to be the case, not after he heard all the commotion in front of his house. Not after he looked out the window and saw those four large SWAT vehicles pull into the driveway. Not after he saw about two dozen men, all fully armed and dressed in black, erupt from the vehicles and swarm the place like ants rushing toward a spilled picnic basket.

This was going to be anything but a one-on-one showdown.

Chambers glanced down at the rifle leaning against the wall, gave a quick thought to picking it up, and then decided not to. This was a gunfight he couldn't win. Better to take a different approach, say, diplomacy, a tactic all but unfamiliar to him.

Opening the front door, stepping outside with hands buried in his pockets, he walked off the porch and toward the guy he assumed to be the leader. It took all of Chambers' effort, but he finally managed to work up a smile. He was quick to note that the leader's expression was a long way from warm and friendly.

"Show me your hands please, Mr. Chambers," the leader ordered.

Chambers raised both arms, palms open, turning them back and forth as if to prove that his hands were empty. That gesture was enough to get the cops to lower their weapons. *So far, so good,* he thought. Looking past the leader, Chambers could see Dantzler working his way to the front.

"You are not taking my daughter anywhere until my attorney arrives," Chamber said.

Dantzler eased past Commander Todd and closed in on Chambers. At six-three, Dantzler was a good five inches taller than Chambers, who had a wide, thick, almost simian-like physique. Dantzler had made up his mind that if this turned into a battle of wills, he would emerge the winner. Getting in Chambers' face was the best method for taking charge.

Leaning down, Dantzler said, "Morgan is coming to the station with me. I have some questions she needs to answer."

"Not until my attorney is present."

"By all means, call *your* attorney."

Dantzler emphasized *your* because Chambers was overlooking an important point: His daughter was an adult, not a juvenile. If Morgan wanted an attorney present, she needed to request it, not her father.

"If she goes with you, does she have to be in handcuffs?" Chambers asked.

"If Morgan comes in willingly, then I see no need to cuff her."

Hearing that, Morgan opened the front door and came outside. Behind Dantzler, every weapon was raised and aimed at her. Not a single weapon was lowered until she showed that her hands were empty.

Dantzler nodded at Morgan as she walked past him and toward his car. As she did, Dantzler turned, smiled at Todd and winked, both men entertaining the same thought.

A full-out show of force usually gets the job done.

*****

On the ride back into town neither Dantzler nor Morgan spoke. In situations like this, Dantzler normally didn't speak. Silence, he felt, oftentimes triggered a suspect's urge to talk, to get a conversation going, to be his new best friend, which was precisely what he was hoping for. Suspects invariably let something slip out that worked to his advantage.

As they reached the edge of town, Morgan said in a quiet voice, "How did you know I was at my father's house?"

"Grace West. She was very worried about you."

"Grace isn't my attorney anymore."

"So I heard."

At the station, Dantzler situated Morgan in the War Room and got her a bottle of water. Then he found Sergeant Marlene Marie Murphy-Martin—"4M" to her co-workers—to handle the video equipment during the interview session. With Eric helping Jake and Arnie and the crime scene folks at the house on Old Ironworks Pike, 4M got the call. She had done it plenty of times in the past, so Dantzler knew he could count on her to do good work.

Taking a seat at the table, Dantzler turned on the tape recorder and said, "Before we get started, do you have anything to say to me? Any questions you'd like to ask?"

"Am I under arrest?" Morgan wanted to know.

"Not yet."

"What does that mean?"

"It means everything hinges on what happens in the next few minutes."

"What do you think is going to happen, Detective?"

"To begin with, I'm going to tell you everything I know."

"Oh, yeah? What do you know?"

"I know about the escort service business you and Suzanne Worley started while you were still in college. I know Sahid Hassaine found out about it at some point and was blackmailing you. I know you guys paid Hassaine ten-thousand dollars at the beginning of each month . . ."

"How'd . . ." Morgan started but didn't finish the question.

"I know you and Buddy Raymond are lovers. I know Buddy hired Mark Banks to murder Sahid Hassaine, those other five poker players, and the two young kids on Lansdowne. I know you, Suzanne and Buddy paid Banks somewhere in the neighborhood of eighty-five thousand dollars for those jobs. I know Buddy killed Mark Banks. I know Thomas Worley was becoming suspicious of what was going on, so you and Suzanne had Buddy take him out. As you can see, Morgan, I know a lot."

"Did you talk to Buddy about any of this?"

Dantzler shrugged.

"I want to speak to . . ."

Here came the dreaded L word—*lawyer*, Dantzler thought. But he was wrong.

". . . Buddy."

"Not gonna happen."

"What do you mean, it's not gonna happen? I want to speak with him."

"You can't."

"Why not?"

"Buddy is dead."

Dantzler expected this bit of news to bring on a flood of tears, screaming, cursing, pounding the table with her fists, all the typical hysteria normally associated with a moment like this. He was waiting for Morgan to crash and burn. But none of that happened. Instead, she took the news without so much as a flinch. Watching her, Dantzler could almost hear the thoughts in her head spinning like a roulette wheel, going round and round until they finally landed on the one she felt was a winning number.

Dantzler knew with the certainty of an algebra formula what the next words out of her mouth would be.

"It was all Buddy," Morgan said, predictable as fog in London. "Buddy *and* Suzanne. They were behind everything. It was Suzanne who told Buddy that Hassaine was blackmailing us. Buddy said we were nuts to pay him a dime. Said he would put an end to that nonsense. And he did. He paid Mark Banks all that money to kill Hassaine and those other men. Those innocent kids, too. Buddy said they had to be eliminated because they might try to blackmail us sometime down the road. And you're right about Tommy Worley. Suzanne got Buddy to kill him. And Tommy was a really good guy. Real kind and sweet. Nice in every way, you know. And Buddy told us he killed Mark Banks. He said Banks was antsy, unstable, someone who wouldn't hold up if the cops ever caught him. It was all Buddy and Suzanne, I'm telling you. All of it."

"Come on, Morgan. You knew about everything that was

going on."

"Yes, I knew, but there was nothing I could do to prevent it. Buddy and Suzanne made it clear that if I didn't play along, I would be the next one eliminated. I had no choice, don't you see? They threatened me with my life."

"Let me get this clear in my head. What you are asking me to believe is that you knew about everything that was going to happen—and did happen—but you were powerless to stop it? Is that accurate?"

"Yes, powerless, that's the perfect word." Morgan was almost jubilant, as though she had just been handed the keys to the kingdom. "I was powerless."

"Powerless to stop what you knew was about to take place, right?" Dantzler repeated. "Like the murder of those six poker players?"

"That's correct."

Bingo. That was it. Morgan Ballard had just climbed the scaffold and placed the noose around her neck. She had just admitted to being part of a criminal conspiracy to commit murder. And even if she didn't take part in the actual murders, her knowledge that they were going to happen made her as guilty as the person who pulled the trigger. In the eyes of the law she was as guilty as the shooter. The rest of Morgan's life would be spent behind bars, and nothing she or Richard Chambers, or whatever famous lawyer they retained, was going to change that fact.

Dantzler turned off the tape recorder, stood and moved behind Morgan. He asked her to stand, told her she was being arrested for conspiracy to commit murder, and then he rattled off her rights while placing the handcuffs on her.

"You will be escorted downstairs, where you will be booked for the charges I just mentioned," Dantzler informed her. "Do you understand everything I've told you?"

"Don't you think I need an attorney present?" Morgan asked.

"Yeah, about thirty minutes ago."

*****

After 4M took Morgan away, Dantzler went to the break room, bought a can of Pepsi, then trudged down to his office. He had calls to make, first to Grace to let her know that everything turned out okay, then to Eric to find out how things were proceeding at Buddy Raymond's house. Before making either call, though, he just wanted to lean back, close his eyes, and take a few minutes to relax. These past two weeks had been eventful, and all the work and strain and thinking and planning and worrying had taken a toll on his mind and body. He couldn't recall ever being more tired and worn down than he was right now.

Fifteen minutes later, far from rested, Dantzler spent the next hour questioning Monica Plemmons, who, not surprisingly, wasn't at all pleased with having been made to wait "an interminable amount of time in such shabby surroundings" before someone finally had the good sense to "realize that I'm still alive."

After speaking with her, Dantzler came to the conclusion that, yes, Monica was aware of certain minor matters, but she had been kept in the dark on the major issues. Murder, for instance. In Dantzler's view, Monica was a high-class prostitute and nothing more. He advised her that she would almost certainly be called to testify during any trial proceedings, then let her go.

Dantzler opened his cell phone and called Grace West to let her know how the day's events unfolded. Too weary to offer lengthy details, he gave her the abbreviated version of what had transpired. Grace listened, asked no follow-up questions, thanked him for calling when he concluded his presentation, said goodbye and hung up.

And that was that.

Dantzler was about to phone Eric when the door opened and Eric himself entered. He had a smile on his face, and he was holding a clear plastic bag in his right hand. Inside the bag was a single light blue envelope. Falling into a chair, he leaned back and nodded. He looked as tired as Dantzler felt, but his energy level was sky high.

"It's a done deal," Eric announced, waving the bag. "Everything we need to know is in this envelope."

"Tell me what you've got."

"Buddy was hiding in a small tunnel-like place that had once been the opening to a bomb shelter. We found a big safe in there. Inside was the rest of Buddy's money—what he had in the duffel bag amounted to about half of the total—along with some high-quality pot, about ten bags of pills and a ledger of some sort. Most important to us, though, was a box containing a bunch of letters to Buddy from Morgan Ballard. I scanned through a couple of them, didn't find anything of interest until I read this one."

Eric unzipped the bag, plucked out the envelope, opened it, removed the letter and handed it across the table.

"You read it, Eric. I'm too damn tired."

Eric pulled the letter back, and said, "I don't have to read it all. These two sentences are all we need. 'Buddy, love: Now that I have removed Deke from our lives, if you will follow through and rid us of the Hassaine problem, then we can live our lives openly, and not fear showing our love for one another. My sweetheart, my sexy darling, I can hardly wait until that day arrives.' She goes on to joke that she's now a happy widow, just like Suzanne is. With the evidence we already have, along with this letter, Morgan and Suzanne are going away for the rest of their miserable lives."

"You know, Eric, the sheer stupidity of criminals never ceases to amaze me. Why would Morgan ever put such incriminating evidence on paper? How dumb was that? And for Buddy to keep it? That's nuts. I really thought he was a smart guy, which, as it turns out, he clearly wasn't. If I'd been in his shoes, I would have burned the damn letter, and then I would have been all over Morgan for sending it in the first place. I suppose we should be thankful they aren't nearly as intelligent as they think they are."

Dantzler took the letter from Eric, wanting to make sure Morgan had signed it. She had, her name written in sweeping, curling letters at the bottom of the page. Below her name was a long line of those X's and O's that meant I love you. Junior high shit.

"Are Jake and Arnie still out at Buddy's house?" Dantzler asked.

"Yeah, but they should be wrapping up fairly soon. Want me to go back out there?"

"Nah, they can handle it. Go home, get some rest."

Eric stood, said, "You gonna give the counselor a call, maybe go consort with the enemy tonight?"

Dantzler laughed.

"Did I say something funny?"

"Eric, I think my days of consorting with the enemy are finished. The war is over."

CHAPTER THIRTY-FOUR

The arraignment for Morgan and Suzanne quickly dissolved into a three-ring circus, with Richard Chambers serving as circus master. When Judge Lincoln Alexander informed the two women that they would be held without bail, Chambers exploded out of his seat, pointed a finger at the judge, and began rattling off a profanity-rich tirade that lasted almost two minutes. He concluded his vitriolic outburst with a final statement that he "hoped you get a bullet in your head just like that goddamn Jew Kurtz did."

With that last line, Judge Alexander, an amiable black man known for having the patience of a saint, had finally heard enough. Speaking in a firm, still voice, he said, "Mr. Chambers, I am holding you in contempt of court. You will be a welcomed guest in our jail tonight. And from this point on, a day of jail time will match each word you utter. So unless you want to stay with us for a while, I would advise you to remain silent. Do you have anything else you wish to say?"

When Chambers shook his head, Judge Alexander told the bailiffs to take him into custody. As he was being led away, Chambers looked back at Morgan. She was not looking in his direction.

The early morning proceeding also offered a preview of what was sure to be a world-class catfight between Morgan and Suzanne. Judging by those intense I-will-kill-you-bitch stares they were aiming at each other, it had the potential to go down as one of the classics. Suzanne was the one whose glare radiated the most anger and hatred. Had there been a kernel of truth to the old saying, "If looks could kill . . ." Morgan Ballard would have dropped dead right on the spot.

Upon hearing that Morgan laid all the blame at her feet, Suzanne, ignoring her attorney's stern objection, wasted no time giving Dantzler her version of how things went down. In Suzanne's re-telling, everything Morgan said was accurate, with a lone exception—the roles were reversed. Naturally, it's what Dantzler expected. If Suzanne were to be believed, it was Morgan and Buddy who set up all the murders, including Thomas Worley's. They were the ones who paid Mark Banks to kill the poker players, Stick and Darlene. It was Morgan and Buddy who threatened Suzanne with her life if she dared break ranks and go to the police. Yes, Suzanne admitted that she knew what was going to happen, but fear for her life prevented her from stopping it.

"So you knew about everything, including the murders, but you were powerless to stop it, correct?" Dantzler said, repeating the line he used with Morgan.

"Yes, that's it, powerless," Suzanne answered, echoing Morgan. "I was powerless to keep it from happening."

Listening, Dantzler was reminded of something Cynthia Purcell told him about how the bond between Morgan and Suzanne was unbreakable. Everything Cynthia said turned out to be accurate, except for that one single point. On that one she couldn't have been more off-base. The bond between Morgan and Suzanne was more fragile than a piece of expensive china. And it had clearly been shattered to pieces. Well, Dantzler thought, those two have a lifetime in prison to work out their issues and mend the deep fissure now separating them.

On the flip side, it wouldn't trouble him in the least if they remained life-long bitter enemies. Dantzler had no interest in that feline fight. As far as he was concerned, they could rip each other to shreds. It's what they both deserved.

For the next three days, the mood among Dantzler's homicide crew, the crime scene folks, and virtually everyone else in the building was joyous and upbeat, not unlike a group of athletes celebrating the winning of a championship. Lots of laughs, back-slapping, toasts, atta boys, and offers to buy the next round. To the astonishment of everyone, even Captain Bird, a notorious tightwad, said he would spring for a round of drinks.

There was plenty of reason to celebrate. Two murderous women turned on each other, and a treasure trove of evidence had been uncovered in Buddy Raymond's safe, including dozens of letters to him from Morgan, all of which offered some insight into what was going to happen, and what eventually did happen. Also found was a small notebook detailing payments Buddy made to Mark Banks, and the money Buddy received from Suzanne and Morgan for killing Thomas Worley. There was so much evidence against the two women that they would be foolish to do anything other than plead guilty, express remorse, and pray the judge had mercy on them.

Considering everything, Dantzler and his crew didn't care in the least what was in store for Morgan and Suzanne. For the moment, with the fate of those two now in the rear-view mirror, all was right with the world. The good guys had prevailed. And because of that positive outcome, everyone involved was more than ready to enjoy the sweet taste of victory.

Everyone . . . except Jake.

Because Jake was involved in an officer-related shooting that resulted in a death, there had to be an internal investigation to make sure everything was on the up and up. This was a mandatory process, one Dantzler and Eric had gone through in the past. While the investigation was on-going, the officer involved was placed on modified duty. What this translated into was the officer sitting at a desk, answering phone calls, and shuffling through a mountain of paperwork, some legit, some given simply to annoy him.

It also meant being razzed by co-workers. During his time in exile, Jake answered to "Mr. Secretary", "Prince of Paperwork", "Desk King", and assorted other monikers, none of which did anything to lift his spirits. This went on for three days. What Jake didn't know was the investigation cleared him of any wrongdoing after day one. However, since Jake, still a relative newcomer to the squad, had never been subjected to an official initiation, his co-workers decided the additional time behind a desk would serve as his rite of passage.

Dantzler made it clear to everyone that he didn't want to be within a mile of the office when Jake was told the truth. "Think Godzilla stomping all over anything in his way," Dantzler said. "That'll be Jake when he finds out he's been played. I value my health and well-being far too much to be around when that happens."

"Who will tell him?" Arnie Edwards asked.

"Captain Bird. Who else? That's why he gets paid the big bucks, and why he has the better life-insurance policy."

*****

One day after the arraignment Dantzler got a call from Grace. The two had not seen or spoken since she phoned to let him know Richard Chambers might be a problem. Dantzler was surprised—and pleased—to hear from her.

He was not pleased with what she had to say.

Grace said she enjoyed the time they spent together, thanked him for his kindness and understanding, told him she was heading back to Chicago, said goodbye and ended the conversation. No I'll see you in the future, no invitation to come visit her, and no mention that she was still entertaining the idea of opening an office in Lexington. Just a simple adios.

And that was that.

*****

At five o'clock Dantzler picked up a sack from under his desk and left the station. With thunder booming in the distance, he walked down East Main, turned onto South Upper, went one block, made a left, and headed toward Park Plaza.

After taking the elevator to the top floor, he got off, went to a familiar penthouse apartment and rang the bell. The door opened almost immediately.

"Homicide, not Vice, correct?" Cynthia Purcell asked, grinning. "Did I get it right this time?"

"You did."

"Come in, Detective Dantzler."

Stepping inside, Dantzler looked around, said, "You alone?"

"Until six."

"You're continuing to play a dangerous game, Cynthia."

"Not to worry, Detective. I'm planning on making a few changes. You know, meet clients in other cities."

"Smart. I don't want to see you behind bars like your two compatriots."

"How are they holding up?" Cynthia asked.

"I would say they are not very happy campers right about now. And they won't be for the rest of their lives."

"Wish I could feel sorry for them, but I can't. Not after what they did." Cynthia motioned toward the sofa. "Make yourself comfortable. Want me to take the sack?"

"Actually, this is for you." Dantzler handed her the sack. "I didn't get you a case of Four Roses Single Barrel, but here are three bottles. This should be more than enough to get you started."

"You didn't have to do this, Detective. I really didn't do anything to deserve it."

"You were honest with me, Cynthia. And contrary to what you might think, what you told me did help solve the case. You filled in some important pieces of the puzzle. We all owe you for that."

"Will you have a drink with me?" Cynthia looked at a clock on the wall. "My client isn't due for another forty-five minutes. We have time for one drink together, don't we?"

"Maybe some other time, Cynthia." Dantzler said. "But right now, with all that's going on, and with you sure to be called to testify against Morgan and Suzanne, it's probably not a good idea. Best to keep things kosher until all this plays out. Then, maybe . . . who knows? We'll drink a toast to the good guys."

"Am I one of the good guys, Detective?"

"In my book, you are."

Cynthia leaned up and kissed Dantzler on the cheek. "Take care, Detective Jack Dantzler. And remember, I'll be here when you get ready to have that drink."

Dantzler left Park Plaza and walked down Vine Street, heading one block toward McCarthy's. Thinking about what he and his team had accomplished in the past two weeks, bringing about justice for nine innocent murder victims while getting bad people off the street, was the reason why he loved his job. It was stressful, difficult, tedious, and, yes, at times dangerous. But none of that mattered, because all of those things, the good and the bad, were included in the job description. It all went with the territory.

At the end of the day, when he closed his eyes at night, the only thing that truly mattered to him was that a time of reckoning had arrived for four violent, greedy, evil people. They were gone, washed off the street like yesterday's garbage, and the world was a safer place because of it.

A better place, because of what Dantzler and his fellow detective were able to achieve.

And for Dantzler, that was the reason why he proudly carried that gold shield.

Smiling broadly, Dantzler drew closer to the big green sign that said McCarthy's Irish Bar. Inside, old friends and drinking pals David Bloom and Sean Montgomery were waiting for him.

Also waiting . . . the good Guinness.

Acknowledgments

Thanks again to the usual gang of family and friends who have always supported me and encouraged me throughout the years. This group includes Julie Watson, Ed Watson, Wanda Underwood, Denny Slinker, Suzanne Slinker, Christina Young, Scott Boggs, Chris Boggs, Bonnie Vincent, Jim Vincent, Grant Sparks, Jimmie Nell Jenkins and my aunt Bobbie Watkins. Thanks to Patty Urfer Holland for her advice regarding Four Rose Single Barrel, one of the premier bourbons in the world. As always, thanks to Frank Hall for giving me a permanent home at Hydra Publications, and thanks to Tony Acree for taking over as publisher and lifting Hydra to even greater and higher heights. Finally, thanks to Marilyn Underwood for her keen proofreading ability, and for putting up with a writer who tends to get grouchy when he can't get a sentence to read the way he wants it to.

About the Author

Tom Wallace is the award-winning author of five previous Jack Dantzler mysteries, including *The Fire of Heaven, The List, Gnosis, The Devil's Racket* and *What Matters Blood.* He also wrote the thriller, *Heirs of Cain.*

Tom, a former award-winning sportswriter, has written several sports-related books, the most-recent being *Golden Glory: The History of Central City Basketball,* an in-depth look at the great hoops tradition at his old high school alma mater. In addition, he wrote the highly successful *Kentucky Basketball Encyclopedia,* a history of the University of Kentucky's basketball program.

Tom, a Vietnam vet, lives in Lexington and is a member of Mystery Writers of America.

His website is www.tomwallacenovels.com.